VILLAGE

VILLAGE

a novel

STANLEY CRAWFORD

LeafStormPress

SANTA FE, NEW MEXICO

Published by Leaf Storm Press
Post Office Box 4670
Santa Fe, New Mexico 87502
U.S.A
leafstormpress.com

Jacket image: Andrew Dasburg, Taos Houses (New Mexican Village), 1926, oil on canvas, 23 1/8 × 29 1/4 in. Collection of the New Mexico Museum of Art. Gift of Mrs. Cyrus McCormick, 1952 (111.23P) Photo by Blair Clark

Book Design by LSP Graphics.
Special thanks to Sarah Armstrong at Ingram for jacket image sourcing.

First Edition

Printed in Canada

10 9 8 7 6 5 4 3 2

Library of Congress Control Number 2017932675
Publisher's Cataloging-in-Publication Data

Names: Crawford, Stanley G., 1937- Title: Village : a novel / Stanley Crawford.
Description: Santa Fe : Leaf Storm Press, 2017.
Identifiers: LCCN 2017932675 | ISBN 978-1-9456529-5-0 (hardcover)
Subjects: LCSH: Small cities--Fiction. | Hispanic Americans--Fiction.
   | Water rights--Fiction. | New Mexico--Fiction. | Satire. | BISAC:
   FICTION / Literary. | FICTION / Satire. | FICTION / Small Town &
   Rural. | FICTION / Hispanic & Latino.
Classification: LCC PS3603.R3974 V55 2017 (print) | DDC 813/.6--dc23.

For Lyn and John

The king has asthma, and the queen's impure.

—PETER LEVY

dawn

When the first gray light of dawn fanned up over the flat horizon of the western edge of the Great Plains, it was scarcely perceptible within the depths of the narrow San Marcos Canyon, blocked by an intervening range of low hills, and the range of peaks to the west loomed as only a shadowy presence. Within the canyon, lights were on within a few of the adobe houses and mobile homes, which were strung out along the highway winding through San Marcos de Arriba. Here and there toilets were flushed by the very old or the newly hungover, who hurried stiffly across cold floors and down drafty hallways. Roosters crowed to each other from nearby henhouses, a relay of calls up and down the narrow village. Down near the Río Sucio, a meandering stream, a chorus of coyotes held forth in a string of high-pitched squeals. A clunking splash suggested that beavers had finally felled a cottonwood after three nights of gnawing. A brief but strong gust of wind through the cottonwoods, freshly leafed out, suggested a windy April day ahead, the sound momentarily overriding the soft rush of water over rocks and gravel. Several vehicles raced through the village at twice the speed limit on the long two-hour commute to Santa Fe, while somewhere near the center of the village came the droning idle of a diesel engine. As the gray sky to the east turned pink, smoke began spiraling up from metal stovepipes and brick chimneys, diffusing the fragrance of burning piñon and ponderosa pine. A back door slammed as someone headed out to or returned from their *excusado*, or outhouse. As the light grew stronger and the pink faded into a light blue over the hills to the east that separated the village from the Plains, the sun finally illuminated the snow-spotted range to the west. Robins began to titter in apple trees and pigeons to coo in the attic spaces of the Catholic church in the center of the village and the adobe school buildings down the highway to the south. In other attics mice quieted down, and rats and packrats and squirrels and a raccoon or two stopped gnawing and scrabbling.

With the early morning light illuminating drawn curtains and shining through cracks in blinds and holes in shades, the older residents—except for two bedridden octogenarians and the oldest man in the valley—rose and wrapped themselves in bathrobes and ran showers and baths and dressed. The unemployed middle-aged lay longer, some couples wrapped in warmth-conserving embraces, and thought about the day ahead and studied their fears and hopes and desires, many of which were about money. A few sneezed, blew their noses, wondering whether this would be another spring allergy day. A younger couple or two vigorously finished what they had started the night before, while solitaries fondled themselves. Others invited dogs or cats into their beds, or pushed them off onto the floor. Alarms sounded, buzzers, bells, cheerful wake-up music broadcast from Santa Fe. Televisions were turned on briefly to the news, which always seemed to come from another planet of well-dressed people who never stopped smiling, before being switched to the new soap opera from Mexico City, where they all talked too fast in Spanish.

The young slept on and on. By the time the sun crested the ridge, toasters glowed all over the village, griddles sizzled, tortillas warmed, and cereal bowls were filled with blue corn *atole*, corn flakes, tiny O's, granola, milk, yogurt.

With that, another ordinary day began in San Marcos de Arriba, population 763, altitude 6006 feet, a village founded by a ragtag group of Spanish colonists on land granted by the King of Spain to Anastasio Moro and his extended family. This present day within the last decade of the twentieth century promised to be little different from most of the other days leading up to it since 1771, when the colonists began digging their first acequias, or irrigation ditches, and mixing mud for their first adobe bricks.

There was the sound of a shotgun from somewhere back of the village store. Perhaps someone shooting at a coyote near a henhouse? Or maybe someone trying to scare off dogs tearing apart a garbage sack put out for Monday's garbage collection? This idea reminded a few of those who had forgotten that today was garbage day. As if in echo, an extended gust of wind banged loose pieces of corrugated metal roofing and loose gutters and drain spouts all over the village.

By the time the postal van had made its morning delivery to the post office and the school bus had made its rounds and deposited the students from kindergarten through twelfth grade at the combined knoll-top elementary and high school, the sun was rising high and the village was fully awake.

CHAPTER 1

The Notice

Monday, Porter Clapp murmured as he pushed open the door of Moro Mercantile and stepped inside. He mouthed the word slowly, trying to place it. Monday, he said to no one in particular. Monday.

Porter had fixed on the word only an instant before, while standing in front of the telephone pole outside the store, where he had read a notice that had apparently just been put up. The lettering on the pink sheet was not yet faded and the paper had not yet been splashed with rain or scribbled on by local vandals or cynics, nor had it been torn down and wadded up and thrown into the trash barrel chained to the telephone pole by any of those who for some reason or other might be outraged by either its message or by the simple fact of the presence of such a notice in the village by a suspect government agency.

Porter had stared at the pink sheet for a good five minutes, not because he was unable to grasp its simple statements—that there was to be a meeting at seven in the evening in the elementary school gym, a meeting about water—but because he was trying to weigh the import of this latest message from the outside world to the tiny settlement of San Marcos.

For Porter, the outside world started at many places, depending on his mood. Sometimes it thrust itself right inside his forehead, just above his eyebrows. At others he was able to push the boundary out to his front door, his driveway, and sometimes—more rarely—it extended as far away as Moro Mercantile and the San Marcos Post Office and even to the north and south boundaries of the narrow San Marcos Valley. In euphoric moods such as those that flooded his body immediately after sex or while first lying down for his afternoon nap, the outside world rushed away in the manner of a rapidly receding wave and vanished altogether, and for a few brief moments there was no distinction between Porter Clapp and the world—the nonoutside world—that remained. At such moments, the distended warmth of his being encompassed and forgave all, even the catastrophic bad habits and cruelties and injustices of the age itself.

.   Porter had taken refuge in San Marcos from the outside world, from mainstream America, with his partner, Stephanie Wachler, and her two children a half dozen years before. The Hispanic village attracted him because everyone looked different and spoke different and behaved in unpredictable ways, which for a time he found charmingly incomprehensible. His new neighbors found it equally incomprehensible why anyone from the outside world would move to a place like San Marcos, to which nobody had moved in living memory, probably not even since the place was settled back in the late 1700s, not unless you counted the handful of Anglos, Vietnam draft dodgers and refugees from urban strife, who had stumbled into the valley in the late 1960s. The only reason Hispanics ever came back to San Marcos was to be buried.

For Porter, the refuge lay not only in the fact of San Marcos's geographical remoteness from any mainstream American city and its sprawling suburbs but also in the way that his Hispanic neighbors lacked the middle-class American templates by which to measure his degree of success or failure as a father or stepfather or as a producer of income or as a discriminating connoisseur of consumer goods and insurance policies and investments. He felt safe. They couldn't type him. They wouldn't judge him for his tangled graying blond hair, always too long, or for his clothes that were never quite clean and never new, for his and Stephanie's constant financial worries and their too-old station wagon and his lack of a regular job. The local people had always lived that way, on the edge. They wouldn't even judge him for the silly little thing he'd done in Berkeley years before that had changed everything and haunted him ever since.

The pink announcement on the pole, flapping this way and that on its two thumbtacks in the brisk April wind, brought it all back. Its words were simple: *All residents of the town of San Marcos are invited to attend A MEETING, Monday, 7:00 p.m., San Marcos School Gymnasium, concerning the establishment of WATER RIGHTS by the State Water Office.* As Porter read them and re-read them, the words tugged the boundary of the outside world back in like a returning wave, first past the entrance of the valley, the notch through which the state road passed on the way down to the main highway leading west to Santa Fe, and down the twisting state road, to wash over the old adobe plaza and then over the knoll-top post office and then over the high second-story roof of the Moro Mercantile building, to crash at his feet and rise up behind his eyes.

He gasped for air. Official notices all affected him the same way. Each one was a sign that the outside world was moving closer, staking its claim. Lately his naptime fantasies had woven themselves around visions of perfectly flat desert landscapes that radiated in all directions from a simple wooden hut where days would be spent thinking up ingenious ways to make small quantities of water last, and where you could see a plume of approaching dust miles away against a backdrop of distant purple mountain ranges.

The meeting was Monday. But what day was today? Standing before the pole, hand on a corner of the notice to steady it, he had worked out that yesterday had been Sunday because the day before he had gone for the mail early, making it Saturday, and meaning that today would be Monday, unless somehow the day had slipped by him without his having noticed, which was sometimes the case. He was always disturbed when he miscalculated and drove into the village on a Sunday morning to find most of the village cars and pickups crowded around the church, the people inside engaged in religious business he had no feeling for.

These thoughts had carried him inside Moro Mercantile to a position in front of the dairy cooler. Another mystery. It would be no good in the shadows of the store to try to make out the date on his digital watch. Yes, milk, that was it. He opened the glass door and pulled out a half-gallon carton. Stephanie had sent him out for it, to make up for having forgotten it Saturday afternoon. Assuming it's Monday, he said to himself. Monday.

So, Monday, he said, setting the milk carton down on the counter of mottled green-and-yellow linoleum held down with brass upholstery tacks, vaguely aware of a figure in a gray apron standing on the other side.

Bueno, bueno, the figure said.

What time did it say? Porter asked.

What?

Porter looked up. Onésimo Moro was staring at him. Today is Monday, Porter suggested.

Sí, claro. Look at the paper. Onésimo Moro placed a finger on the stack of newspapers on the counter. That's what it says.

Porter looked down. The newspapers were turned toward him.

Headline words stung his eyes. *Rape, murder, prison riot, car theft*. Onésimo's fingers obscured the day of the week.

The misery of human life washed over Porter. Another episode in the great battle was about to be engaged. It was to find him tired and disorganized and weary of even the smallest struggles that were needed to convey him from day to day, out of bed in the morning, into bed in the evening, in and out of this dark still store, in the car and out of the car, which was falling apart and got so few miles to the gallon. He looked up at Onésimo Moro. He was a short, potbellied man, almost bald, with pointed ears and drooping eyelids over quietly watchful brown eyes. He and his people seemed so immune from it all.

The meeting, Porter said.

A dark, flashily made-up young woman stuck her head in the door and thrust a twenty-dollar bill at Onésimo. Ten dollars of super unleaded, she said. A whiff of an apple-scented perfume teased the air an instant before dissolving in the odor of kerosene that had inhabited the interior for generations of Moro shopkeepers, who used the fuel to settle dust and discourage bugs on the plank floor, whose boards here and there were worn an eighth of an inch below shiny nail heads. After she had pushed the sticking door closed, the vision of her darkly smooth cheeks hung suspended at a point both Porter and Onésimo were staring at, her glistening lips, the sparkle of gold bangles on a wrist.

Porter absently watched Onésimo Moro insert the twenty-dollar bill between the jaws of a large fluorescent green plastic clamp that hung suspended by a string just above the cash register and give the string a tug. *Bajes diez*, he called up as the bill took wing toward a large round hole in the pressed tin ceiling. Porter had never been inside the upstairs apartment where the Moros lived and where Isabel Moro did the accounts and kept an eye out for shoplifters below through several holes in the ceiling.

I don't know what meeting you're talking about, Porter.

Porter stared at him, then looked at a handful of rumpled bills and change he had retrieved from his pocket. He sorted through his most recent recollections, which had an odd antiquity to them. Perhaps he had only imagined Onésimo tacking the notice on to the phone pole. He saw himself standing outside staring at it. Had he not looked at it only a moment ago, before coming out of the wind? He saw himself reading the notice.

He stepped over to the window and looked out. The pink sheet was flapping in the wind. That one, he said, pointing.

Onésimo craned his neck. Ten-dollar bill in its jaws, the clamp swayed down from the ceiling. Well, I didn't read it, Onésimo said, releasing the ten-dollar bill. I just told them to put it up. They were in here this morning and asked me to put it up. I said sure. I mean, there was only one of them. I think he said tonight at seven.

That's what I said.

Porter thought he heard whispering noises coming down from the hole in the ceiling.

The young woman getting gas pushed the door open. The wind swept past her like a dog pushing its way indoors. Onésimo, that pump, she said, with a backward toss of her head.

Onésimo stepped out from behind the counter and went outside and pulled the chattering door closed behind him, leaving Porter to count out the amount that glowed in green letters atop the cash register. He did so slowly, straightening out and smoothing the bills and laying them down on the linoleum. The carton of milk seemed heavy when he picked it up to leave. He disliked buying milk in cartons because of the time he'd found two drowned mice in a milk carton on a family camping trip when he was ten. He wondered whether he would be able to accomplish the vast labor of climbing back into the station wagon and then driving back to the house and walking in the back door, whether he would even be able to remember to find a scrap of paper to slip into the bathroom mirror to remind him of the meeting tonight.

Above his head, from the direction of the ceiling, there came some creaking noises and a light thump. Mrs. Moro would be looking down at him through the hole, he guessed. He glanced down at the bills and coins he had spread out on the counter. And a puzzling puddle of milk. He was seven cents short.

A prickly flush worked its way up his neck. Quickly he counted out another nickel and two pennies and noisily dropped the coins on the counter, funneled the rest of his change back into his pocket, and pulled open the door.

CHAPTER 2

Moro Mercantile

On this April morning the breeze flowing down from the distant mountains showed signs of working its way up into a good strong wind that would soon be whipping the apple and cottonwood branches of new clear green leaves into long swaying arcs. Already bits of paper and plastic from garbage bags heaped along the roadside and torn open and strewn about by the village dogs were blowing around. Monday was garbage day in San Marcos. The orange garbage truck would soon be coming down from Los Martinez to pick up the black bags and cardboard boxes. The village always looked worse after garbage collection, a fact that never bothered Teofrasto Vizarriaga, the head garbage man of the route. He regarded the eddies of blowing trash in his wake as signs of his strength and virility.

It's all yours, said Onésimo Moro, having given a sharp kick to the base of the aged mechanical gas pump, and handed the nozzle back to Brenda May Serrano, who had stood there inspecting her shiny nails freshly painted a dark rose as if she expected him to do the pumping like in the old days. The glinting synthetic fabric of her black skirt and her flawless makeup said as usual that he should keep his distance and that

she was in an important hurry to some scheming meeting. He
handed her the ten-dollar bill and headed back into the store,
catching the door as Porter was leaving. He wiped up the
puddles of milk with a sense of satisfaction: the leaky carton,
gone at last. A creak next to the wall upstairs told him Isabel
would be upstairs leaning over to peer through the slits in the
blinds to see who was getting gas.

Like his father and grandfather before him, Onésimo Moro
was unusually possessive of his shop goods, as announced
by a slight hesitation in handing them over to the customer
once they had been paid for. To have his inventory daily
dispersed throughout the village disturbed him. Whatever
the impracticality, he would rather have a customer enter
his shop and look around without touching anything, like in
one of those pretend shops he'd seen at a historical display
in a museum in Santa Fe. The only exceptions were gasoline,
which would go bad if you kept it in the underground tank
too long, and things like the leaking half-gallon carton of milk
he'd just sold to Porter Clapp, who never noticed anything. He
despised the large retail outlets in Santa Fe and Albuquerque
because those people didn't care about their stuff, they just
wanted to get rid of it as fast as they could, which he and
Isabel were quite happy to help them do on their weekly trips
to town.

And though he regarded shoplifting as the ultimate crime,
he was perhaps more interested to know who submitted to
temptation in the darker aisles and blind corners at the back
of the store and other places not visible through holes in the
ceiling. His father had kept a ledger of such events, which
Isabel now maintained from her upstairs peepholes, a detailed
record of seventy years of shoplifting from Moro Mercantile.
Onésimo often thought that one day he would drive the two
hours down to Santa Fe and Xerox up the whole volume and

hand out the sheets at a large public meeting in the school gym called to deal with just that problem. He could imagine the passion with which one by one he would denounce his customers, his neighbors, even his closest relations, venerated ancestors long deceased, and children especially. But then what? What would come afterward? Silence? A riot? Or, his secret hope: the people of the village lining up, heads bowed, to make amends for their pilfering, and for that of their parents and grandparents. One by one writing checks, emptying their wallets of cash and food stamps, jars of coins, socks full of banknotes.

Milk puddles wiped up, he realized that he hadn't finished dealing with the two large tissue-paper cartons filled with trash around the side of the building. He dragged them out past the gas pumps and the old Chevy Carryall station wagon where, front door open, Porter was standing and staring into space, to the farthest point of the store's peninsular parking area, where he surveyed the apron of crumbling asphalt and hardened red mud for bits of trash that would have blown down the road. None had yet arrived. Brenda May Serrano hung up the nozzle and climbed back into her new black Ford pickup with its smoked glass and matching camper shell. She and her wheeler-dealer husband, Manny, were always buying new cars and pickups and mobile homes and clothes. The only way they could get that much money that fast was to rip people off. Onésimo thought he could make out her bright pink lips through the glass as she roared away.

A car door slammed. Onésimo turned and watched Porter Clapp lean over the wheel and start the engine. He wondered whether Isabel had let Porter get out of the store without paying his bill.

The clear morning light had begun to yellow. The breeze was becoming frisky and colder. The wind was probably going

to keep blowing again all day. On the way back inside
Onésimo paused at the phone pole and studied the flapping pink
State Water Office notice Porter had tried to say something
about.

Good riddance, he thought. They're going to try to take
our water away at last. It would be good to dry this place up.
Onésimo was tired of growing a garden every year and then
seeing Teofrasto Vizarriaga's uncle's cows trample his chile
just as it was getting ripe, if an early frost didn't get to it first.
And last summer the irrigation ditch overflowed and flooded
their garage, and he had slipped on the wet cement and come
down on a pile of old newspapers. He still felt that swooning,
backward, that spinning plunge every time he thought of it,
which was at least once a day. Then the acequias and all the
arguments about who gets the water when from the ditch, don't
talk to me about that. And then the boys were never going to
come back from Denver and Chicago to work the field out
back and the bottomland fields below the highway. Dry the
valley up. Sell the water, sell the land, send all the water down
to Texas for all I care. Sell all the water—the thought slipped
through his mind with an ingenious innocence—and then
everybody would have enough money to pay all their back
bills at the store, even Porter Clapp. Why not?

He pushed through the dragging, chattery door. From the
hole in the ceiling, Isabel's muffled voice called down, Did
you ask el Porter to pay his bill? *¿Por qué no?*, she immediately
answered, knowing that he had not. Her p's and t's were
sharp, a sure sign that she was angry. But at least Abundio
Moro was paid up, she added, that's something.

Did he finally die or what?

Esta mañana, she called down absently. *Pobrecito*.

Onésimo stared up at the round hole cut in the tin panels
embossed with fleur-de-lis patterns and ringed by an old tin
lampshade that served as a funnel to guide checks and food

stamps and bills up into the opening. After a village shootout forty years ago, his father had rigged up the arrangement, also lining the floor of the upstairs apartment with eighth-inch steel plates in the kitchen and living room and in the two bedrooms. For a radius of ten miles at least, everybody owed Moro Mercantile money. Some just a few dollars, some nearly a hundred, like Porter Clapp, and more than a few, three and four hundred dollars which had been carried on the books since Onésimo's father's time. But Onésimo knew he couldn't ride around town with a shotgun like his father used to, to repossess the worst of the debts, coming back with a pickup loaded with washtubs, wheelbarrows, chairs and tables, saddles and harnesses, even sinks and doors, to be resold out of the back of the store, sometimes a month or two later to the very neighbors who had defaulted on them, but this time for cash. That was back when you knew who had a gun and who didn't. Now the question was what caliber and how many of each.

And now it wasn't just the store that everybody owed money to. Everybody was in arrears with their ditch dues to the acequia. Nobody had paid their water bill to the mutual domestic water association, which ran the village well pump and storage tank for drinking water. Nobody had any money to pay for the television translator station electric bill, which the electric co-op was supposed to cut off today. There wouldn't be any TV tonight. Why should I pay when nobody else does?—this was the excuse. Forget the doctor bills. The hospitals in town. Nobody ever paid those. The only undertaker who would still serve the valley, Zepeda's, now came with both a hearse to pick up the body plus a pickup to take away the furniture to sell off to pay for the funeral.

How did you get good people like Porter Clapp to pay their bills, people you thought of as almost your friends? Onésimo considered that maybe he should try saying something to

Stephanie. She was the one with a regular paycheck. She would probably be in later in the day to pick up whatever Porter forgot. Onésimo would drop a hint. He would start asking about their children, Krishna and Athena, who, like all the other kids in town, Isabel had tried to discourage from shoplifting by lowering pieces of candy down from above. Porter's kids had only shoplifted once, as far as he knew. Page 379 of the ledger, line 17.

They're good kids, he might try saying. They've only shoplifted from me once, as far as I know, he would say, hoping Isabel wouldn't start thumping around upstairs. He could almost hear her correcting him from above, shouting down through the hole, No, those kids of yours do it all the time. Why do you think we charge such high prices?

No, he thought, he'd have to try some other angle. But what?

CHAPTER 3

Dos Equis

From the other side of the bank of brass post office boxes came the frantic scrabbling Postmaster Morales recognized as the sound of one of his so-called patrons, *esos cabrones*, who had either forgotten their combination lock number or who had picked the wrong box to try to open. He looked up at the clock. From the time and the direction the noise was coming from, the lower left-hand corner of the partition just behind his chair, he guessed it would be *ése el Porter Clapp*. A heavy orange plywood board covered the service window at the tiny counter, with the letters *O-U-T* splashed in black across it, though everyone in town knew that Mr. Morales was probably inside sorting the mail or, some thought, drinking or napping or reading his postal patrons' girlie magazines. If you knocked long enough on the plywood board blocking the grilled window, softly and insistently, not loudly, eventually you would hear a chair scrape inside and heavy footsteps on the old wood floor. The plywood panel would vibrate as the postmaster unhooked it and slowly took it down. *¿Qué quieres?* Can't you see I'm busy?

Mr. Morales was in fact up to more serious business behind the blocked window and behind the gray curtain that screened his mail sorting table from the window, at the far end of which sat a hotplate and a tea kettle. Years ago he had advanced from thumbing through the villagers' magazines to reading letters that arrived torn open or were never properly sealed in the first place, to steaming open with his kettle a sampling of letters that flowed in both directions through the tiny post office, and the occasional bill, particularly the credit card bills of the few people in town lucky enough to have them. This place is always so humid inside here, he heard Onésimo Moro virtually shout into his open box door as he was withdrawing his mail one day. Somebody else going out the door cackled: I wonder what goes on back there, take a bath or what? After that Mr. Morales brought back a two-burner hotplate from Santa Fe and took to boiling onions during his inspection of the mail, hoping that suspicious customers would figure he was keeping his lunch warm. He steamed open and glued closed envelopes at the rate of a dozen or so a week. An envelope or mailer that was sealed with non-soluble adhesive Mr. Morales would throw down on the floor and with the toe of his left boot holding it in place he would rip it open with the heel of the other, then rub random black marks on it from an old tire he kept in the back room just for that purpose, completing his work by stamping *DAMAGED IN TRANSIT* in red ink liberally on both sides. Very occasionally, whenever it rained or snowed, he would plunge an entire envelope or package into a bucket of dirty water after first inspecting the contents. Mr. Morales had become proud of his artistic defacing skills, and he encouraged his neighbors to believe that the United States Postal Service employed such antiquated equipment all over the country that accidents were the rule, not the exception. No point complaining, *primo*, he often observed to his customers. It will just get lost in the mail. Lucky anything gets here at all, *sabes?*

As a result of his investigations Mr. Morales had assumed the burden of knowing more about his fellow villagers' private affairs than anyone else in town. He considered his neighbors fools and madmen for throwing their money away for the breakable gadgetry and alcohol-laced elixirs that came through the mail, and on cars and trucks they couldn't afford and which wore out just as the payments ended. And because he studied medical and dental bills and lab reports with special care, he was convinced that all but two or three families were inflicted with incurable diseases and conditions. One day he would wake up to find the entire village dead or dying, neighbors staggering down the dirt lanes toward the post office, gasping, clutching their chests or throats before toppling over into the mud or snow or dust, depending on the season, as they attempted to reach their cars and pickups and drive somewhere for help. This was the unspoken burden he nursed within himself and which peered out of the steady gray eyes transfixing all those who dared come to his window and knock before noon, and which had earned him the nickname of X-Ray Morales, most often shortened to Ray or Rey and then inflated to Dos Equis. I tell you that guy X-Ray knows everything that's in the mail—a remark passed around the village with ritual regularity, most often earning the rejoinder, Yeah, that's Mr. Immorales, that's what I think. Mr. Morales did not permit the use of his first name by anyone addressing him, and he answered his phone with either a severe "Postmaster Morales" or "Mr. Morales," and as a result only a few old timers new his first name, Irwin.

The sad knowledge of the village was not what he had had in mind as a child with a burning desire to work in a post office when he grew up, perhaps as a way to stabilize the oscillations between village and city that he had experienced from age five to fifteen. His father was a cook, or a chef, depending on his drinking, and when his drinking was under control the family lived in Albuquerque, Las Cruces, or Phoenix. When not, he would find himself jobless and the family would move back to San Marcos and pry the boards off the windows of their small adobe house and stay until he was dried out enough to place a collect call to a café or restaurant where he had worked five years before and whose owners had forgotten or forgiven his earlier lapses or whose new owners had not known of them.

Young Mr. Morales learned how to ingratiate himself with the gringo kids at the city schools, at whose hands, or at whose parents' hands, he inevitably suffered some sort of vague humiliation. When Mr. Morales was seven, an earnest phlegmatic gringo kid by the name of Wayne invited him home to help build a cardboard post office in his bedroom and glue his collection of cancelled stamps onto envelopes and scrawl out penciled addresses. In the course of this exercise, Mr. Morales couldn't resist pocketing some of the brightest stamps, a fact noted by Wayne's observant, possessive mother, who finally called Mr. Morales aside and said that maybe such things were okay among "his people" but they certainly were not okay among hers, and she asked him to empty his pockets before going home. This was the first of what came to seem an endless string of embarrassments Mr. Morales associated with gringos, the worst of which came during a particularly prosperous period when his parents sent him to a military academy near El Paso for a year.

Mr. Morales had nothing personal against any of the dozen gringos who had moved into San Marcos within the past ten years, though experience had taught him never to trust them, not even the seemingly inept ones like *el Porter Clapp*, whose scrabbling had now abruptly stopped on the other side of the bank of postal boxes. Mr. Morales listened as the sound resumed more slowly and methodically after a pause. He could hear the mechanism click into place. Then a snap and a scraping sound as the brass postal box door opened, illuminating the inside walls of the box, which grew brighter as Porter pulled out the catalogs and bills Mr. Morales had stuffed so tightly from his side, having used his knee to cram all the mail into the tiny cubicle. Some of it was last week's mail. Mr. Morales had fallen behind on the soap opera of overdue notices, threats of cancellation and legal action and visits from bill collectors and repossessing firms, not that they would ever bother to drive out this far. What he couldn't figure out with *esos Clapps* was why she got all the mail; it all went to her, Stephanie Wachler, and never to him, though she never came here to get it or mail anything, only him, Clapp not Wachler. It was like he didn't exist legally. Maybe he had his own box up in Los Martinez or even in Santa Fe. To stop defections, Mr. Morales spread the rumor that they burned mail in those other post offices when it piled too high, especially at the beginning of the month when all the *cheques* went out from the government, Social Security, retirement, welfare. He had even taken to singeing a few letters to make his point. That one must have got past the fires, *que bárbaro.* He also blamed delays on *el otro,* the other San Marcos, San Marco Abajo, seven miles downstream and with a zip code only two digits different, where some of the real San Marcos mail went by mistake. His wife's ancestors had been part of the group that left the original San Marcos in the 1800s to found a new settlement only seven miles away, which they arrogantly gave the name of San Marco. A hundred and fifty years later her relatives still weren't on speaking terms over the "theft" of the name of the village and church. But he sometimes thought the only customers he frightened into staying at his post office were the *viejitos* and *viejitas* who didn't drive anymore and who all had heart conditions and diabetes and cancer anyway.

The splashing sound of letters and magazines spilling on to the linoleum floor came through the wall, once, then twice,

then a third time, probably at the threshold of the entrance
door. Mr. Morales thought he heard el Porter gasp—or was
it a whimper? Then he realized he had failed to hear the
definitive slap of the postal box door latching closed. Porter
would have left it wide open, *ese cabrón*, disturbing the tight,
secure symmetry of the wall inset with a hundred tiny brass
doors and small squares of beveled glass and little knurled
knobs with pointers on them angled at any one of the numbers
from one to ten. Mr. Morales's early morning ritual was to
turn each of the hundred pointers vertically to zero, like an
airline pilot adjusting the gauges before flight.

Porter's open box door aimed a faint shaft of light toward
the back of Mr. Morales's chair. He feared the day when
someone might enter the narrow post office lobby and insert
some kind of mirror on an extension shaft through an open box
door and catch him with the curtain inadvertently left open
and in the act of steaming open an envelope. A cousin who
was a postal inspector out of Albuquerque sometimes stopped
by to say hello and catch up on the family gossip without ever
commenting on the tattered remains of the American flag that
flew above the rusty tin roof of the adobe building or on any
of the other irregularities that demonstrated Mr. Morales's
contempt for his employer, the United States of America.
His inspector cousin came through regularly on Fridays every
couple of months, a day that Mr. Morales was careful not
to fly the spotless silk flags of either Mexico or Spain, the
raising of which was usually inspired by newspaper articles in
which the venerable traditions of Chicano New Mexico were
ignored or ridiculed. On Fridays, he was also careful to take
down the framed 1848 Treaty of Guadalupe Hidalgo, texts in
Spanish and English, and replace it with the official portrait
of the president, *ese cabrón Clinton*.

The open postal box door nagged at him. *El Porter*. Finally
he stood up from his chair and reached up and pulled down a

length of baling wire bent into a hook at one end. He crouched down, peered into the box, inserted the wire, snagged the latch mechanism, and gave it a sharp pull. The little brass door slammed with a satisfying snap.

He returned to his chair and pulled the curtain closed behind him. On the counter was a small cardboard carton addressed to Ricky Salcedo and containing the pornographic video *Miranda's Memories*. That teenager Ricky had a reputation as being a too-bright troublemaker, confirmed by how he had figured out how to order and pay for the video without arousing the suspicions of his parents, *esos Salcedos*, who thought themselves better than everybody else. With his wife having gone to bed early, Mr. Morales had spent the evening watching the movie, stretched out in his recliner in his bathrobe with a margarita in hand but puzzled why the images of Miranda's dozen partners penetrating her, male and female, in countless ways, had failed to arouse his pipi, which had remained small and shy throughout. *Es verdad*, Erlinda and me don't bother with that stuff anymore, they say it's all over when you get to sixty-five. Then toward the end of the hour-long video he finally realized what it was. They were *todos güeros*: all gringos.

On a shelf above his workbench was a row of specialty glues. He pulled down a yellow tube, uncapped it, and carefully smeared the flap of the carton, sealed it closed, and · slid it into the Salcedo box.

CHAPTER 4

Spilt Milk

To her friends, Stephanie Wachler's name had long ago devolved into Steph or Fan, as she was not the type for the full treatment. Not pert, not bright, not efficient, in no way fashionable, which is what she thought a Stephanie should be. No Stephanie would ever deliberately move into a mud house in a remote Hispanic village. Family tradition was to misname children, which she herself had let happen not once but twice. This morning Krishna and Athena had nagged her again about having named them for dead gods who didn't even speak English. Why would you give a *baby* a name like that, the usually vague and otherworldly eleven-year-old had snapped, the she. The names had been bestowed by a Jung-reading father, who eventually had drifted away to become a professional tornado- and storm-chaser for a cable channel.

Steph was lying on the couch, her feet up, staring at the buckling yellow-painted Masonite that passed for a ceiling, as she mulled over the chain of events that had led up to this dismal moment. Above the Masonite, or on top of it, she pictured beaded ribbons of mouse turds, the accumulation of decades, and a labyrinth of dusty cobwebs between the Masonite and the sagging beams and planks the paneling had

been tacked up to conceal a generation ago. She could feel
the beginnings of the drilling sensation that always indicated a
headache coming on. The tin roof was beginning to flap. The
wind would blow all day.

The trouble was that yet one more time she had made
herself subservient to yet another male. Why did she keep
doing this? Fear? A need to cater and coddle? Where did it
come from? The village was coming to seem to her a refuge of
male stupidity and denseness and obstinacy. There was Porter.
There was the store owner, Onésimo Moro. That postmaster,
Mr. Morales. Even Lázaro Quintana, the mayordomo of their
irrigation ditch. Len Mott, even. All of them. Males. Where
did they come from? Periodically the three that she had lived
with, two of whom she had actually married, had all said in
so many words, I'm a man, a male, I need this or that to prove
my maleness, and if I don't get it then I will leave you, commit
suicide, or gun down fifty innocent people in a McDonald's,
so do I get the flavor of ice cream I want for dessert or not?

She squinted and closed her eyes tight. Definitely a
headache. She could hear Porter coming in the kitchen door.
Why? She had hoped that he might decide to drive to town,
leaving her at home for the day. His noises in the kitchen at first
puzzled her. Then she understood that he had taken a plate
out of the dish rack and had set it down on the table, no doubt
to catch the drips from yet another of Onésimo's damaged,
leaking milk cartons. When she heard the refrigerator door
open and close, bracketing the sound of the plate being slid
across the wire shelves, she was certain. Another leaky carton.
Rapist toad, she muttered.

Coffee? Porter called out.

She remained silent for a moment. That meant he wanted
to talk.

No, she said.

Nothing?

An aspirin.

Oh.

No, two.

She heard him disappear into the bathroom. For a moment she dozed off. She was on a sailboat cutting through the water, a cooling breeze washing her forehead. There was a bang. Something was about to capsize. She awoke with a start, her arm falling off the edge of the couch. Porter was handing her a cup of coffee.

No, he said, pulling it back, this is yours. He handed her a bright green plastic tumbler of water, then opened his palm for her to pick out the white pills.

She let the aspirins tingle on her tongue a moment and grow furry, then swallowed both together, washing them down with a long gulp. Porter's breath had been bad for two days, a sign he might be coming down with something. She hated spring, a tricky, nasty time of year. Only the Spanish people had it right, slogging around with crosses on their backs and beating themselves with chains, or whatever they did around Easter. And the kids had worn nothing to school. They'd all be sick by the end of the day.

No mail?

Junk, catalogs, he said. It's Monday.

There was never any decent mail on Mondays because Postmaster Morales needed more time to fondle it or whatever he did in there. Porter perched on the edge of the couch, sipping his coffee.

There's a notice at Onésimo's, he said vacantly, staring across the room at the bumpy plaster painted in glossy white. Through the gaps in the windowpanes where the putty had fallen out, a draft was toying with the burlap curtains. A mufflerless car roared by on the state road above their house.

She said nothing. The leaking milk carton meant that she'd

have to go back in the afternoon and lecture Onésimo about passing off damaged goods yet again, that maybe he should send somebody over to the house to clean up the refrigerator after the carton had dripped all day, overflowing the saucer. And then when the kids got home they would spread the drips all over the kitchen. Or refuse to drink the milk. There's a hole in the carton, Mom. Germs can crawl right up in there, Krishna would say, making an upward screwing gesture, worm-like, with his index finger. Lately she'd heard that at school he'd taken to pronouncing his name "Kroosh" and saying it was Norwegian. She could hear one of his Chicano playmates saying, No, bro, that's just plain puro hippie. Playmates? Tormentors, more likely.

Porter was talking. She had missed the beginning. When he talked it was like some friendly old machine droning by in the distance, something like a tugboat, reassuring in its rhythms and regularity, predictable where it would begin and where it would come to rest. This was one of his end-of-the-world musings. A piece of rusty tin roofing gave a particularly vicious bang. The TV antenna moorings whistled. She had heard that there might be no TV tonight because nobody had paid the translator station electric bill, though the real story, she had also been told, was that Manny Serrano, the treasurer, was trying to sell more satellite dishes for the business he owned in Santa Fe, and to that end he had engineered the whole crisis. Word had it that the down payments on the new maroon Chrysler sedan and new Ford pickup he was driving around had come out of the poorly supervised and less understood translator treasury, causing the last and most loyal or naive subscribers to suspend their monthly payments. And once he had saturated the village with satellite dishes, then he would make money a second time by bringing cable into the valley and making the dishes obsolete. He had connections on the county commission. People said this with the rubbing of thumb and fingers together. Money Man Manny they called him. M&M for short.

So it looks like this is it, Porter said. She could tell he was winding up. It was bound to come home to roost sooner or later. I'm trapped. He let his words hang in the air. Steph suspected he wanted her to say something reassuring. Porter was always saying he was trapped. He loved to announce that any minute now the car would be coming down the drive to take him away. How they would make him just disappear like they did in—well, wherever they did that. Argentina, Chile. In this hypothetical drama of his, Steph wondered whether she would fling her body down on the driveway to stop them or just stand back and wave good-bye with a neutral smile, suppressing a sigh of relief.

How bad is the leak in the milk carton?

Abruptly he stood up. I forgot, I've got to wipe off the front seat of the car.

Bad, she thought, turning her head and staring out the window at the apple trees, whose branches were swaying back and forth, their new leaves fluttering in the wind. She wondered whether or not to let herself be moved by the painful beauty of the season and put down the anger she carried within her. She lay there rigid, unblinking, waiting for the answer, the decision, while the wind blew and blew.

CHAPTER 5

The Ditch

Lázaro Quintana had been in charge of San Marcos's largest irrigation ditch for most of his adult life, starting at age eighteen, when his father was injured by a horse. And though his father had remained titular mayordomo another ten years with his bad leg, Lázaro had become the one who actually regulated the water at the headgate and distributed it among the *parciantes* up and down the long ditch, the one who supervised the work crews in the spring and again often in mid-summer and whenever the ditch banks broke or the old cement WPA diversion dam needed to be patched. Fifty-seven years I been mayordomo, he had told an incredulous Anglo not so long ago, though he could no longer remember which one, Porter or Len or that other Americano, who had appeared amazed at this simple fact of his life.

You've been mayordomo longer than Hitler or Stalin, the young fellow had said, shaking his head, or Mao or Trujillo, Batista, or Stroessner for that matter.

I don't know about those mayordomos, Lázaro Quintana had replied, I just know about this one. Fifty-seven years. Since I was eighteen, a *joven* like you.

Lázaro Quintana had no idea who those other fellows were, other than names in the papers he occasionally picked up at the barber shop in town or heard on the radio, some of whom seemed connected with the cyclical conversion of good able-bodied ditch workers into corpses brought home in coffins draped with flags, though that had not happened for a few years now, not since Vietnam, wherever that was. For Lázaro a sense of history lay in his many operations over the decades, appendix, stomach, gall bladder, and chest, back, and neck for various lumps and bumps, and down there, you know, for two hernias, and further down for a bad vein and an ingrown toenail. He had no idea how these got paid for. His father had long ago told him, Just tell them to send the bills to that *presidente* of theirs. The presidents, like the doctors, were all Anglos, and they were probably all related besides. You just go ahead and send the bill to President Bush, he had told him for the toenail. As far as he knew, Roosevelt, Truman, Eisenhower, Kennedy, Johnson, Nixon, but not Ford, who wasn't around long enough, and Carter and Reagan had taken care of his bills up to now, though he wasn't sure that the new fellow Clinton would. The only bill he ever opened and paid was the light bill. And his property taxes, which he went and paid in person each year. His father had taught him how to throw away things without reading them.

Lázaro Quintana had been in charge of the Acequia de los Hermanos for so long that it had become known as Lázaro's ditch or the Acequia de Lázaro. No one else in the valley knew its five-mile serpentine course along the contours of the eastern side of the narrow valley, crossing over and under a half-dozen arroyos and cutting through groves of cottonwoods and through banks of gravel and rich red clay—and no one else besides Lázaro Quintana knew the details of all sixty of the leaky headgates that diverted water down to its members' fields and gardens and orchards. Over the years the long winding ditch had come to inhabit his body like a tapeworm, and when something stirred inside him, some ache or pain, or even some disturbing thought, he would try to translate it into a problem with the ditch channel. Maybe there's some *ratas* working there, he would conjecture, maybe there's some of those *perros de agua*. Whenever he woke with a sore elbow or knee, which was almost every morning now, he would think, Maybe something got stuck at that narrow place by the Arroyo de los Ahogados. Guess I better go see.

This morning Lázaro Quintana had put water into the ditch channel for the first time in the new season and was following it from the beginning, down through the village to the end, where what water was left flowed back into the river. The Mott driveway, where he now parked, meant that he was about one third of the way down the ditch. He sat behind the wheel of his old red Nissan two-door for a moment, pondering the meaning of the fresh aches in his left thigh, up and down which he ran his stiff fingers. These new aches the acequia had bestowed on him in a direct and unmysterious way earlier this morning, when he had fallen down a grassy bank slippery with dew. An old root sticking out of the earth had snagged the left cuff of his Levi's on his way down, pulling him to one side and off balance. His spine still tingled with the sensation of heavy plunging. But he had been able to stand up and walk. No broken bones, at least, he had been muttering to himself all morning since.

He looked down at his Levi's. The faded blue weave of the left pants leg was streaked with black and green. Somebody had burned the ditch bank not long before in order to clear away the dry grass and brush. It was dirty to walk through, dirtier to fall down into. He would have to go back to the house and change his jeans. Walk into Moro Mercantile or the post office like this, with big black smears down he Levi's? He could hear Onésimo's cackle: *¿Eee, qué pasó, primo?* Did you fall down the septic tank?

No broken bones at least. Yet the shame of having lost his balance still stung. And he knew that bank like the back of his hand. He knew that root. He could see it now even though he had missed it at the time. He had been thinking of something else. He shook his head. Never think of something else, *hombre*, or you get in trouble.

He fished out a folded sheet of cigarette paper from his shirt pocket and dribbled sweet-smelling tobacco chips into it. He licked and rolled the paper and lit up. An aching spiral unwound in his chest and then softened and mellowed. No broken bones and not dead yet.

The little car rocked in the wind. He opened the door partway and then gave a more substantial shove, to the sound of metal straining against metal. With a loud pop, the door yielded. He swung his legs out. Then he reached out with his left hand and raised himself up out of the car and stood straight, pressing his gray felt hat firmly on his head. A car roared past, a hand raised in salute. Ignoring a new pain in his back, he bent over and pulled a rake out from behind the front seat.

He walked slowly over to the edge of the ditch, where the water flowed into a culvert beneath the Mott driveway. With his rake he flicked out a small willow branch pinned to the sharp edge of the culvert. He looked down into the smooth flow. There was something untrustworthy about the muddy brown water, or perhaps it was the wind that ruffled its surface. He wondered if he would have the strength to go back before dark to the diversion dam and crank down the headgate handle to reduce the flow overnight. The ditch tended to break within a few days of being reopened each spring. Less water in it would reduce the chances of a break during the night. The morning was turning out to be a hard one, with the wind and then all that *basura* blowing into the ditch.

He hobbled back to the car. The driver's door groaned and popped again as he opened it. Got to fix that, he used to tell himself every time he heard the noise. But now he said to himself, Never going to get that one fixed, I guess. He bent over and threaded the rake to its position behind the front seat. Then he climbed back inside behind the cracked black steering wheel and relit the stub end of his cigarette.

Through the smoke winding upward from the end of the cigarette, he followed in his mind the worm of brown water feeling its way down the sandy five-foot-wide channel, on the other side of the highway, along a fast-dropping stretch where nothing ever got dammed up. It would take him fifteen minutes to drive back to the house, change into fresh Levi's, look in on Ramoncita and have a word with Isabel Moro if she was there yet, drive back and catch up with the water, which by then would probably be back of Lalo Moro's house. The thought of doing all those little things wearied him. And so early in the day.

He puffed on the cigarette. There came a little burst of light-headed hope. He sighed, then coughed. No broken bones at least, and not dead yet, he said to himself, turning the key and starting the engine.

The road was clear. He pushed the blue plastic shift knob into first gear and swung around in a U-turn and headed back up to the house.

CHAPTER 6

Los Cristianos

Porter Clapp opened the front passenger door and stared at the dark spot the size of a dinner plate on the grimy brown weave of the plastic seat cover. The inside of the cavernous station wagon smelled of warm milk about to turn rancid, mixed with the odor of gas from the leaky carburetor. A cold wind chafed his lower back. The damp rag he had brought out from the house was turning icy. The morning breeze had become a gusty wind, and despite the clear sky the wind was cold, carrying hints of a distant snowstorm. He climbed inside, pulled the door closed, and perched on the edge of the seat, arching himself over the wet spot.

He scrubbed. This produced little result beyond spreading the milky area wider and mixing it with previously spilled and now congealed liquids. He knew he should have brought a sponge and a pail but something had hurried him along. The other thing, the water thing. The trick was to involve as many other people as possible. That way they wouldn't single him out. Time was ticking away, and here he was sitting in the front seat of his station wagon trying to clean up a mess. He saw what he had to do as a map on which he had far too many destinations to reach within too little time. He thought of

those miserable rainy days thirty years ago on his junior high
paper route. He felt short of breath, a tightening just below
the sternum. Go for a walk? But everybody had to be called.
He could hear them. He could count on the Vizarriagas only
sometimes. Porter, you can't do nothing against those people.
They're full-time. What are you and me? I'll tell you. We're
part-time. People don't care. They don't want to do nothing.

Porter had never succeeded in imagining the mechanics
of mopping up a mess. He tried to visualize the molecules of
milk and what in his actions was inducing them to depart from
the plastic weave of the seat into the increasingly gray rag he
was rubbing back and forth, which was leaving fuzz balls on
the seat. Was he not simply driving the offending molecules
deeper and deeper into the upholstery, into the foam rubber
padding beneath it?

They would be there in suits and ties. The Anglo lawyers,
maybe a Hispanic engineer, quick talking, quick to move
back and forth from English to Spanish, one of their own
people, one of their young successes, gold watch, dark suit,
winning public smile. They'd be sitting and standing behind
the cafeteria tables set up in the gym with its thick adobe walls
and sagging white sound-proofing ceiling panels, above which
pigeons would scratch and coo during the meeting. They'd
talk a smooth line. Nobody knows how much water anybody
has a right to, is this good? No, of course not. You all want to
know that, just like you want to know where your fence lines
are supposed to be. ¿Sí? Cierto. So to find out how much water
each and every one of you has a right to, we're going to start
by—

Porter looked at the rag. He unfolded it and refolded it.
All sides were equally gray. A sour odor filled the interior. His
fingers adhered to each other with a slight stickiness. He liked
being inside the car when he wasn't waiting for anything and
would be quite happy to spend the rest of the day sitting in

one seat and then another, looking out this window, then that. Steph wouldn't notice until about one in the afternoon. He stared down at the open toolbox on the floor in front of the passenger seat. Toolbox? What was it doing there? Krishna?

It came back to him. The left rear taillight, of course. He had noticed that it wasn't working when Steph last drove up the drive and stopped at the highway. He had got the toolbox out of the shed and then the phone had rung. Better do it now, he reasoned, before it all starts. Because later it would be that head-buzzing, dry-mouth state of too much talking, too many things to do, phone ringing all the time. Though there was something telling him that now wasn't really the best time to fix the taillight at all, that it was really the worst, that the only good reason for fixing it now was to be able to stop thinking about everything else. Still, if I get it done, then it will be done, right?

He leaned over and fished out the multi-point screwdriver and climbed out of the car into the sharp wind. Dust swirled around the driveway. But at least the rear of the car was in the warmth of the sun. He crouched down. Sure, do it. Get it done. The lens was held in place by two Phillips screws, which he quickly backed out. Some gentle prying released the flat red plastic lens without cracking it. So far, so good. Fine brown dust coated the silver plastic reflector, which he blew off. Now: getting the bulb out, he seemed to remember, was the tricky part. Counterclockwise, press in, or something like that. He pressed and turned. Nothing gave. He pressed harder and turned. There was a snap and a crunching sound and his fingers shot into a strange depth. For an instant he was afraid he had cut himself. But no, the bulb was intact, still between them, though blood was oozing out of a skinned thumb knuckle. He peered in. Something in the reflector or bulb holder had given way, and in the center of the reflector there was now a gaping hole that consumed his hand up to the wrist. He released the bulb. It dropped from view into the depths of the fender well behind the fixture.

His chest tightened. The tips of his fingers tingled in the cold, his ears flushed hot, then cold. An angry voice in his brain was shouting, What the hell are you doing this for? If it ain't broke don't fix it. A child whimpered back, But it was broken. He got down on his hands and knees and stuck an index finger into the jagged hole to try to snag the wires to the socket and bulb. But it wasn't long enough. He scanned the surface of the driveway, gravel set in hardened mud. Within reach lay a short length of bailing wire on the ground like a stiff dried worm. He bent an end into a hook. As he set about fishing for the electrical lines, the thought came to him that there might not be a replacement bulb in the toolbox. From the front of the car came a noise like the vigorous wadding up of newspapers. What?

He looked up. Tires were crunching on the driveway only feet away, the whoosh of an engine. Still on hands and knees he craned his neck. A flower of hope blossomed within his aching chest: was a friend coming to visit? But then a stab of fear. He had no friends. Or none who ever came to visit.

He climbed to his feet, brushing off his knees. He saw stars. A plump woman in a pink dress, smiling at him. And a taller fellow in a gray suit and blue tie. Both of them in their twenties. He sensed that the maroon sedan from which they had emerged was too new and shiny to belong to anybody he knew. The woman spoke in a baby-talk voice with a faint Chicano accent. Did he know these people? There was something familiar about them even within the relative formality of their dress. Apparently she was introducing herself. Porter stared back. Then the man spoke. A voice too quick and mechanical, eye contact too fixed and gleaming. Porter could feel something swelling up inside him. His face would be flushing red. He could hardly breathe. This was the moment. They had come for him. Was that why they seemed familiar? They had tracked him down. He had spent so many years imagining them that when they finally arrived, it was almost as if they were neighbors, familiar yet strange. CIA or FBI. Which? Should he bow his head and slowly raise his wrists, joining them together, to make it easier for them, as he had many times imagined?

The man stopped his patter and said in a high-pitched, sing-song voice, I forgot what I was saying.

Porter stared. Where were their guns? He felt his face twist up into a grimace. He thought: At this moment in my life? When I need a friend to come down the driveway and throw his arm around my shoulder and say that everything is going to be all right? To ask, how can I help? Now?

Porter blinked. Should he ask to call his lawyer, even though he didn't have a lawyer, even though he didn't know the name of a single lawyer anywhere? Would they let him thumb through the Yellow Pages?

The man stood immobile with mouth agape, hand clutching his tie. The woman in the tight pink dress gave an embarrassed downcast smile at her partner and then handed Porter a copy of a typed pamphlet with simple line drawings.

For your wife, she said, stepping back. Tell her we'll come back another time.

Porter looked down at the blotched cartoon-drawing cover, showing a man in jogging gear trotting blankly ahead, oblivious to cloud-like headlines inscribed above his head:

TIME IS RUNNING OUT. ETERNITY IS RUNNING IN.

CHAPTER 7

Jesus and the Dolphins

With her elbow, Glenda Louise Serrano nudged back down the front seat armrest, reestablishing a barrier between her and her cousin, Benny Serrano, who was behind the wheel.

I couldn't stand it the way he looked, Benny Serrano was saying. His hands clutched the steering wheel stiffly as he twisted his head around to see out the back window. That's the way the devil looks at you.

The Clapps' old powdery blue Chevy Carryall, a tall ungainly station wagon on a pickup chassis, dented and splashed with rust, was parked at an awkward angle, forcing Benny to back up the driveway without turning around, a tricky maneuver that meant you had to shoot up onto the highway rear end–first and hope that nobody was coming from either direction.

There was a murmur of assent from the backseat. The new couple in town, the Castanedas, were being shown the monthly route. They had just moved back to New Mexico from thirty-some years in a Utah mining town. They were originally from Los Martinez, up the road, but Mrs. Castaneda had inherited a piece of land from a brother in the southern end of San Marcos, which is where they had planted their new double-wide.

She's very nice, the wife, Glenda Louise Serrano chirped. She always talks to me a long time about God. Then she added, My *abuelos* are buried under their house.

Mrs. Castaneda clucked from the backseat, *¡No es verdad!*

Que sí.

Que sin vergüenza, those people.

Oh, they don't know. It's not their fault.

Benny tried to chase Porter Clapp's fixed stare from his mind. He could tell that Porter *knew*. Anybody who stared at him for more than a second *knew*. God *knew* all the details. He stood overhead with a stopwatch and note pad. For Benny, God was a big red-faced gringo basketball coach with a towel around his neck who shouted about how bad it was to play with yourself. But why did he spread rumors? Benny Serrano had joined the Cristianos to find help one way or another from his agonies. They had begun again after his wife had left him six months ago. He had hoped that riding around all day with his cousin Glenda Louise would keep him out of trouble, but she had only made it worse. The suit and the tie didn't help. They cinched him all up, giving him a nice, proper respectable appearance, but underneath nothing changed.

The trouble was that they were too closely related, daughter and son of two brothers. They had gone out a lot in high school but just to be together, not on dates, just to talk, not even holding hands except once, just before she told him she was joining those people who go around and pass out religious pamphlets all day long, and she'd said, Benny, why don't you put that crush you have on me, on Jesus instead?

But Benny thought that her getting religion in such a big way really showed how much she was attracted to him, and he listened to everything she had to say as if it were some elaborate excuse to keep her distance from him because she was afraid of what she really wanted. Glenda Louise told him that she believed that if only people would look long enough at the drawings of Jesus in the pamphlets or read the words over and over enough that they would come to believe, and when enough people believed, then there would be miracles all over the place. That not enough people believed, this explained everything to her. She had left the big national organization for the little local band of Los Cristianos because the national organization was only interested in money and they didn't really believe in anything else. She boasted that she had got five or six people to really believe in the last year, and one of those she claimed was Benny himself. The best thing that ever happened to you, she confided to him between stops the other day, was when that atheist wife of yours you never should have married in the first place finally walked out on you.

So here they were riding around with each other in the front seat together, just like old times five years ago when they'd just drive around for hours going out not on a date, they told everybody, but just to talk and spend time together in his father's Impala. For hours and hours driving around in the dark, hardly talking, not touching, trying to figure out how not to be first cousins. Then he'd go home and take a long shower and jerk off with God standing over him with a stop watch. Some things never change.

Benny didn't really believe, except in Glenda Louise. He was convinced that someday all her warm soft talk about Jesus and the next world was something that sooner or later she'd let drop away to reveal that all these years when she had been talking about Jesus she really meant him, Benny. He only wondered how much longer he would have to wait and how much longer his impatient body would have to seek frenzied substitutes instead of her ripe plumpness. He also wondered if everyone in both their families died whether that would mean that they were no longer first cousins.

So he'd roll down the window or put on the air conditioning on their monthly route through the valley, but then the old people in the backseat would complain and he'd have to turn it off, and then the car would get warm and stuffy again and he'd get drowsy and his little friend would start waking up and stretching its way down inside his boxers. Hey, stop it, man, stay in your little dog house. And Glenda Louise sitting right next to him, though she always put down the plush upholstered armrest first thing when she got in the car, and he'd slowly put it back up every time she got out first.

Benny squeezed the steering wheel and glanced in the three rearview mirrors, all of which were out of adjustment, and gunned his brother's brand new Chrysler sedan up the last and steepest part of the driveway. The car bounded on to the pavement with a screech.

Glenda Louise looked out the window and back down at the Clapp place, adding absently in the direction of the backseat, They were Methodists or something and they had to move out of town and so their little *camposanto* got neglected. Then somebody built a house on top of it. Can you believe it? She knew this was a simplification. The vision of pack horses and mules trampling their manure down into the ground above the graves had always horrified her.

Que bárbaro, Mrs. Castaneda muttered complacently from the backseat. She had heard worse, much worse. Those Catholics are terrible people. They're all going to go straight to Hell for things like that, she knew. She had in mind a particular coal mine shaft near Provo, Utah.

Up on the highway Benny adjusted the rearview mirror to the sounds of a roaring muffler and the hissing of air brakes to the rear. The grill of a Kenworth logging truck on which was affixed a naked woman in chrome, legs crossed, hand behind flowing curls, seemed about to come crashing through the trunk and rear window. He dropped the transmission lever into Drive and sped away to the sound of screeching tires. Pop a wheelie, he chuckled to himself. Down below the highway several San Marcos men looked up from their yard work, while inside their women turned down their TVs and pushed aside curtains and peered up at the highway. Foot to floor, Benny raced away from the semi and passed a half-dozen driveways and rounded the last sharp end before the center of the village, then slammed on the brakes and swung right, down a steep driveway over a culvert. He hoped they were out of sight of the surely enraged driver of the logging truck.

This is my father's uncle's place, he called back to the newcomers. One of the other reasons for joining the Cristianos was to have a reason to talk his older brother Manny into letting him drive Manny's newest car, currently the maroon Chrysler with plush seats and power everything.

No, corrected Glenda Louise, he sold it years ago to some Americanos. She felt the term Americano, which her grandfather used, was politer than *gabacho*, gringo, *güero*, *los de afuera*, hippie, or Anglo.

Tío Porfirio? No, when did he do a thing like that?

Long time ago, she said, when we were in high school. But what are we doing here? She unfolded a hand-drawn map in her lap. We're supposed to go to those other places back there first.

Benny had spent most of his childhood in Califa and had come back with his parents in time for high school, to find the village his parents remembered had changed in countless little ways. It still looks the same but somehow it's different, they were fond of saying. I guess things change. After high school he had gone to work in Albuquerque. Now he was back here on unemployment and disability for lifting too much furniture at Sears, and he was living in his parents' old house that his older brother Manny had bought from the rest of the family when his satellite dish business started taking off.

Their parents were now in Albuquerque living with their sister, who worked for an insurance agency. They all had terrible arguments every time Benny went into town. I don't believe in God, she would say, pacing around the crowded house, I believe in insurance. You should see the things that happen to people. The *viejitos*, sitting on the sofa staring at terrible things happening to people on TV all day long, they would pretend not to hear. Last time Benny blurted out, God helps me, you know, she shot back, Helps you how? Find a new girlfriend? Tell me, what's her name. Maybe you should hang on to her, Benny. She might be good for you. She must be better than that last one who ran off with your double-wide and all the major appliances. He had come home from work that day and there was nothing there but those cheap steps made out of wood and wrought iron left in front of where his PleasantCrest two-bedroom double-wide had been.

He was perspiring as the car bounced to a halt at the bottom of the driveway. A long arbor of some kind of woven net fabric was stretched over the patch of ground where Tío Porfirio had grown chile and corn and beans, to the east of the small upright stuccoed adobe painted yellow. Benny wondered whether the kitchen had been redone. There used to be a big black wood-fired cookstove with nickel trim and a hot water tank painted silver hooked up to it. The green diamond-pattern linoleum floor tilted slightly. The walls were painted a shiny green. He remembered that it smelled of beans and chile and bacon and some disinfectant. Lysol?

A man with mousy brown hair parted in the middle and silver-rimmed glasses emerged from the arbor pushing a wheelbarrow. He set it down and stepped over to the car before any of them could get out. Benny lowered the electric window.

At that moment a woman pushed open the screen door and called out, Len, phone.

The man smiled and turned away. As he trotted up to the house, a short woman stepped out from behind the screen door and walked down toward the car. She was carrying a bundle of papers.

Benny, whispered Glenda Louise just before the woman was upon them. We shouldn't come here. I forgot.

But it was too late. The Castanedas had emerged from the backseat. They looked very sleepy. Mrs. Castaneda smoothed down her skirt. Then the woman from the house was warmly pumping her hand, thrusting papers at her already, folders and pamphlets.

I'm Carrie Mott. How nice to meet you, Mrs. Castaneda. Do you know what dolphins are? she went on. Mrs. Castaneda nodded, smiling. Wonderful. The thing about them is that they're as intelligent as people. It's a crime what we humans are doing to them in oceans all over the world. They're God's beings as much as any of us.

Glenda Louise opened the door and climbed out. With his elbow Benny nudged the armrest up and pushed open the door. As he joined Glenda Louise and the rest of the group, he leaned over and whispered to his cousin, What's she talking about fish for?

Carrie Mott intercepted the remark with a beaming smile. I'm not talking about fish. They're mammals, breathing warm-blooded mammals. They have babies just like us. Christ particularly loved them.

The Castenadas flipped through the glossy full-color pamphlets as if searching for something. Benny chewed at his left cheek, mouth all twisted up. If He loved dolphins, why did He turn them into loaves—or tortillas, as he was supposed to say to the *viejitos*. Glenda Louise tried to remember how to divert the conversation back to the End of the World. But this woman talked too fast. They would be there for an hour.

Next would come the whales. Then the trees, those redwoods or whatever, which had feelings just like us. Then those owls. She was afraid of owls. She had dreams of them swooping down and tearing at her long black hair. She looked at her watch. This would cost them three or four other stops.

Carrie Mott had managed to unload all her literature into the Castanedas' hands. Glenda Louise broke in. We made a mistake. This is not our stop until next week. She thrust one of her pamphlets, suddenly cheap and flimsy looking, in Carrie's direction. Carrie took it, smiling broadly. Glenda Louise gave Benny a piercing look and opened the back door for the Castanedas and quickly climbed in the front seat.

As Benny started the car, she could hear the Castanedas in the backseat bending over to gather up the pamphlets they had spilled on the floor. The armrest was up again. She slammed it down.

CHAPTER 8

Ranch Spanish

Mrs. Morales began each late morning bilingual session with the following statement in what she was quite certain was flawless Castilian pronunciation with thickly lisped *s*'s: *He pasado tiempo en España hace muchos años.* Please repeat after me. *Todos juntos.* With Mrs. Morales exaggeratingly mouthing the syllables, the sixth-grade class would shout out the words, inflating the *s*'s into great windy gusts of *th*'s, *He pathado tiempo en Ethpan-ya hathe muchoth an-yoth-th-th,* so loudly that the five other classes in the knoll-top adobe school building would pause in their work while their own class clowns set about huffing and puffing with tongues between teeth. And when the other teachers went Shhh! even the most timid youngsters would respond with a loud Thhh! The ruckus from Mrs. Morales's room also meant that the lunch bell was only twenty minutes away.

The schoolhouse was a long rectangular adobe spanned by fat thirty-five-foot-long vigas of a size that had long vanished from the forests twenty miles west of San Marcos. The flimsy walls that partitioned the building into six rooms and a small office reception area and a teachers' lounge did not reach to the ancient ceiling. As a result, class deliberations were never very private. When the wind was blowing, as it was this morning, windows rattled and doors slammed closed, and the pigeons that lived in the ceiling were especially restless, cooing and scratching and flying on wheezing wings in and out of the space between the ceiling and the roof, through holes that the principal, Mr. Molinas, had long ago given up trying to plug. Mr. Molinas, who had respiratory problems, wore a dust mask on windy days during those hours in his office he could count on being alone. At last count, ninety-three pigeons lived above the ceiling, and one afternoon he calculated that over the past ninety years they and their ancestors had deposited some four tons of droppings in the ceiling space. Sooner or later, like the straw that broke the camel's back, the whole thing would come down in a great dusty crash. His calculations suggested that this apocalyptic event would take place three years after he retired, so at least he would be spared. The adjoining gym, a somewhat newer structure, was another matter. Sixty-eight pigeons and a flimsy ceiling of something called Celotex, a sort of pressed sawdust, could bring the whole thing down tomorrow. An adjacent modular building, pigeonless, housed kindergarten and grades one and two; it had been added a year ago when the district junior high down river had burned down and seventh and eighth grades were moved into the main adobe school building.

On windy days the sixty-some San Marcos and Los Martinez children in attendance usually behaved like the wind itself: unpredictable, frisky, and often mean to each other and wildly joyful at the same time. Mrs. Morales hated windy days, because they made her already thankless task even more difficult. She had spent two nights in Madrid thirty years before, on a return flight from Greece, where she had been summoned to deal with the death of a brother stationed at an Air Force base near Athens. One Monday a student had asked,

In those days did the planes still have propellers? The hideous reality of her two nights in Madrid, when she was coming down with a cold and where the hotel staff had expressed scornful amazement at her quaint archaic New Mexican Spanish, and where by the end of the first morning she had given up speaking Spanish altogether, had stayed with her for many years, but the passage of time had softened the rough edges of that terrible visit, casting an increasingly warm glow over those forty-three hours on actual Spanish soil—or concrete pavement, cobblestones, asphalt. In time she came to realize that she had heard with her own ears the mother tongue spoken by real Castilians. She strained to remember those sounds that had at first puzzled and then frightened her and then made her deeply ashamed. Such delicate consonants, such finely measured vowels, and so many more tenses than the cramped, degraded San Marcos Spanish, which seemed by comparison like the language of people who had had to burn all their furniture to stay warm during a bad winter or who had thrown all but the bare necessities overboard in order to keep their leaky boat afloat. The pure Castilian of Spain was a language in which every single thing had its own special word and where English words were chased out of the language with the banging of pots and pans and hoots of derision, where consonants were not allowed to sputter and spit, and vowels were prevented from loitering and dawdling, and where each phrase and sentence shot to its destination like an arrow tipped with steel. She loved the saying of the Spanish king, though wasn't certain how it went in Spanish: I speak to my lover in French, to my servant in German, to my horse in English, but to my God I speak Spanish—meaning *Castellano*, she always added, and not that terrible lingo Spanish of this place, let me tell you that.

For her weekly bilingual session for the combined fifth and sixth grades Mrs. Morales, who dyed her hair orange, stuck a large Spanish-looking comb she had got at Walgreen's in Albuquerque into the bun atop her head, and draped over her shoulders her mantilla, a lacy black shawl from Walmart in Las Cruces, with which she alternatively covered and exposed the remarkable cleavage her satiny black dress framed in a tight yet plunging V. Mr. Morales himself had picked the wrap-around dress out of a catalog for oversized women he said some customer had left in the trash at the post office. The fifth- and sixth-grade boys were avid observers of her cleavage, crowding into the front rows. Mrs. V-for-Victory, they whispered to each other, here it comes.

This spring Mrs. Morales had instituted a new project in which she required her nine eighth-grade pupils, the Hispanos, not the two gringos, to bring from home each week words in the local San Marcos dialect, each one to be written on a separate scrap of paper. These she collected at the beginning of the too-short period and would write on the board, that is the ones that were not PG or R, and then with a great chalk-snapping slash she would cross them out and write next to them the modern Castilian equivalent. She would then crumple up the offending word and drop it into the hole of a cardboard box covered with white paper on which she'd lettered *BASURA*.

She was discovering, however, that the exercise was somehow flawed. This lot of kids hardly knew any Spanish at all, or pretended they didn't know any, even though she often heard them out in the hall or on the playground shouting the most awful epithets at each other, like *pendejo* or *coño* or *puta*, or else they didn't know what words were special to San Marcos, the ones that above all needed to be extirpated, and which ones were to be treasured as pure Castilian. She was thinking of adding a second box to put on the opposite side of the *BASURA* box, lettering it *ORO*.

The too-bright Salcedo boy shot up his hand. His friends called him Streak or Streaks, she didn't know why.

Put this word in *el dompe* box, Mrs. Morales.

¿El dompe? ¡Sagrada familia! How do you say "dump" *en castellano, niños?*

There was the usual yawning silence. Somewhere within the clutch of hunched over, sprawled out, droopy-eyed children, a faint voice uttered, *El dompe*, I guess, *qué no?*

Mrs. Morales flicked back her shawl, exposing her cleavage. A silly question, she realized. She herself had no idea of what *el dompe* was in real Spanish. She would have to go home and look it up. Then this Anglo kid, who everyone called Snowman at school, raised his hand.

It says here in my dictionary, bass-bass-your-all, or something like that.

Démelo, por favor, she said, reaching across the heads of the students in front of Krishna, twisting her hand impatiently, fingers spread wide to show off the four large costume rings that crowded her fingers, and her long nails freshly painted in Ecstasy Peach. She brought her reading glasses down over her nose and inspected the entry in the frayed, yellowed, coverless paperback.

We have to be careful. That could be Mexican Spanish, not *Castellano*. *Basural*, it says. Dump.

She scrawled on the blackboard the word *dompe* and then lavishly crossed it out, writing *basural* next to it. A piece of chalk snapped off and spun away over her head.

She put the dictionary down on her desk. *Muchachos*, she began, pulling the shawl tightly across her projecting bosom, what you need to understand is that the so-called Spanish you speak at home, it is not good. It is bad Spanish. Pure and simple. I cannot even bear to call it Spanish, this lingo of yours. It is so bad it is like . . . Here she groped for words, wondering whether the comparison might somehow be not quite fit for the tender minds of her eighth graders. It's like the words have got cancer. The *lenguaje*, it's rotting away, sick to death, with these bad pronunciations and terrible words.

A few heads were looking up. She was encouraged. This *vocabulario* that you hear at home, with *dompe* and *trocka* instead of *camion* and *estafeta* instead of *correo*, what do you expect? They're rotting away. They're smelling. One of the boys whistled softly. There was a snort. Did somebody whisper, Way to go? Maybe she had better stop.

Órale, niños, mi hermana in Califa, I mean California, she lives in California, in a nice suburb with a swimming pool, you know what she says you talk? She rearranged her shawl. She says what you talk back here is *puro* ranch Spanish, not the real thing at all. Ranch Spanish. You hear that?

The bell rang. The echo of her last words was drowned out by desktops opening and closing. She wasn't quite sure whether she heard right when the Salcedo kid yelled at the Quintana boy across the room, but it sounded like, Mrs. Morales, we don't speak ranch Spanish around here, what we speak is Thousand Island. There were peals of laughter as they crowded out the door.

Hablas Thousand Island, bro?

No, hablo solamente ranch.

The Clapp boy was standing unusually close to her, inspecting her cleavage, which he towered over.

Can I have my dictionary back, Mrs. Morales?

CHAPTER 9

Pistol, Pruning Shears

While putting on his last pair of clean Levi's, Lázaro Quintana remembered the bridge. It was a small wooden bridge, just wide enough for a tractor, which led across the acequia from the fields to the west to the rocky slopes to the east where people used to drive wagons and later tractors up into the hills to cut juniper for fenceposts and piñon for firewood. The log and plank structure had settled over the years, and deposits of silt and gravel had raised the ditch bed. In any case, when the water finally got there it would wash against the underside of the sagging logs.

The bridge was a cramp in Lázaro's right calf that had grabbed him sharply last night in bed. After he finally quieted the spasm and turned on the light to look at the clock, which said three a.m., he lay back and saw it all again, under the milky sky of last Tuesday afternoon. The old *puentacita* with its rotting planks, the barbed wire gate overgrown with gray strands of Virginia creeper not yet in leaf, the windless sky fast losing its blue. And the dark shapes of the low green juniper trees up on the gravelly hills, which always invited him to put aside his shovel and climb up and lie down in their dusty fragrant shade and gaze out across the valley, which he hadn't done since he was a boy. And then there they were, the two *muchachos*, the troublemakers standing there, and the black shape of a small pistol gripped in an outstretched hand.

They had not seen him bend down and crawl beneath the rusty barbed wire, where he had inspected the bridge while kneeling, noting how low its logs had sunk down into the channel. Then he had stood up, knees aching. The scene was at first puzzling. He had been warned by the grumbling of the work crew that something was up. Then the two troublemakers had held back, becoming separated from the others. Putting the spring cleaning crew in charge of his *ayudante*, Lázaro had backtracked along the ditch to find them.

The two youths stood facing each other. Benji Guerrero was holding upraised a pair of long-handled pruning shears, one of whose wooden handles had apparently come apart or broken off. The other kid, Leandro Salcedo, the one with the gun, had his back toward Lázaro. He had showed up for work in the morning with beer on his breath and circles under his eyes, his sullenness silencing the early-morning wisecracking.

Lázaro called out, *¡Basta, jóvenes!*

The two turned toward him. Their eyes locked briefly on his. The gun slipped away into a pocket of the leather jacket Leandro Salcedo had carried with him all afternoon despite the warmth of the day, and in one of those other zippered pockets there was probably a pint of Four Roses. Eyes cast rigidly down, the two young men walked past Lázaro to join the others, both panting faintly, with a hiss of rubbed denim, boots creaking. Lázaro's dulled nose scented their acrid sweat. A chill ran down his spine.

Nothing else happened. But the incident opened up searing memories of shootings and knifings and killings that passed beyond even the memory of Lázaro's own father. There were those at the cantina before it finally burned down last year, and on the highway at night, at the old dance hall up in Los

Martinez, in the plaza, and on the ditch banks, one every three or four years, generation after generation. He didn't know how close Leandro Salcedo had been to shooting Benji Guerrero. Hey, man, pull the trigger, see what happens next. There were always fights. But if somebody had a gun or a knife, then somebody got shot or got stuck in the ribs. *Con armas*, that's the way it's going to happen, *siempre*. Guns. *Que bárbaro*.

He peered through the screen door at the little red car out in front, rake handle sticking out of its rear quarter window. He checked all the buttons on his Levi's and patted himself to make sure wallet, change, keys, and comb were all in the right pockets. The jeans felt fresh and stiff. They would hold him up and keep him going no matter how tired he was. He pressed his gray felt hat firmly on to his head.

Forget about that, he said to himself as he headed out the front door toward the rusty Nissan. Forget about those old things. This acequia is giving me too much aches and pains.

Una hora, maybe *dos*, he called back toward the bedroom where Ramoncita lay.

He listened absently for her Don't be too long, but the only reply that came from the small adobe house was the shot-like report of the screen door slamming.

CHAPTER 10

Money Growing on Trees

The discreet, almost camouflaged brown-and-green sign reading "Trees & Trees Landscaping" was more for the benefit of those from afar who had been given directions to the Mott place than to attract business from San Marcos or Los Martinez or the other villages farther north along the county road. Len and Carrie Mott had bought the old ten-acre Serrano place a few years before when land prices were still relatively low, as a way to expand their nursery and landscaping business without going as deeply into debt as they would have had they bought a place close in to Santa Fe, which was the source of most of their landscaping contracts. The far-flung branches of the Serrano clan had finally agreed to sell the property when the death of the last brother, the caretaker of the place, precipitated a financial crisis after none of the survivors was willing to come back from California or Utah to take care of the place. Part of the ritual of establishing a relationship with a new client, or renewing an old one, was for the Motts to invite them out to the country, to their place in San Marcos, to inspect the prospective shrubs and trees and perennial beds for front and back yards.

Invited prospects arrived at the rate of one or two a week, finding their way at the appointed hour down the steep drive to the small nursery and display gardens of raised beds and flagstone walks and rock gardens, which were small versions of the ideas the Motts could execute in much grander dimensions. Perhaps one out of three or four such visits would result in a contract that could keep the Motts going for anywhere from a week to months.

Most San Marcos residents didn't understand this kind of business, and when they saw the Trees & Trees Landscaping sign first appear somewhat furtively planted in a thicket of wild plum bordering the top of the driveway, they were both curious and suspicious. After several years the Motts had become used to unannounced visits at odd hours by their neighbors, either too early in the morning or too late in the afternoon. Their typical visitor was a Hispanic man in his late fifties or early sixties, sometimes a couple, who would quickly walk through the nursery with a frown, picking at leaves, shaking heads at price tags, and saying things like, We used to dig those out down by the river for nothing, or, They say money doesn't grow on trees, you know, but maybe you've got that figured out, eh?

Len and Carrie had long ago decided that these visits were probably not about shopping for trees and shrubs so much as about estimating whether these new gringos were going to fit into the community or move on after a couple of years when they became bored with the place, as a few had in the past. The Motts had become experts in guiding conversations away from the nursery business to local lore and family relationships, children, grandchildren, neighbors and feuds. With religious and political proselytizers, who called in at least once a month, and more often just before elections, Carrie had taken to trumping them with environmental pamphlets and related petitions, enabling Len to keep going about his work in the nursery. On the morning of the visit of the Cristianos, he was pleased to be called out of the wind to the phone just as they arrived.

You saved me from the Cristianos, he spoke into the receiver as he sat down at the kitchen table, embraced by the steaming warmth of the room.

Porter Clapp was on the other end. He said, What? But they were just here.

At your place?

Two minutes ago.

Why did you send them to me?

What?

Len had befriended Porter not long after moving to San Marcos, and then the two couples had become close, the Motts and the Clapps, which sounded vaguely comical. The first labor of friendship had been to guide Porter out of a so-called business relationship with Boots Clippenger. Porter and Clippenger had a combined interest in what they called the Plantation, down in a southern New Mexico county known for its fulminations against any kind of federal regulation. Through excessive investment in drip irrigation, plastic pipe, well pumps, caves, and grow lights, all charged to credit cards, the Plantation had possibly become one of the few money-losing dope-growing operations in the country. The situation got worse when much of the equipment was "seized" in what turned out to be a bogus nighttime raid by rival growers dressed up in rented uniforms and with flashing lights on the roofs of their old pickups. Clippenger had promised Porter a share in the profits in exchange for his labor during three- and four-day stays every two weeks, but fortunately Clippenger hadn't been clever enough to pin an equivalent share of the large losses on Porter. The relationship had come to an end. That was three years ago.

Now Porter was carrying on about a water notice he had seen at Moro Mercantile earlier in the morning, about a meeting to be held tonight by the State Water Office in the school gym. Len could hear him becoming overexcited, arabesques of alarm and indignation spiraling up out of Porter's hunched-over form—or the form Len imagined to be hunched over, sitting on that sagging living room couch of theirs that gave everybody a backache after five minutes. Porter was reaching into his storehouse of apocalyptic words for terms like *hamstrung* and *death blow*.

Wait a minute, Porter, Len said, knowing that in calming down Porter he might also soothe that part of himself prone to such panics. Then he insisted. Porter, stop. This is a long, long process. It goes on for years. Once started, it is apparently unstoppable. But appeals and more appeals drag on for decades. By forces greater than us, something has apparently been started. But what is in our favor is that once started, nobody seems ever able to quite finish the process. So the trick is to keep everybody well informed, united, and calm for the next twenty years. It's that simple.

How reasonable he sounded to himself. And perhaps how wrong.

A slightly hysterical giggle came over the line. Twenty years?

Maybe more. Look at that water adjudication going on down near Santa Fe, now the longest suit on the federal docket. The point is, I think, to go to the meeting pretending you are completely ignorant and to sop up as much information as you can. For the moment, be the little willow that bends in the wind.

An unfortunate choice of words, Len realized, peering out the kitchen window at the flapping black netting on poles that shaded some of his trees and shrubs. The wind was settling into a late morning blow. He would have to finish going around the place and righting blown-over pots and anchoring them down. He hoped the netting would last one more season.

So do nothing?

Such has always been the wisdom of the great wise men, including most of the old Chicano guys in the valley, Len said happily, pleased that Porter had for once actually heard what he had said. Wait and see should be your motto.

Wait and see? Even when somebody is trying to take away your water?

No, Len said. Perhaps truly wise men never have anything to do with water in the first place, especially around here.

Advice I myself long ago should have heeded, Len added to himself.

At that moment a gust of wind whirled sand and dead leaves and a tumbleweed across the driveway. The maroon car was gone. Len Mott watched the netting billow up and strain against the ropes. He expected to see it rip loose. It held distended against the sky for a moment. Then the wind dropped. Nothing had given. He could hear Carrie stamping her feet on the mat outside the back door.

Gotta go. Gotta lash down the decks.

CHAPTER 11

Call Zip Zepeda

Zip Zepeda Jr., Zippy or Zipper or Zippers to his friends, sat in the front seat eating a tortilla rolled around two slices of baloney and a smear of green chile that his mother had fixed for him early that morning, when it had become clear that the family business was going to need his help and he would have to miss school. I can handle two in a day, his father had too often said, pointing a nicotine-stained finger at his son's chest, but when it gets to three or four, then I got to have you too.

I need to get back by five to take a shower, Zippy retorted this time. It's my first date with her. His father had snorted.

Zip was a skinny sixteen-year-old with lank black hair and a sallow complexion and dark rings under his eyes. The black suit he'd been given for the work was a size too large, in the expectation that he would fill out into its bagginess, as was the white shirt, whose collar could be closed around his long neck only with bunchings up to either side of the metallic blue tie upon which was painted a rainbow trout being lifted out of the water by a taut line and arching pole.

He was eating his lunch seated at the steering wheel while waiting for his uncle Rudy to show up to give him a hand. Zippy had been sent to Los Martinez to pick up old Eugenia Pomona, but the competition had got there first because of some argument in the family. He got there too late, and they had already whisked her away. He knew his father would carry on about it all through dinner, never taking off his dark glasses in their heavy gold frames. What do you think I spend all that money on advertising those three words for, Call Zip Zepeda? Because I want to convey the impression we're finally going to get around to picking up your loved one next week or next month? Zip means fast. Now what did you do, pull over and have a nap on the way?

So Zip Jr. had telephoned back to Santa Fe to ask what to do, and his mother had told him to come back by way of San Marcos and pick up Abundio Moro, he was finally dead, the old man.

What, again? I been there five times already.

Actually, only once, but he still remembered where it was, at the Los Martinez end of the San Marcos Valley, the old guy who lived in a cave dug out of the red clay hillside with the front mortared up in black stones and a small low door and a single, dirty four-paned window, not far from a fancy adobe with tile roofs and bars on the windows. Just like the last time, he drove the Cadillac Fleetwood hearse up to the front of the cave and lowered the electric window. His mother had told him to wait for his uncle Rudy to arrive to help him out.

You're sure he's dead this time?

Of course I'm sure. They just called. He's dead, Zippy's mother protested.

Last time he was with his father. He still broke into a sweat at the recollection of how they had driven up to this same spot and his father had honked the horn, and then after about five minutes the door to the cave rattled for a long time and then slowly opened, and there came out this old guy bent over double with age and with a drooping black suit coat hanging from his bones and an aluminum walker that looked like it had been run over once or twice. That was when Zip Jr. was still riding with his father, just before he got his license.

¿Qué húbole, Mr. Moro, how you doing, *cómo estamos?* his father had called out the open window.

It took a while for the old man to clear his throat. Zippy had seen a lot of old dead people but he had never seen one who looked as old as this one, who actually looked pretty dead too. His father had told him that Abundio Moro was the oldest person alive that he knew about between Los Martinez and Santa Fe, maybe a hundred and twenty. He was so old that he had never had to learn English. Zip Zepeda's grandfather had sold him a complete funeral contract sixty years ago. We're going to lose money on this one, I tell you.

The old man spat. He wiped his lips with a black sleeve. *¿Quién es?*

Zepeda, his father bellowed out the window.

The old man twisted up his eyes toward the sky. *Ya no estoy listo.*

The father turned to the son. He says he isn't ready. Should I tell him we can wait? he added with a cackle before turning back to the open wind. *No te apures, viejito.*

Ya mero, the old man called back with his hand lifted a couple of inches in what perhaps was a wave.

That had been a year ago. Now the door remained shut. A stout woman in a flowery apron was walking over to the hearse from the large white house across the dirt road. Zippy opened the door and got out.

He passed away some time this morning, I don't know, she said. I was just about to call somebody. She waved back at the house. Isabel Moro, you know who she is? He nodded no. Mrs. Moro who owns Moro Mercantile, she brought him some food to eat this morning and said he was still asleep and that maybe I should look in on him later this morning, which

I did. She waved back down the valley toward the village of San Marcos. He's not related to anybody anymore, not any of the other Moros. They all died. He didn't even speak English.

Could I use your phone?

Long distance or local?

Eight hundred number.

Oh sure, come on over.

She wore heel-less house slippers. He followed her across the dirt road and inside her house, which was all Mexican tile and vigas so shiny with varnish that they looked like they had just been washed, and black knobby furniture with lots of red leather, from what he could see from the glaring white kitchen where the wall phone was. His mother told him she didn't know what was holding Tío Rudy up but he should be there soon to help get the old man into the hearse, in about half an hour, she thought.

But you said he was going to be here when I got here. He hung up without waiting for an answer.

He thanked the woman and went back to the hearse to eat his lunch and think about the new girl in class, Patsy, a *gringa*, who had surprised him by saying yes, she'd go out with him but not too late. She was tall, blond, and skinny like him. Where? she wanted to know. She was so new in class that maybe the others hadn't got to her and told her, You know, you're going out with the undertaker's son. Yuck.

Colonel Sanders or McDonald's? You pick.

Is there a Pizza Hut here?

Sure, lots.

But he had to figure out what to say when she asked, like they all asked, as if they didn't know, So what does your dad do? He knew he couldn't say like his mother told him, Just tell them that we're in the bereavement business. What if he told the truth? Maybe she'd get off on it. Yeah, I'm really into death myself, Zippy could hear her say. Then she would say, What's it really like?

But then what would he say? He finished the last of his bologna tortilla. He reopened the paper sack. Inside there were some biscochitos wrapped in waxed paper and an orange.

Oh, you know, you get used to it, he could hear himself say. Or maybe he would say, I hate it. I really hate it. I don't think I ever want to see another dead body as long as I live.

Zippy bit into a biscochito. He wasn't sure. Maybe it would kind of depend on what she said.

I guess we're all going to die, sooner or later, maybe she would say.

Yeah, I guess so, he should say, I guess we're all going to die. He knew he definitely shouldn't say, Call Zip Zepeda, which she had probably already seen in the papers and maybe even heard on the radio. Maybe that's when he should lean over and draw her near and pucker up his lips.

Call Zip Zepeda. Shut up, he snapped at the phrase rattling around in his head.

CHAPTER 12

Spilt Milk Again

Stephanie Wachler swung open the refrigerator door. On the top shelf a half-gallon milk carton listed to one side on a saucer. The saucer was filled with milk and dripping onto the lower shelves and collecting a pool atop the cracked plastic vegetable crisper, the milk working its way through the cracks to drip onto the fresh head of lettuce she had paid far too much for on her last visit to Santa Fe. Her temples throbbed. The wind was making the back door rattle. She inflated her cheeks and released a hissing sound—at all of them, at Porter for having bought a damaged carton of milk, at Onésimo Moro for having sold the milk to Porter, at the faceless chain of men in their trucks who had brought the carton to San Marcos from God knows where, slamming the fragile container against floors and walls so it would reach her tired old Kelvinator in the weakest possible condition.

Porter had taken over her place on the couch. He was talking on the phone. His hands were shaking. His right hand was bleeding at the knuckle. She didn't have the energy to ask him what he had done to his hand or who had come down the drive a few minutes before.

She pulled a plastic shopping bag from a drawer and inspected it for holes. And holes it had, of the sort to keep small children from suffocating and perhaps even mature healthy adults who had simply had enough, like right now, this very minute. She pulled out another. The same. Then she unrolled a new bag of clear plastic, re-opened the refrigerator and slid out the saucer and carton. An arc of white drips made a trail across the linoleum to the sink counter, where she slipped the carton into the bag. More milk on her hands and down her jeans. Then she emptied the saucer into the bag on top of the carton, closed it with a twistie. The carton swam in its own white effluvia. She snaked it into a plastic shopping bag.

Porter was talking to Len Mott. She could tell. They could carry on for hours, those two, about how the country and the world were slipping into the abyss. Those were the large sweeping conversations in which countries and continents were flung about in a loud but-first-let-me-finish voice. They discussed local topics in a lower tone, almost a hush, as if the neighbors might overhear. This was a local one, the same conversation he had tried to have with her half an hour ago. She thought she heard the words that always made her want to leave the house, *water rights*, and that always led to a conversation about how the government was going to come and take away everybody's irrigation water and charge them for the favor, which meant she wouldn't be able to plant her melon patch next year or the year after next or maybe it was twenty years from now. She could never understand how the government people could come and physically take away the water. In what, tanker trucks? An ugly black pipe? Even though she had asked Porter about this a half dozen times. The little stream that meandered around sandbars along the north side of the narrow valley didn't have enough water most of the time to fill the valley's two community irrigation ditches completely full, so how could anybody else take anything at all? Each time, Porter had given a longer and more complex answer. The trouble was that lately she couldn't bear to listen to him. Her mind wandered. She began thinking of other things. Money. The kids. Once, while he droned on, she remembered a dream of bare-breasted women in bright blue shawls standing in the dusty post office parking lot, dark faces turned toward the sky, mouths wide open, all waiting for rain. Later she thought that if you were really thirsty that was the last thing you would want to do, stand in the hot sun with your mouth wide open.

From the direction of the couch she thought she heard the murmured words, It will be the death blow . . . , as she slipped out the front door. Death blow? This place is already dead. She pictured a white rabbit her father had once killed with a karate chop to the back of the head.

From her right hand swung the plastic shopping bag, milk carton safely enclosed in yet another layer of plastic. Or so she hoped. She held it up to see if there were any drips. None.

The toolbox, open, sat on the ground behind the station wagon. The tail light red lens cover was off, also lying on the ground and cupping four screws and rocking back and forth in the wind. There were smears of blood on the rusty white bumper below the taillight. She wondered whether she should go back inside and ask him if it was all right to drive it. No, she decided. If it breaks down, so what? She climbed inside and started the engine.

She could see herself circling Onésimo's gas pumps in low gear, holding the carton out the window and emptying its contents onto the dusty parking lot. No, she would have to go inside and have words with him. She would begin, "I'm sick and tired . . ."

No. She'd have to begin more inventively. He had probably heard "sick and tired" too many times by now. Even if she was actually sick and tired this actual minute, probably developing a brain tumor.

Onésimo, it's a real asshole thing to do. . . . But that would depend on who else was in the store.

She guided the wallowing station wagon up the steep drive, steering with one hand while the other steadied the carton. The car stank of fresh kid vomit.

As she turned onto the highway, a little red car passed by going the other way. She saw an index finger raised in salute, the blur of a hat pulled low, a wooden handle sticking out of a side window. That would be Lázaro Quintana, she thought, the mayordomo. Perhaps he'd finally put water in the ditch. She'd forgotten to look. Her peas were now a week late getting in the ground because she'd been waiting for the water, held up by some internal dispute on the ditch.

She had only a minute or two to figure out what to say before she reached the store. Maybe she would just set the carton down on the counter and let Onésimo figure it all out, and not budge until he had replaced it with an intact carton with an expiration date well into the future. Maybe she should try to be polite. Reasonable. Understanding. Running a store is such a hard business, being here twelve hours a day, six days a week. But, Onésimo, you're not giving this stuff away. We pay for it. The customer is always right, fucking right. She could hear him weaseling out. Not my customers, he would say, to be perfectly honest. She could hear Isabel Moro calling down from that hole in the ceiling, You want to know the truth, Mrs. Clapp? The truth is that our customers are the scum of the earth. Stephanie had given up trying to tell them she wasn't Mrs. Clapp. If they wanted to be fancy, she was Ms. Wachler, thank you very much.

She pulled into the unpaved parking area, a blunt finger of reddish earth spotted with islands of muddy gravel that stuck out into the crook of the elbow of the hairpin turn that

marked the center of the village, a deformation of the winding highway route that was the outcome of an ancient feud
between the Moros and the now extinct Robles. She shut off
the engine and twisted the rearview mirror to look at herself.
A watery blue eye stared back. How could she forget? This
was not her day. Every now and then something in the air
made her sag and droop and her eyes and nose run and gave
her a headache and puffed up bags under her eyes. Her head
throbbed dully. A curtain of dust scampered past the nose of
the car. This was one of those days. Her period must be on the
way. When was the last one?

She climbed out. A metallic blue hearse purred around
the hairpin turn, its chrome hubcaps gleaming in the sun.
That's what I need, she thought. A mere boy was slouched
behind the wheel. Three other cars were parked at odd angles
on the narrow space. She would not be alone with Onésimo.
She went around to the other side of the car and opened the
passenger door and lifted out the bag. A handle abruptly gave.
A slithering, ripping sound, then a splat. She jumped back.
The carton lay in the reddish dirt, now quite broken open, its
contents fanning out and darkening the mud. She bent over.
I simply cannot believe this.

From the doorway there came a piercing wolf whistle.
She wouldn't look. That would be Lucido, over-medicated or
under-medicated as usual, who whistled at every woman who
walked in and out of the store, sometimes right in your ear, so
loud once her right ear had not stopped ringing for an hour
afterward.

She snaked the carton back into the shopping bag with its
one good handle and strode across the parking lot, trailing a
stream of drips. She glared at Lucido, who was standing at
attention next to the door, a dirty American flag draped over
his shoulders, a corner of its material elegantly flowing from
his mouth. She pushed open the chattering door and pushed

it closed with her right foot, holding the dripping bag out far from her side.

She flushed as she realized she would have to wait her turn. That kid who had already been in jail a couple of times was standing at the counter.

Those pruning shears I bought last week, they're no good. I want a credit.

Onésimo Moro stared across the counter at Benji Guerrero's puffy reddened face. The dark prickles of a two-day growth of beard ringed his mouth. His breath stank of sweet wine. His stare was fixed and angry. Young punk, Onésimo thought. The family had been on food stamps since the days of Coronado. He pursed his lips and calculated the damage Benji was likely to wreak on the store if refused. His mother owed a hundred and seventy-five dollars on her account, the limit, plus another fifty his grandfather had run up the week before he died.

Where are they? Onésimo demanded.

At home, broken, like I told you.

I can't just give you a credit like that. Maybe you ran over them. Where's your receipt?

I got to go to town, I told you.

The floorboards above Onésimo's head stopped creaking. Isabel had thrown herself in a rage over his failure to dun Porter Clapp and had set about pacing back and forth. Most of their customers were used to her muffled shouts through the ceiling when she was in such moods. But suddenly she was quiet again. Onésimo turned. There was Stephanie Clapp standing next to Benji. He hadn't noticed her coming in. He turned back to Benji.

I'll give you a credit to pay down your mom's bill but I won't give you any gas until I see those clippers. Bring them in. Go home and bring them in and then maybe I'll give you some gas and you can go to town and spend money there in Walmart you should be paying off your mom's bill with, OK?

Benji turned and slouched out the door. In the moment before it chattered closed, Onésimo heard the gasp of a car tire hitting the pothole at the sharpest point of the bend, meaning either a newcomer or old Mrs. Vizarriaga was driving past. He craned his neck in time to see a big state sedan, silver-gray, negotiate the curve. Some government bigwig burning up tax money. Maybe it was that young fellow from this morning.

Stephanie stood opposite him holding up a mud-smeared plastic sack in which was encased a split-open half-gallon carton of milk inside a second clear plastic sack, with a residue dribbling out of the torn corner of the bag on to the counter. There was a nasty gleam in her blue eyes. Her chin was thrust forward.

Refund, Onésimo. It came this way, she said, leaning over the counter and tossing the sack past him into the trashcan he kept next to the wall. A trail of white drips marked the trajectory. Slowly he bent down and reached into the box under the cash register where he kept a large rag for emergencies. He wondered. Came that way? Sure, maybe it had a little leak, but it wasn't like that, all squashed and muddy. But he decided it would be safer not to get into an argument about the carton.

Why don't I just give you a credit for it, he said with unexpected pleasantness as he wiped off the linoleum counter.

A credit?

On your bill. You have a bill, don't you? he asked with feigned innocence.

Not that I know of.

Yeah, I think you do. He nodded toward the ceiling. I think it was Porter. He bought lots of gas that week when you were helping the Clippengers out, long time ago. Maybe he forgot.

Isabel Moro's scratchy voice called down through the hole. He forgot, Mrs. Clapp, and then he forgot again. Then he forgot some more. Sixty-three dollars and fifty-one cents is what he forgot.

Fuck, Steph said to herself. Yeah, she said, head turned up toward the ceiling. Yeah, he forgets all the time. She swept out the door past Lucido. Like some ill-mannered bird, he whistled loudly, but only after she was halfway to the car. She answered with a loud slam of the car door. Out of the corner of her eye, the dark spot on the dirt told her that she had only done half of the errand. She had failed to get a replacement carton. Yet she couldn't go back inside there. She couldn't face the humiliation of having to pay him again. A credit! She would make Porter take care of it, he was the one who ran up the bill without telling her, just after they'd agreed they wouldn't do that anymore. No, she'd drive to town, all the way, a hundred and twenty miles or whatever it was round trip, for that half-gallon of milk. She'd spend three hours driving before she went back in there again.

She pulled out to the pavement. Involuntarily she glanced back at the hateful little store. Lucido was leaning against the doorjamb next to the pay phone booth, wiping his nose on the flag. Inside, through the glass, she could make out Onésimo's face, that bald head, those hooded eyes and pointy ears. He was turned in her direction. Upstairs, fingers parted the dirty blinds.

No one was coming. She pressed the accelerator to the floor. The wheels spun and then screeched as they grabbed on to the pavement.

Maybe she would just drive and drive and never come back.

CHAPTER 13

Obstruction

A few feet beyond Onésimo Moro's west fenceline, there grew a large tree on Teofrasto Vizarriaga's place, in his backyard, next to the Acequia de los Hermanos, where it crossed under the dividing barbed-wire fence. It was a wide branching broadleaf cottonwood with deeply furrowed gray bark, one of many that followed the meandering shallow track of the Rio San Marcos down through the valley and stationed themselves in clumps here and there along the two community irrigation ditches that fed off the river and up arroyos where they marked the existence of numerous springs. This particular cottonwood was among the largest in the valley. It had fattened itself to five feet in diameter near the base of the trunk and reached sixty feet into the air, becoming as it grew a greater and greater source of contention between the Moros to the east and the Vizarriagas to the west.

The Moros believed that the Vizarriaga *alamo*, as they called it, sent roots under the fence and way out into their field, roots that had been robbing their soil of nutrients for generation after generation, in order to provide increasingly lavish shade to the Vizarriaga backyard. Proof of this lay in the long orange roots snagged by Onésimo's plow every few years when he put in a new feeder ditch, roots exactly like those his father-in-law had brought up every spring when the field had been planted in chile, corn, squash, and beans. Worse, the Vizarriagas used the shade of the quaking round leaves as shelter for their growing collection of expensive lawn furniture, a propane barbecue, a trampoline, a Ping-Pong table, a croquet set, and other games that they too noisily enjoyed on weekends like some family on one of those TV soap operas. Onésimo had even heard Teofrasto calling it "the family tree," with that barrel-chested laugh of his that carried right up into the upstairs Moro back porch and kitchen, which looked out over the Vizarriaga backyard and into the middle reaches of the offending tree, along with the barbecue fumes and screeching of their grandchildren and yapping of their three Chihuahuas. In the autumn the Moros regarded the large yellow leaves that came to rest on the floor of their back porch as a form of pollution that had to be swept away immediately. They suspected that the crop of leaves the prevailing wind blew on to their field further debilitated the soil.

From the tree's invading roots suckers also sprouted. Onésimo used to cut them back in the spring, at least until he rented out the back field to a nephew who used the alfalfa for a few cows he kept down the road. Sometimes the nephew trimmed back the suckers in the field itself, but never along the fenceline or around the little wooden bridge where Leandro Salcedo had recently pulled a gun on Benji Guerrero.

As a result, for two or three years, a thin gray-green whip had been allowed to swell into a fat sapling that emerged at an angle from under the footbridge to reach out across the ditch channel. It was the thickness of this particular sucker that finally loosened one of the wooden handles of Benji Guerrero's brand-new pruning shears, an event that had prompted him to whoop with laughter at precisely the moment when Leandro Salcedo decided to unwrap his new .45 pistol and put an end to Benji's disrespectful remarks, which had been emerging from his tight little sneering mouth at the rate of one every fifteen minutes or so since early that morning, about how much Leandro drank, and what he drank, or smoked, or snorted, and with who, and who or what he ended up in bed with every night, like they were old compadres still in fourth grade or something, and all the while hinting that they should step into the bushes or fall back from the rest of the crew and smoke some weed or "whatever else you got." None of your business, Leandro had snarled in reply. Just keep out of my face. And then the whole crew had taken to calling Leandro Walgreens that morning, source of all your drug needs.

But Benji's sarcastic whoop had not been directed at Leandro at all. He had bought the pruning shears new from Onésimo that very morning at quarter to eight so he could work on the ditch. He held them high, now in two pieces, and laughed partly in relief, because he would have an excuse to leave the ditch crew and go get a Coke or something at Onésimo's and argue with the old man about replacing them and maybe even throwing in a little extra to compensate for lost time on the acequia. But then suddenly the pistol, and the mayordomo coming around the cottonwood and climbing up out of the dry ditch and first sending them back to join the rest of the crew and then a few minutes later ordering them to leave without pay. So Leandro and his gun and then the mayordomo took care of all that.

And the cottonwood sapling under the bridge remained unpruned, or half unpruned, or cut into just enough for it to droop a little lower into the ditch, with two thin branches dragging on the sandy earth of the waterless channel. Six days later, Lázaro Quintana, the mayordomo, opened the headgate and sent the first water of the new season down the five-mile long ditch, empty since the November before.

When the brown water finally arrived four hours later at the bridge, the tip of its foamy tongue was bearing along a small plum branch that a ditch worker had thrown on the upper side of the ditch bank, where the wind had blown it back down into the channel. It was one of many such prunings that Lázaro had inevitably failed to catch with his rake, but it was the first one to snag on the cottonwood sapling at the mouth of the small bridge. The splayed structure of its short branches provided a fine armature for the next arrival, some plastic wrap and a Styrofoam meat tray that the village dogs had fished out of a Clapp garbage bag. Next came a small tumbleweed, or half of one because a passing car had clipped it while it was blowing across the highway into the ditch. Next, in short order, a flotilla of Greenpeace pamphlets and bumper stickers bearing images of whales and dolphins and seals and sea birds in blues and greens, just beneath the surface of the brown water, some of which flattened themselves against the sinking tumbleweed and plastic wrap and the prongs of the plum branch.

The obstruction slowed the water only slightly at the entrance of the wooden bridge. The ditch was wide here, almost five feet, and there was plenty of room for the water to flow to either side of the little dam, and even over the top, as it continued to collect items throughout the afternoon. And though the water slowed only slightly, it still slowed, inducing some of its silt to precipitate out of it, weighing down plastic, paper, tumbleweed, twig, and branch, anchoring them more securely in place.

The bit-by-bit accumulation of debris was a slow and by no means certain process, a dry leaf here, a tuft of grass there. A surge in the flow, from a similar such dam, an *atarque*, breaking somewhere upstream in the ditch, could be enough to sweep away, downstream, the incipient dam under the bridge, and

that would be that, or at least until the next rolling bolus
of twigs and dry grass encountered the next obstruction or
narrowing in the ditch channel, such as the too-small culvert
under the next arroyo, behind Lalo Moro's house.

And it might well hold throughout the day, gradually
tightening up, becoming dense enough to cause the water
to overflow at the bridge, if nobody noticed that the water
was running high over the next day or two. In the meantime,
nothing would happen. There would be a little turbulence
at the entrance to the low log bridge, but no more than the
sound of gently splashing water that now and then might be
heard over the wind.

It was cold outside that Monday. The wind had
discouraged Lázaro Quintana from crossing the highway and
following the ditch across the top of the alfalfa field spotted
with rounded clumps of green, to check the entrance to the
bridge. Lázaro knew that unless you absolutely had to be
outside, it was the sort of day you'd stick your head out the
door and see all the newly leafed-out trees tossing back and
forth in a wind not of spring but still quite of winter, and then
you would pull back inside and figure out how you were going
to ignore the rest of the day. But he couldn't. He had to keep
following the water to the very end of the ditch, raking out
branches and bits of trash, wind or no wind.

CHAPTER 14

A Delivery

Myrna Clippenger had spent over a year calculating that she would most likely live to the age of 83, seven months, and two days, and that she would die in perfect health and in a good mood, on a September nineteenth, in a year well into the twenty-first century. Her tools in this calculation ranged from astrological charts to the Harvard Wellness Letter and those tables that appeared now and then in the health sections of the daily papers with which you could estimate your life-span by factors such as how much money you earned and whether you lived in the city or the country and how many strips of bacon you ate each week and how many parents, siblings, and aunts and uncles had been victims of heart attacks, cancer, strokes, or other forms of unpleasantness. But from what? She was still uncertain. Probably cancer, some undetectable painless form she might never know she had even had, until the final terminal twinge.

Myrna Clippenger lived in the southern end of San Marcos, where she believed the air was cleaner by some small measure, since the southwesterly winds and breezes had not yet entered the village proper to pick up the smoke of woodstoves and fireplaces or burning trash and other household vapors generated by what she regarded as the bad habits of most of the valley's inhabitants. She lived in a small three-room adobe house, which was occasionally the talk of the town for how sparely it was furnished and how uncluttered it was kept. While most other residents of the San Marcos Valley put out swollen black plastic bags of trash for the Monday collection every week, suggesting that abject poverty and conspicuous consumption might not be incompatible after all, Myrna set out only a little white plastic sack of trash once every two or three weeks, and most of that was bits of plastic and tin cans and aluminum beer cans she picked up on her daily walks down the arroyo to the river.

She was a small, slight woman of quick and efficient movement, the envy of larger, clumsier humans, or so she thought, with round green eyes and prematurely gray hair. The centerpiece of the largest room in the house, which normally would have been the living room, was a loom on which she wove with painstaking slowness woolen rugs sold by an exclusive outlet near the plaza in Santa Fe, with dependable regularity. Whenever her bank account shrank to just enough money to get through the next six months, she knew that there would come a call from Santa Fe asking her to bring in the next rug and pick up her check.

Weaving gave her ample time to reflect on the course of her life and its inevitable outcome. She detested messiness of any kind, material, emotional, bodily, or spiritual, and would never forgive herself for inviting Boots Clippenger into her life four years ago during a lapse in judgment she later attributed to a viral infection and for letting the relationship drag on for seven whole months. She had even, now unbelievably, married him. She would continue to bear his name as a perpetual reminder never to get involved with a man ever again. His main function in life seemed to be to go out in the world and come back with some kind of illness or injury or condition

picked up at construction sites where he worked as a carpenter.
It had been a cold autumn. She had been weak from the
viral infection and unexpected loneliness and a deep vaginal
hunger for sex, in the piercing low light of early December. She
had allowed, indeed invited, his at first charming, shambling,
noisy, creaking, rattling presence to fill up her small house
and trip over the loom. Sex with him was noisy, shouting,
slapping, headboard banging against the wall so loudly she
was afraid they were heard way up in the center of the village.
When the weather warmed he favored mid-afternoon alfresco
sessions on the back porch glider, where once they had been
surprised by the UPS man delivering a package, fortunately
not one to be signed for. Soon she came to look back fondly
on her own gentle self-administered glissandos. Like a clumsy
boy attracted to a bright Christmas ornament, he could not
believe his good fortune in being allowed into her charmed, if
cramped, world. He entered on tiptoes of amazement, almost
of admiration, a condition of restraint he could hold for only
so long, or exactly one month after they were married in El
Paso. Chickpeas and lentils were for her the universal foods
that guaranteed vigorous health. They gave Boots stomach
cramps and loose bowels. A kingdom for a steak and mashed
potatoes, he was heard shouting up at the cantina in Los
Martinez the night she kicked him out. For your own good,
she concluded sharply while pushing the front door closed,
after nudging out onto the snow the last of the black plastic
bags of his too many belongings and tools that had come to
clog the passageways of her small house.

The secret of long life, or of a life of just the right length,
was mood, she'd decided after many years of reflection.
Keep in a good mood and you will simply never get sick. The
terminal feat would be of course to remain content even when
you knew the end was at hand, in order to know the blessing
of dying in a state of perfect bliss. Myrna had bought her

little house in San Marcos because it was cheap, believing that the village was an even-tempered place, one in which a good mood would be easy to maintain. Only after a year or two did she discover the truth, which she saw as being quite the opposite. San Marcos now appeared to her to be an ill-tempered place, in a collective bad mood most of the time, particularly when the seasons changed, but also when they settled into what they were supposed to be, freezing and icy in the winter, hot and dusty in the summer, and windy and snappish on an April day like today. She knew that the only way to keep in a good mood today was not to go to the village store or post office, where everybody would either be complaining or else quibbling, and where they were likely to turn on her for her calm expression of somewhat faded radiance and try to prod her into complaining about something. San Marcos had become a test. If she could stay calm and unruffled in a place like this, then surely she could face death itself with that firm and confident smile which everybody so resented.

Just to be safe, she decided to unplug the phone today. She saw the main problem of San Marcos as being inhabited by the wrong kind of people. At first she'd seen her Spanish-speaking neighbors as happy-go-lucky souls who flirted with catastrophe for the fun of it, like kids daring each other to take foolish chances at the village swimming hole. And while they killed themselves off at an alarming rate through bad driving and bad eating and drinking habits, at first this seemed like a colorful melodramatic backdrop to her quiet and hermetic life, even a kind of entertainment. On the whole, people deserved what they got, a sad fact of life. But in time she came to resent the way her neighbors seemed to draw misery willfully into their lives with their bad habits all perfectly capable of being corrected and improved. So much misery so close was threatening to impinge upon her sense of well-being. As a result she found herself at times vaguely wishing that all her Spanish-speaking neighbors would move to Albuquerque or East LA or even Mexico, allowing the village to be repopulated with people more in control of their own lives. She wondered at times if this was being racist.

Surely ill health was a sign of moral decay, if even remotely, and that included so-called accidents, though such beliefs had been shaken by her sweet and innocent niece Nora during a visit when Nora abruptly came down with appendicitis at precisely the moment when Myrna's car and the car of her former husband down the road had both refused to start. Myrna had to draft those messers, the Clapps, and their large, allergenic truck of a station wagon, to run Nora and her to the hospital and back, plus a post-operative visit. Myrna had thought of offering to pay for the gas and certainly would whenever her sister, who lived in Iowa, finally forgave her for the episode and sent the money Myrna was too proud to ask for.

Gate closed, door latched, phone unplugged, these were the thoughts that Myrna Clippenger wove into the morning's band of greenish blue she had planned to complete by about one. A quick lunch of hummus and raw cabbage, perhaps a brisk walk, smiling into the wind, down to the river and back, and she would resume sitting at her loom until almost sundown, when the wind would probably drop. The thought of the course of the remainder of the day pleased her. Her mood would hold. And tomorrow she could drive into the village to the post office and the store, perhaps encountering a few people by then purged of memories of the wind of the day before.

From outside her door came a long, flat honk. She pulled the shuttle to the end of the weave and stood up. Through the plasticked-over windows, she could make out a square brown form. She blushed. She couldn't see well enough to know whether he was the driver who had seen them making love. She wondered what she was expecting from UPS. She hoped not the one who always insisted on carrying even small parcels to the door and even, if they were large, who would push his way inside and set the package down on the floor and then slowly look around at her simply furnished rooms but say nothing. She could ignore the truck, not open the door, and sit back down at her loom. But the brown-uniformed man waved in her direction. He had seen her though the milky windows. She unlatched the door and stepped outside. Of course, it would be that special wool she had sent for a week ago. The wind tugged at her baggy cardigan.

They were always men, the drivers, and always Chicano, dark brown as if to match the truck, and black hair, and so was this one, a young, short, pudgy fellow with an oddly sweet smile and an almost wounded look. She didn't think he was the one. He was angling an awkwardly large carton out of the back and down the step to the ground, where he balanced it on a corner. He handed her a clipboard to sign.

You want the gate closed, ma'am?

If you could, please.

No problem, he smiled, bounding back up into the truck.

A horrible job, Myrna thought, bouncing around on back roads all day long. Terrible for the kidneys. She was momentarily confused by how cheerful the fellow seemed to be. As he backed up and turned around and flashed a smile and a wave out the side window, she felt a small pang. Perhaps she wasn't the only one who could keep smiling into the teeth of it all. The thought trailed after her in the wind like a loose strand of hair as she walked around the back of the house in search of a handcart.

CHAPTER 15

Cash or Credit

One of those lulls descended on the store. They could last anywhere from five minutes to an hour, usually around lunchtime or just after, a time that could also generate a flurry of activity when passersby stopped for soft drinks and chips and a stale sandwich or burrito warmed and toughened up in the microwave.

But today was a lull day. The wind was keeping people inside. Upstairs Isabel Moro leaned over the end of her grandfather's roll-top oak desk and peered down the hole in the floor, directly under which Onésimo's bald head wavered, slowly rocking back and forth. From decades of staring down on it, Isabel knew this part of her husband better than any other. His pate had two expressions, wrinkled and unwrinkled, and onto either she could project whatever she wished, to the point that it was always a shock at the end of the day when he came upstairs for her to encounter his actual face and its unsmiling downcast expression, gloomy yet watchful, which never directly assented to any of her sharp commands. She knew now that the nodding back and forth meant that he had gone to sleep in one of his stand-up siestas.

She turned back to the ledger. She had just completed the monthly calculation of how much their nearly three hundred customers who charged items to their accounts, from San Marcos and three outlying hamlets, owed the store. The number had reached a dangerous new level. Part of the total was thanks to the recent consolidation of two village stores, one owned by Onésimo's family, and the other, the one that had always just limped along, by Isabel's own parents, when her parents finally decided to retire from retailing in their nineties. Her business sense told her it was madness to acquire their stale and antiquated inventory that in no way corresponded to the little store's debt in the form of unpaid accounts of all kinds. Yet she also couldn't see letting her own parents, the sweet old *viejitos*, spend their last days fending off bill-collectors and filing for bankruptcy. She worried that she was becoming soft like they had always been.

She had finally talked to a nephew who worked for their bank in Santa Fe. I'm not here to borrow any money, she said right away as she sank down into the too-soft leather chair in front of his desk. I don't borrow money, period, she said, adding with somewhat less certainty, and Onésimo, he doesn't either. So if he comes in here and asks, don't you lend him anything.

So, Tía Isabel, you just tell me why you're sitting in that chair where only people who want to borrow money sit. Here, I just got some new photos of Consuelo.

She cooed dutifully at the framed photos of the spoiled ugly child and then unburdened herself. In response the nephew played the same old broken record about how she and Onésimo should finally break down and accept credit cards. Too many people had been telling her to do that. But the idea just made her close her mind. She understood columns of numbers in pen or pencil, and coins and bills and checks and food stamps, but there was something about this new way where people just pass back and forth plastic cards that she didn't like at all. But each time she listened a little more. This time she understood that by accepting credit cards the store would cleverly pass on the villagers' indebtedness to those big banks in New York or wherever, meaning she wouldn't have to deal with it anymore. The thought of those big banks having to lose sleep over how to get the likes of Benji Guerrero and Porter Clapp to pay their bills suddenly pleased her. She could see well-dressed men behind large desks in the tops of skyscrapers dialing numbers, like in that terrible movie her other nephew had taken her to one afternoon where people got killed before they could even open their mouths, and calling the governor to send out the state police in their long black-and-white Chevy sedans all the way up to San Marcos. She could imagine the satisfying sound of the sirens howling through the village on the way to the houses of the *delinquentes* to collect their overdue bills.

So how much do I pay for this service? she said a little more sarcastically than she intended.

Less than what it's costing you to carry the accounts yourself given where interest rates are, he said. He went on to work up some hypothetical numbers, in the course of which he asked, voice lowered, head thrust forward over the desk, How much are you carrying? How much do your customers owe you?

She feigned ignorance at first. How should I know?

Tía Isabel. Don't tell me you don't know.

You promise not to tell?

He promised. She told. He frowned. He said they could install the latest new electronic gizmo in about three days. She said she would think about it.

That was two weeks ago. She was still thinking about it.

She decided that she would call him at the bank this afternoon, one way or the other. She looked at her watch. She'd have to make up her mind in an hour or two.

Afterward she would slip out to continue her daily village rounds, to check in on Mrs. Quintana first, poor Mrs. Quintana, and quarrelsome old Mr. Serrano. She had just heard she had lost Abundio Moro, who was also the oldest man in the village, so old he wasn't related to anybody anymore, worse than the Anglos being like that, though he was still alive early in the morning when she had carried a Styrofoam bowl of warm *atole* into his cave, where he was snoring away under a mountain of old army blankets. He must have passed away a little while later. Finally, she thought, though he had been very little trouble. She wouldn't replace him. She only liked to have two at a time at the most.

Village gossips, Isabel Moro knew, insisted that she took an interest in the terminally ill, the bedridden, the paralyzed, for purely business reasons. She didn't want them to die on her without making certain their bills were all paid up. In this they were partly right. It seemed to her that dying with a clear conscience was better than the other way, and she had seen plenty of that. It had happened more than once that the last face an elderly San Marcos resident peered into in this life was that of Isabel Moro as she leaned over the bed and said, forcing what she hoped was a radiant smile to unloosen her normally expressionless thin lips, Your bills are all paid. Thereby granting them permission to enter the next world.

But it was also just one of those things you did, even if people did shoplift and cheat and steal from the store and piss on the front walls at night, because it had to be done, whether you liked it or not.

As she stared at the old black telephone on the desk, wondering when to call, her main worry was that if the store accepted Visa and Mastercard it might have some effect on that other work of hers, of helping the old people leave this world. If they all had those little plastic cards, would they still need her to make her rounds with bowls of *atole* and posole, to change bedding and bedpans? She didn't know. Nor was it something she could ask her nephew about.

Then she decided. She would do it next year, January first, almost eight months away. That way she could start telling people that their bills needed to be paid up by then. After that, she would hint, those New York bankers would start sending the state police out to collect.

Below, the door chattered open. She nudged a red cushion on the floor into position and slowly dropped to her knees to have a better look through the hole.

Her knees. She didn't know how much longer she could do this. Thirty years of kneeling down to peer through the various holes in the ceiling was beginning to take its toll.

CHAPTER 16

Pumping

From the number of times he had seen Lázaro Quintana's little red car up on the highway, Len Mott had guessed that Lázaro was finally bringing the water down—and about time, because the holding pond east of the drive was about empty under the plastic tarps, and the well pump was beginning to suck air if it ran for more than a half hour at a time, as it always did in the weeks just before the mayordomo put water back in the ditch. He turned on the pump every night after he and Carrie finished the dishes, illegally topping up the pond in the dark. The brown woven mesh plastic tarps on the surface, held up with plastic buoys, served to minimize evaporation of the precious liquid and to camouflage the pond from the highway above during the winter, when the overhanging weeping willows were bare of leaves. As soon as the ditch flowed again, he could pull off the tarps and resume replenishing it in an entirely open and somewhat more legal manner. Always at this time of year Len Mott felt that a few more days of no water in the ditch would make it conspicuous that by some means the laws of nature were being altered and that he had another source of water than the acequia. Most of his neighbors probably knew, he guessed, that he was supplementing acequia water to the pond with well water he pumped into it every night, but few perhaps guessed the extent of the illegal pumping. And certainly the State Water Office knew nothing about it. Or so he hoped.

Len Mott argued internally and explained his views to Carrie whenever they began to trouble him, that the illegal pumping was a minor matter because most of the water they used did in fact come from the acequia, and most of that, or at least quite a lot of it, seeped back into the ground and eventually back down in the first and second water tables, all nicely purified, or so he hoped, as it filtered down through strata of soil, sand, gravel, and rocks. In the large sense he reasoned that he was only taking what he was putting back in. There was some self-serving sophistry here, he also knew, but how much? And how much did it count that their nursery and greenhouse operation was scrubbing carbon dioxide out of the air, on land that without it would be almost barren and lifeless.

But he was too preoccupied by the problem of getting through the next few days to worry about the finer distinctions. He and Carrie had a large landscaping order to get ready this afternoon for delivery tomorrow to Santa Fe. They planned to stay overnight. The drive home after a long day of planting trees and shrubs, probably in the wind and cold, would tire him more than he wanted to think about. But now a water meeting had come up for tonight; somehow he had missed seeing any announcements of it, and it was one he shouldn't miss, however much he had tried to find justifications for doing so. It was probably going to be a preliminary public relations meeting where the State Water Office bureaucrats would try to sound sincere by saying things like "We haven't made any decisions about anything, we're here to find out what the people of this community think." In other words, to scope out how much and how well organized any opposition was going to be. From his limited experience of public meetings and hearings, Mott knew they were a way to obliquely announce what had already been decided in some office somewhere. Enough people were sure to be there that he could count on getting a fairly good report of what was said. But most appealing excuse for skipping the meeting was that he didn't want to know about why the State Water Office was suddenly taking interest in the piddling waters of the San Marcos Valley until the last possible moment, preferring to live in that state of blissful ignorance—or was it paranoia?—so often commended by local lore. What you don't know can't hurt you, or the Spanish equivalent, that was the traditional way. He suspected that many of his older Hispanic neighbors were ignorant of the existence of the Internal Revenue Service and other federal institutions that had come into existence since the 1848 Treaty of Guadalupe Hidalgo ceding the former Mexican territory to the US. Or, more likely, that they felt quite protected by that document.

An exception was the State Water Office, which seemed to enjoy a reputation akin to God itself as arbiter of petty local disputes and as putative owner of all waters, as vengeful patriarch who would one day take it all away, despite little evidence for any of these beliefs. Most irate landowners and water users who took the trouble to drive all the way to Santa Fe and ask about some minor dispute with a neighbor about garbage thrown into the ditch returned with a Delphic pronouncement that usually suggested, on close reading, that neighbors had to figure out among themselves how to live with each other.

Such were Len Mott's ruminations following the phone conversation with Porter Clapp, to whom he had revealed none of his own doubts and insecurities. During the call he had been aware of the maroon sedan climbing back up the driveway and heading west. The squeak of the kitchen cupboard doors told him Carrie was back in the house. He decided he had better get the difficult moment over as soon as possible. He was going to have to tell her that their long-awaited night in a Santa Fe motel, following dinner and a movie, was going to have to be put off.

There's a water meeting tonight, he said from the kitchen door. I need to be there.

She was sorting through her pile of environmental pamphlets in a large glass bowl on the kitchen table. She was never without them. She left a few on the table at the post office every time she went in, much to the irritation of Mr. Morales, and on the counter of Onésimo's store, where they sometimes sat for several hours before he slipped them into the trash, and on the couches and kitchen tables of friends she went to visit. Carrie's been here, I see, had become a village refrain.

She looked up across the green linoleum at her husband. He had moved over to lean against the cooler end of the wood cookstove, which was quieter than it should have been. She strode across the room and picked up the curved stove tool and flicked open the ornately nickeled firebox door. A few large coals were still glowing. The wind blew a puff of ash out into the room. She rummaged around inside the copper kindling box next to the stove and threw a handful of thin pieces of wood into the firebox and then inserted a split cottonwood log through the narrow opening. With the edge of the tool she lifted up the door and dropped it closed with a clatter.

This is the third time we've put it off, she said. No.

We'll pack the truck this afternoon and go tomorrow and spend the night and then start early the next morning, how's that?

I've got everything lined up for tonight for the kids.

Can't Porter and Steph take them tomorrow night instead?

She grimaced. Something's going on with them. With Steph, at least. Since she quit her job.

Something was always going on with them, he thought.

Sometimes a couple more kids in the house actually helps.

She looked up at him to see if he was serious. He was. And perhaps he was right. Steph had quit her job to spend more time with the kids only to discover that they had all become more dependent than any of them had realized on the money she had brought in as a secretary in town. At the time this had seemed obvious to their friends though not to them. Porter's handmade wooden toy business was not something they could depend on. Perhaps they were nursing some secret hope of sudden wealth. And then there were the contortions Porter always worked into their lives.

I don't know why he persists in that Social Security number business.

Who? Porter?

But Len knew perfectly well who Carrie was talking about, only her comment had interrupted thoughts about the kitchen and when they were ever going to get around redoing it. In gentle mockery they called it a classic Chicano kitchen, replete with linoleum in a pattern of little green squares and glossy light green stuccoed walls and a kitchen table with a yellow Formica top and tubular chrome legs and four chairs with tubular chrome legs and yellow plastic cushions. The vigas and latillas at least had not been covered over with dark wood-look paneling, but they had been repeatedly varnished. They hung overhead like the underside of a raft of logs nailed together with boards, a dark sticky molasses-colored mass. The Motts had left the kitchen relatively untouched in deference to old Mr. Guerrero, who had sold them the place ten years ago. He still dropped by now and then to have a cup of coffee whenever he could get somebody to drive him back up to Los Martinez, where he lived with his youngest daughter. He liked to remind the Motts of all the relatives he had refused to sell the place to, specifying the amounts of each of the embarrassingly low offers. He concluded the catalog by raising an index finger and saying, I want you to keep this kitchen just like Ramona did, just like. The Motts felt he had said this a few too many times by now. His wife had died twenty-five years before in the next room. It was now their bedroom.

It's probably too late now, Len said after a time. Porter has built his whole life around that number. Back in the sixties, at the peak of the draft-card burning frenzy, Porter had mistakenly ignited his Social Security card instead. It was dark, he once explained, he was stoned. As the result of a convoluted but logical train of thought, Porter had refused to use his Social Security number from then on, which meant that the burden of official paperwork had to be carried by a succession of partners, the latest and most long-standing of whom was Stephanie Wachler. Porter had shaped his official existence to preclude the necessity of ever having a bank account, a credit card, a passport, cheating in only the one matter of a driver's license, for which he used the Social Security number of his twin brother, who lived in Argentina.

Small miscalculation compounded with interest over the years, Len Mott had once remarked, although knowing, as he said it, that their own more palpably successful life was built on miscalculations just as shaky. The holding pond, for example, and the secret pump.

Will you call her to at least remind her about tonight? he asked, bringing the matter back to the more immediate question. He knew better than to try to argue with Carrie anymore. They would leave late this afternoon as first planned.

She bent down and looked in the firebox again. No, I think it would be better to leave them here. They're old enough to take care of themselves. I'll make lunch for them before we leave, she said. She straightened up. I think there's water in the ditch.

Yeah, I saw Lázaro's car. I'll go up and see.

CHAPTER 17

Esquire

Martin Caudell sat slumped down in the passenger side of the front seat of the enormous state Ford Crown Victoria, thumbing through the San Marcos pages of the county phone book. He had no idea what he was looking for. He was parked at the lower end of the Nuestra Señora Cemetery and had dutifully trotted around the alarming graveyard as fast as he could before regaining the safety of the large silver sedan. No grass, no trees, he thought as his eyes searched for something known and familiar among the wooden crosses and small red granite monuments and tiny wrought-iron fences planted in the sand—sand!—and everything festooned with fading plastic roses and daisies, no benches, not even any squirrels, just sand and gravel and cactus and blackened root-like shrubs that twisted up out of the ground and were fringed with a blue-green fuzz instead of actual leaves. Back at the car, climbing inside, he stepped on a cactus and several spines penetrated his new cowboy boot, the right foot, at the instep.

The Old Man had made some suggestions. Go talk to people, walk the ditches, check out the church, the cemetery, get to know the place a little, he said. Study the phone book.

You know, the basic stuff. Martin Caudell had been warned in the office that the Old Man's "suggestions" were in fact exact orders, signed and sealed. The Old Man had added, You know Spanish?

Martin Caudell knew hydrology, his undergraduate major until he switched to law. He had just passed the bar exam. He knew law. But no, he didn't know Spanish. The things he didn't know still weighed on him in the form of all those libraries he had studied in without ever knowing what was truly in them. Did anyone?

Then pick up some of those tapes and get going. You ought to be able to make some progress in one night, the Old Man said. Was he being sarcastic? Immediately he had reached into the folds of his gray suit pants pocket and pulled out a set of keys. Here, young fella, take my car. Then he added, Just make sure you go to the right San Marcos.

The right San Marcos?

Yeah, the right San Marcos. There are two. Long story, the Old Man said before trotting off down the state office building hallway.

Martin wondered, But how will I know which one is the right one?

A paralegal working in the office finally sorted him out. The upper one, she explained, San Marcos Arriba. You go through San Marcos Abajo first, about seven miles before. There are two because of some dispute going back to Spanish land grant days.

Normally this was the sort of field trip the Old Man loved to do himself in the company of one or two of his young assistants, but all had been called away to Washington to testify to a House committee, so through some arcane bureaucratic logic within the State Water Office, the newest kid on the block, Martin Caudell, his freshly minted law degree allowing him to add *Esquire* to his business card, was handed the assignment to spend a day in the San Marcos Valley, inspecting the inhabitants and their irrigation works prior to the public meeting that evening in the village school gym. He was also to check that notices about the meeting were still up at the village store and post office. Does that mean I'll be running the meeting, he wondered? He broke into a cold sweat at the thought.

The car was the first problem. A second-hand BMW had seen him through his law school years, and compared to it the mammoth six-passenger Ford with government plates felt like piloting the window display of a furniture store. Between Santa Fe and San Marcos he had been given the finger three times by drivers of pickups with double gun racks across the rear windows, and the passenger of a lowered hardtop had emptied the contents of a large-size Pepsi cup into the turbulence as the car had overtaken his, splashing the hood and windshield with the syrupy brown liquid and crushed ice. Thereafter the heater smelled of Dr. Pepper.

And at the San Marcos Post Office, Martin's first stop, he had stepped from the car just as an older man, perhaps the postmaster, was raising what appeared to be the tattered half of an American flag. Martin had walked over to him. He wondered whether he should try out one of the three short Spanish phrases he had finally memorized the night before. But the man's cold gray eyes, revealed in a quick furtive glance in his direction, suggested perhaps not. Martin began with an ingratiating sally, offering his hand:

That's a very historic-appearing flag you've got up there.

The postmaster ignored him. He didn't look at him, pretended not to see the extended hand, and started walking away around the small adobe building toward the back.

Excuse me, wait a minute. Could you put up a notice for me?

The man stopped and turned. In a strange staccato accent, he said, You want me to put up a notice for you who I don't know from a hole in the wall?

Martin nodded hesitantly. This was not going well. Martin Caudell, from the State Water Office, he offered snappily.

The postmaster retraced a few steps, coming closer.

Look around you, he said with a tight turn of the neck. Martin obeyed, looking around him, though with no sense of actually seeing anything. Later, as he drove back down through the village he slowed near the post office and glimpsed the low adobe houses with tin roofs, many with boarded up windows.

Tell me where you see water, the postmaster demanded. Then he added. Tell me what you know about the Treaty of Guadalupe Hidalgo.

What?

Nothing, of course. Nada. You call yourself an educated man, I suppose.

The postmaster turned and strode away. Martin wondered, Do I call myself an educated man? Well, I do, yes, but on the other hand I don't really believe that. He heard the hollow banging of a wooden door somewhere in the back and then some more crashings from inside. The front door remained locked. He stood waiting for ten minutes. "Hours: 8-5," a hand-painted sign said on the door. It was almost eight fifteen. He eyed the tattered scrap of flag. He pondered. This is a United States Post Office? Several cars and pickups swung into the dirt parking area and paused and then sped away, sending up clouds of dust. Finally, he went back to the car and retrieved a notice for this evening's meeting and slipped it under the door. If someone from the office had succeeded in leaving one ten days before, it had probably not been put up by the postmaster. This one wouldn't be either.

The village store was up the road a quarter of a mile, on the inside of a strange hairpin turn, the outside of which gave an excellent view of the narrow little valley and a line of cottonwoods that suggested the presence of at least a little water. His experience at the store was just as odd. Once inside the chattering door, Martin sensed that everything abruptly went into slow-motion. A woman standing in front of a shelf of non-prescription drugs just kept standing there, now and then turning around to look at him. Two other customers assumed the poses of undecided shoppers, one at the dairy cooler, the other at the magazine rack just inside the door. Was it his tweed sports coat? His rep tie? He drew a deep breath and decided to be forceful, even aggressive. After all he was an attorney working for the people of the state. All three million of them.

Martin Caudell, from the State Water Office, he said, thrusting his hand straight across the counter, forcing the shopkeeper to intercept it if he wished to avoid a poke in the ribs. He engaged in a fleeting, limp handshake and raised his baleful eyes, offering no name in return. From above Martin's head there came a clatter. He looked up. In the middle of a metal funnel affair set in the pressed tin ceiling, there was a large hole that framed a wide brown eye, heavily made up with black eyeliner and long black lashes. Martin suddenly struggled to remember what he was doing in this particular place, a little too early in the morning, after a nearly sleepless night.

To put up a notice, could you possibly put a notice up in your window? he blurted out. The shopkeeper took the sheet of paper from him. From the ceiling a woman's voice boomed down.

Three dollars, unless you're a customer, the voice said.

A customer? Martin wondered what that involved.

Sure, said the shopkeeper. That will be three dollars.

To put up a notice? Three dollars?

A dollar a day, three-day minimum.

Martin had never heard of such a thing. To put up a notice? He looked around the store. Perhaps the people standing there were really mannequins, like in the Whitney or MOMA or wherever it had been. Hey, he said to himself. I'm an attorney now. This kind of shakedown doesn't happen to attorneys. But even as he was thinking these words, his hand was fishing his wallet out of his right rear pocket. He opened it and pulled out three one-dollar bills and set them on the counter. Do I get a receipt? he asked. He suppressed the urge to add sarcastically, What about a warranty? What about a service contract? Are they included?

The shopkeeper snatched up the bills and stuffed them into the cash register and pushed the tray closed. Back to Martin, he answered, No.

Martin turned away and walked out the door. Actually he was relieved. He couldn't have brought himself to put down on the expense report a "charge for posting notices," which he would then have to explain to somebody in the office, explaining how he had been taken for a ride by the village yokels. He broke into a cold sweat at the close call. He could hear them cackling in the men's room. You mean you actually paid money to those people to put up a notice? Ha, ha.

He found himself behind the wheel of the big car. A couple of mannequins out in the parking lot slowly raised their eyes and watched him drive off.

After that he had driven up and down the valley, explored a couple of dirt roads down by the so-called river, where he came across a party of young men simultaneously drinking beer and urinating and waving at him as he swung the car around. Finally, he located the headgate of the largest of the two ditches in town, whose name he couldn't pronounce, at the end of another dirt track that wandered through the willows. On the way he encountered a leathery old man walking with a rake over his shoulder who looked like the murderer on the old silent film Martin had absently watched on TV a few nights before and who had stopped and rolled down his window and advised him not to leave his car unattended along here, Unless you don't mind driving home without your wheels, if you see what I mean. Sometimes they take the seats, too, and the motor, and the windshield, but not always.

The last dirt road he had explored led up to the school, a long adobe building with small high windows behind gray wire netting, from which emerged the bird-like chatter of school children. The taller gym was tacked on to the south end, alongside two newer modular units. The cracked brown stucco walls of the older structures were patched with a lighter plaster, suggesting major subsidence issues. The whole was set in a roughly circular patch of bare ground serving as playground and parking lot, across which a dust devil was scattering dead leaves and scraps of paper. A basketball hoop was attached to the outside wall of the gym.

As he turned around in the bare parking lot, the cemetery below revealed itself. He had missed it on the way up into the valley, hidden as it was by a cut in the road. Driving back out, it was the last feature of the village over to the left, on a shelf of barren land with an excellent view up the narrow valley and the glinting tin roofs of the village itself. Martin reluctantly turned off the pavement, wondering what unpleasantness was in store for him here as he parked at the closed barbed-wire gate of the cemetery.

Cactus, of course. And why not, he muttered to himself as he gingerly pulled off his boot in the front seat. The interior of the car filled with the sweet, acrid odor of sweaty sock. He peeled back the woolly fabric. The stubs of three spines glinted from the white flesh of his instep. His bare foot looked breathtakingly vulnerable. It seemed to cry out, Why have I been treated in this way? With his Swiss Army knife tweezers, he extracted them one by one, holding the pinkish-brown spines up to the sunlight glaring through the windshield.

After that he thumbed through the phone book. So many Moros, Serranos, Morales, Vizarriagas, however you pronounce that winner, one after the other, probably two or three generations, and then only one listing each of the few Anglo names, Borstad, Clapp, Clippenger, Mott, Rawlins. He had rushed through the sandy cemetery too quickly to notice much about the names except they all seemed Spanish, or strange, in any case. The oldest date he saw was 1823. Born or died? He couldn't remember.

What would the Old Man ask him back at the office? Would he want details? All he could hear himself saying in reply was, That's a really weird place, really weird.

He could see the Old Man in his light gray suit and close-cropped gray hair and florid face looking down as he stood in the doorway, asking in some sly way how the visit out in the "field" had gone. What could be the quick yet casual-seeming question that would tell Martin that he was still just a kid, just out of law school?

He could feel another cold sweat coming on. He slid across the seat and inserted the key in the ignition, started the engine, and dropped the shift lever into reverse.

It was seven hours before the meeting. Out of the question to stay here the whole time. Seven hours in a place like this? What could he possibly do? Door to door? No thanks. He decided he would drive back down to the Interstate and then drive east to the nearest rest stop and spend the time going over some briefs he'd brought along.

CHAPTER 18

A Speedy GasMart Epiphany

The kid looked about sixteen. Inside the Speedy GasMart checkout island, he was darting from gas pump control panel to cash register to credit card machine, keeping up a cheerful patter with himself and whoever cared to join in, in a mock tremolo.

Okay, next shift, where are you? Half an hour overdue now, he now almost sang as he looked out through the glass and switched on pump number nine. He swung around to the counter. Now will everybody please, pretty please pay for your gas today? he called out in a jokey high-pitched voice to the half dozen people milling around the store.

Stephanie Wachler held out a candy bar and a dollar bill.

Eighty-nine cents. Anything else? Please tell me you don't want anything else. Do not buy a money order at this particular moment, for example.

Reluctantly she smiled. Then she remembered. Oh my god!

The clerk's hands stopped scrabbling for change. You mean you do want a money order?

Oh, no. I just remembered something. Can you add a half-gallon of milk? She rummaged around in her purse for a five-dollar bill that was supposed to be there somewhere. Yes, found.

· Anything but a money order, ma'am, is yours, he said. Handing her the change, muttering. Paperwork is awful. Gotta write stuff down. Where the hell are those people?

She picked up the milk on the way out and climbed back into the Chevy Carryall and unwrapped the candy bar behind the wheel. She knew she should get gas, but there were cars at all the pumps and people walking back and forth from the pumps to the convenience store and more cars driving in, and the inside of the store was filled with customers with staring, twisted-up expressions at having to wait, while the poor kid behind the counter was trying to keep track of ten things at once.

Coming into Santa Fe, into the traffic, into the confident bright rush of cars that seemed to bully her to go faster and make up her mind about changing lanes and making turns, she suddenly didn't know what to do. Without thinking she had stopped at the first GasMart and parked at the end of the store parking lot. She was too confused to call any of her town friends who would be rushing off to pick up kids or take them somewhere or would be getting ready to go out for dinner or to have a drink with a new friend or somebody they didn't want to talk about just yet. It was the life, or an oblique version of it, she'd given up only a month ago when she'd quit her secretarial job to spend more time with the kids and Porter and not be on the road all the time and to finally face what she was going to do with her life. And she had burned her bridges by immediately selling her little Toyota, her reliable commuter car, to get out from under the monthly payments.

She and Porter had moved to San Marcos because it was quiet and beautiful in a spare, almost austere way that shocked some of their city friends, the ones who had visited once and had never come back, saying things like, There's just a little too much sky out here, or, This place must be directly under the hole in the ozone layer. They thought it was going to be a good place to raise the kids, or finish raising them, away from the multiplying forms of urban craziness, which of course was just what the kids now craved, throwing them back into the yo-yo existence of all the other commuters, with far too many trips back and forth.

Like this one. Krishna and Athena would not fail to let her know how thoughtless she had been in driving to town all by herself without them, and they wouldn't accept the excuse that she'd left San Marcos well before school was out. The motherly thing to do would be to bribe them off by bringing them back a present. She chewed on the candy bar defiantly. No, she thought, this is *my* crisis, thank you. She would leave the bright orange-and-blue wrapper on the dashboard just to make it clear to them. The foot traffic in and out of the store seemed in some imperceptible manner to be no longer ill-humored. People were walking less stiffly and more swingingly. Perhaps the next shift had finally arrived. What an unpleasant place, all asphalt and fumes and the noise of traffic and cars stopping and starting up, doors slamming and slamming and the wind driving thin clouds of dust across the pavement. She wondered what she was doing here.

She should of course go back and throw herself into helping Porter with his always limping business. Should? Should. With his too-sophisticated wooden toys he was trying to reconstruct a childhood he felt cheated out of by a severely doctrinaire left-wing father, who had managed to turn the son into a bumbling, impractical radical. She had long ago realized that Porter had to solve that problem himself, that she might only complicate it, and also that his problem was large enough that he might have no energy leftover for any of hers.

She was on her own. Why didn't candy bars ever taste as good as their wrappers looked?

She thought of her own mother, who had been pulled around the country by her mechanic father and car-obsessed brothers until they were all exhausted to the point of settling in a cheap old abandoned mining town in southern Arizona, where she had no hope of growing the lush and bountiful flower garden, like in those catalogs, that had been her one simple but always frustrated ambition. African violets. A few pots of African violets on the narrow little windowsill of the rattling old aluminum motor home they lived in, in an RV park where you had to haul your own water.

Suddenly it became clear. None of it was new, it was just that she had never managed to put all the pieces together until this particular moment. She would grow her mother's flower garden. And then?

She looked around the parking lot, such a desperate place only a moment ago, in some wonder. The mid-afternoon sun, glinting off the wind-shuddering canopy over the gas pumps with its blazing red plastic letters, shot into her in a piercing way she had never experienced before. Two men and a woman, all huddled up against the cold wind, seemed to be fueling their cars with an attentive joy, as if this could be the finest thing a person could be doing at this particular moment in life. And then?

She rolled down the window and looked up into the sky. Such fine round clouds, moving briskly. And then? They had the land, they had the garden plot, though her melons never tasted as good as they should have, discovered in the jungle of tall weeds that were a casualty these past years of her job in town. This summer she would finally deal with the weeds. She had the catalogs, the flower seed and bulb catalogs, which arrived from late December and kept coming until May. She had quit her job in February, mumbling to somebody about wanting to plant a really nice garden this spring, while knowing this sounded like a lame excuse to her boss, whose calendar had more to do with skis, hang-gliders, mountain bikes, and climbing gear.

And then? She would grow her mother's garden and then she would paint it or, more likely, make prints of some kind, dabblings and experiments she had given up when the kids were born. There was something surprising and unexpected in the reversals and indirectness of prints that she could never catch by slapping images directly down on paper. She would sell the flowers—somehow, somewhere. Then she would sell the prints.

The San Marcos she had just fled from, a cramped narrow place inhabited by small minds transfixed by trivial obsessions, now returned to being a place where you could realize your dreams without anybody seriously suggesting that you ought to spend eight hours of every weekday at what everybody called a "real job" and where nobody would try to tell you how to run your life, not even in that indirect way of people rushing around and trying to be fashionable in what they wore and what they served for dinner and the color of the car they were going to buy this year. San Marcos was its own little place, barbed, contentious, mean-spirited, envious, and yet you could charge things at that wretched store when you were out of money, and people helped each other out when things were really bad, and half the year water splashed down from the acequia in an abundant, generous way that laughed at the dry sandy cliffs that enclosed the valley. And now there would be lots of flowers, a great circular bed of gladioli and phlox and zinnias and marigolds and peonies and dahlias that people could look down on as they drove by on the highway above or sometimes strolled on foot on warm summer evenings. She could get Carrie Mott to order some of the bulbs and tubers more cheaply.

A teenage boy dressed in a too-thin T-shirt and khaki pants ran past the front of the station wagon and jumped into a doorless Jeep a couple of spaces away, and in almost one motion started the car and backed out and shot away. She realized he was the beseiged clerk, finally relieved.

She woke to the fact that she was sitting in a parking lot on the outskirts of Santa Fe. She hadn't even locked her door when she got back in, which she now did. All she wanted now was to be home. She started the rough-running V-8. There was just enough gas to get back to San Marcos.

Not my problem, she decided. Porter can take care of the bill at Onésimo's store, and all that.

She didn't care that she was talking to herself out loud.

Got to get my garden planted.

noon

Twelve noon was not marked in any formal way within the village of San Marcos, though on quiet windless days, in moments when there was no traffic, the tingling of distant school bell could be heard as far as the center of the village. It summoned students to the gym, which also served as a cafeteria, for a lunch this particular day of rubbery hamburgers and limp french fries. But most days no one heard it in the central part of the village, a good half mile away, and certainly no one indoors, where TV sets murmured throughout the day in kitchens and living rooms and bedrooms, absently watched by women ironing clothes, setting out lunch, washing dishes, sweeping and vacuuming, and by those men too old to work outside anymore, and by the bedridden. The church bell could have been heard by all, but it had not sounded the hours for a generation or more. The priest who came up from Santa Fe now and then to preside over Sunday mass would give a few desultory tugs at the rope to announce his arrival, and it was still the custom of local teenagers to break into the church late on the night of March thirty-first and ring in April Fool's Day at midnight. The most memorable of these pranks occurred back in the 1950s, when a goat was tied to the bell rope.

The ringing went on for hours until someone got out of bed and went and freed the bleating creature.

Around noon each day, the village paused for lunch in the form of hot sit-down meals, in the case of the older generation, consisting of posole and beans and tortillas, sometimes enchiladas and tamales, downed with a Coors or a Coke or 7UP or coffee. The younger generation, at least those out of school and those not fed by grandparents and aunts and uncles, were more likely to go for the quick bologna or cheese sandwich on white bread, either slapped together by themselves or in the form of staler versions purchased at Moro Mercantile, followed by sugar-coated donuts.

Not drinking water, or drinking as little as possible, had become almost a folk tradition within San Marcos, on the theory that the more you drank the thirstier you would become. Given the aridness of the climate, it was considered appropriate to abstain as much as possible from drinking water, a rule that did not apply to beer drinking, at least among young males. Water is for washing and for irrigating, many a young person was scolded by his or her elders. Drink any more of that and you'll spend all day going *pipi*.

By noon the water flowing down the Acequia de los Hermanos, as nursed along by Lázaro Quintana, was more than halfway down the ditch channel. For the rest of the season, through spring and summer and early autumn, the water would meander through front yards and backyards and along wild stretches of cottonwood trees and squawberry bushes and New Mexico olive, reflecting sky, sun, moon, stars, and the muzzles of coyotes and bobcats and foxes and dogs and cats and goats and sheep and cattle that dipped their heads down to drink from it. Its waters would be swum by the odd beaver exploring dam locations at the mouths of culverts and other narrow spots in the channel, crossing paths with muskrats and water ouzels and small water snakes and crayfish. Here and there, now and then, its waters would reflect the form of its tender, Lázaro Quintana, leaning on his shovel and assessing the size of the flow. Occasionally a brown trout would make a wrong turn at the diversion dam and find itself trapped in the narrow flow, though with luck, no one irrigating that day, it could follow the channel to the very end where it could rejoin the cooler waters of the stream at the south end of the narrow valley. Late at night the acequia's waters would be pissed in by a drunk or two at the Upper Shooting Gallery, amid the cottonwoods. One of them might even stumble and fall into the ditch, filling the night air with curses and splashing sounds and laughter from his more fortunate drinking buddies.

Time did not exist for the waters flowing through the village, either in the acequia or in the small river, the stream from which it was diverted—or else the movement of the waters was a representation, a mirror, of time itself, pure time, time without the markers of dawn, dusk, day, night, or noon, time unadulterated by the many forms of human clocks, time as flow without beginning or end or middle.

CHAPTER 19

The Plaza

What was left of the old fortified plaza of San Marcos, once self-enclosed, consisted of an L-shaped collection of adobe house and buildings, with the open sides facing southwest and overlooking the valley toward the mountains. A dirt wagon track used to approach the plaza from the south and pass along its west wall to what a few old timers still remembered as a *portal* with huge wooden gates. But then the large Salcedo houses that made up the west wall of the plaza burned—hay was being kept in a room next to the stables—which is to say that the vigas and latillas of split cedar covered with straw and dirt and the wooden window and door frames burned, leading to the collapse of the heavy dirt roofs. Over the years the walls began to slump. When it became clear that the Salcedo family was unable or unwilling to rebuild, the old walls were mined for the still intact adobe bricks within them. The dirt track became a road, and then the road was widened and paved and realigned over the site of the former west side, and several houses on the south east corner were bulldozed out of the way. The Salcedos granted easements in return for a little money, but the more prosperous Moros, by means of a well-placed relative in the state highway department, defended their store parking lot on the outside corner of the old plaza, around which the new highway was forced to make a hairpin turn. The Morales house, a quarter of a mile east of the plaza, the destruction of whose neighboring structures had opened up a view to the west and access to the highway, eventually became the post office.

In the old days, the Acequia de los Hermanos passed both behind the plaza to the east, where it brought water to the long narrow fields and small garden plots that fed the plaza's inhabitants and to their cattle and sheep, and into the plaza itself, through rock- and timber-lined culverts that entered under the Moro house and exited under one of the Salcedo houses. This last spur, which kept besieged inhabitants in water during Comanche raids, was abandoned when the raids had become a memory of the past and after the fire.

A hundred yards away from the plaza, at the higher end of gently sloping fields back of the six adobe houses that leaned against each other, against the last intact wall of the old plaza, Lázaro Quintana propped himself up on his rake and watched the muddy water of the acequia drop with a gurgling roar into the mouth of a siphon that snaked under the Arroyo de los Ahogados. He had just finished raking out a pile of branches and tumbleweeds and assorted plastic trash that had caught on the steel bars of the sloping trash rack. Had he not done so in time, the water would have jumped the bank. When he'd arrived it was just beginning to dribble through the grass atop the bank.

He knew that the close call was because he had dawdled back at the house. Pulling off his cracked black boots and the slipping off the dirty Levi's and putting on a clean pair and then getting back into his boots was a slow process, requiring him to stop and reflect about something with every gesture. His joints and muscles were sore, he was winded, and what was the hurry anyway? Getting old, got to slow down, that's what they say anyway, he thought. Then he realized he was hungry and couldn't wait until later to eat some of the posole Mrs. Moro had left on the stove after feeding Ramoncita. It was still warm. And then one thing led to another and he had to sit in the *excusado* for ten freezing minutes while the wind through the cracks in the boards blew wood ashes onto his clean Levi's and tried to roll the toilet paper out the door.

Yet all the while he could feel the water moving down the acequia a mile away, nudging at his aching body, and he couldn't keep from wondering what obstacle it was encountering. By the time he got back into the car and retraced his path through the village, the water had outrun his expectations by a hundred yards or so and had reached the mouth of the siphon. Trash was jammed so thick against the steel bars that it took a quarter hour of heavy raking and pulling sticks with his bare hands to clear it. Had he been another few minutes late, the water would have overflowed the bank and run down into Lalo Moro's field.

Lalo Moro lived in one of the old plaza adobes. Lázaro knew he was home because he had seen his car parked in front, but he also knew not to expect any help at all from him, even though he was a ditch commissioner and therefore Lázaro's titular equal or boss, depending on how you looked at it. Lalo was his boss because he was one of the three *comisionados* who signed his always-late paycheck, but he was also his equal or less because he was decades behind on his ditch dues and was showing no signs of paying up. Despite his *delincuencias*, Lalo Moro had been elected along with Lázaro at last December's annual meeting in a stumbling, accidental way, because all the other likely candidates for the position of commissioner had refused, opening up the way for Panchito, who was maybe sober but then maybe not, to jokingly suggest Lalo Moro, whose main achievement in life besides never paying his ditch dues was to survive a succession of spectacular car wrecks. A half dozen twisted carcasses decorated his backyard.

The other commissioners were the *güero* Porter Clapp, who kept talking of quitting, and Arturo Mesta, who had just left one job in town and was never at home because he was looking for another. Lázaro's solution to the disorganized, disunited commission, which paid him his monthly salary and was supposed to advise him on problems when they threatened to become overwhelming, was to ignore all three of them. With time Lalo Moro might even forget that he was in some way responsible to his neighbors for the flow of water. Mesta would be in the village so little that he too would let it all slip from his mind. That left Porter Clapp, who Lázaro figured he could probably talk into letting him do whatever he wanted. Then Lázaro would have the acequia all to himself, though he hadn't yet worked out how to get himself paid each month. Maybe he could just pay himself. *¿Porqué no?*

He gazed back down the slope, getting his wind back. The six houses huddled against each other in a row, their rusty tin roofs at irregular heights and angles. One of the gutters was loose. It swung and banged in the wind. All had been plastered in cement at varying times and in different ways, and on the empty windowless house at the far end of the row, the gray plaster had dropped off here and there in large circular slabs, exposing even rows of brown adobe bricks. The gutter had also fallen off, and water splashing along the drip line of the overhanging room had begun to cut a potentially fatal gash along the wall just above the foundation, or the piled rocks that would pass for one. It was the last house owned by the once-prosperous Salcedo family. Those people, he thought, just moved from house to house until they wore them out and they fell down, like the way some people wear out cars because they never change the oil or fix them. Lázaro guessed that unless the gutter were put back, the thick wall would begin to pull away from the rest of the structure in a year or two and would fall in three or four years, leaving vigas and ceiling boards dangling over thin air before they too collapsed.

The east-facing backyards and fields were divided into strips by sagging barbed-wire fences. In one, inside a small pen of boards and corrugated tin roofing and old car doors, a sow grunted and then fell silent. In another yard, chickens scratched fitfully, brown feathers ruffled in the wind, beneath a clothesline hung with flapping white long underwear. In the field Lázaro had just walked up, which belonged to Lalo Moro, there sat the smashed and rusty remains of his wrecks, the most recent of which was a red Ford Torino from which he had emerged with scars down the side of his face. Its lidless trunk and hoodless empty engine compartment were filled with empty beer cans. The wind brushed across a fringe of short grass, bright green, where gardens had once grown. Lázaro wondered whether any of them would be planted this year, or ever again.

He began walking back down toward the plaza where his car was parked. The plaza had been whole when he was a kid, at least until the fire that gutted the long Salcedo house. Lázaro remembered the summer evenings when he was carried on the back of his father's horse into town and was allowed to play in the plaza with the other kids, among the horses and wagons, while the women talked inside open doorways by candlelight and the men stood around a bonfire of chamisa and juniper branches in the middle of the dusty square, before anybody had electricity or cars or pickups, except Onésimo's grandfather.

They would come down to the plaza on evenings when the moon was bright enough to see by for their return home, along the track that was later to become a road and then a highway, to the choruses of dogs barking from nearby houses, and to the noises of cattle and sheep and goats and pigs settling in for the night, and coyotes and foxes chattering from the hills above and the banks of the river below. You could still hear from a distance the slow wash of water over the stones, at night, and even the slap of a beaver tail a half mile off, when no radios or TVs chattered through the night, no cassette decks blared from open car windows. His father even told him you could stand at certain points in the valley and listen to all four acequias murmuring in their channels at night, for this was when there were still four, not just two like now, and you could even hear where one was having trouble, where it was beginning to overflow its banks where a branch had fallen across it, or where the water was gurgling out of a gopher hole, or where some *parciante* was cheating by using the water at night when it had been assigned to somebody else. Lázaro wasn't sure whether to believe him or not, and in any case couldn't remember where those special places were anymore.

Órale, mi hijito, his father liked to tell him on the walks back to the house at night, when he would slow the horse to a stop and still the creakings of the saddle. Listen to that sound. And in the crepitations of the evening he would pick out a new sound, the regular chirping pulse of the crickets that announced the end of the summer and the slow conquest of autumn, and his father had told him about the distant pulsing he had heard once or twice as a young child, the sound of a ragtag band of Indians up on the bluff to the west beating on their cottonwood and deerskin drums.

But work in the mines had messed up Lázaro's hearing, and now sometimes through the ringing in his ears he only picked up the dull muffled noises that came from machines and the whining voices of his fellows.

He swung his legs over the low barbed-wire fence and walked down past the three houses that had once made up the south wall of the plaza, and where once there had been twice that many. The survivors stuck up like teeth in a jaw on its way to becoming toothless.

With a rasping pop, he pulled open the door to his Nissan and thrust the rake into the backseat. Maybe, he thought, it's time to get another car. Maybe he should go to the doctor and ask him whether he was going to live long enough. I feel fine, he would say. You know lots of things, doctor, he would say, shaking a finger at the young fellow. They were all young fellows now, gringos most of them, or Spanish people who might as well be gringos, *gringos ahumados*, smoked gringos, they were. You know lots of things, you young doctors. I need a new car, I think. What do you say about that? Should I get one or not, doctor?

He climbed inside. Maybe it's going to start, he considered, and maybe not. He put the key in the ignition and turned. It started. He chuckled, then coughed. Maybe you still got some life in you, not dead yet.

CHAPTER 20

Naps

The sun was beginning to move into the south window frame of the living room when Porter Clapp returned from the kitchen where he had warmed up a bowl of chile and beans for lunch.

The day's most important ritual was his afternoon nap. This he invariably took on the hard wooden *banco* opposite the east-facing window that looked across their garden and up at the steep bank of the acequia and the highway above. He first slipped off his boots and then wrapped himself up in a thick woolen afghan of thrift-store origin and then flopped over onto his left side. Once in position he pulled the blanket up under his chin just so, not quite touching, but with so little gap between blanket and chin that no air would circulate. This last arrangement was absolutely essential, just as was that of having his toes firmly wrapped up in the blanket and pulling away slightly over his folded knees in such a way as to place a certain tension on the other end of the afghan loosely wrapped around his wrists.

If he did all this just right, he would doze off in a matter of seconds. If not, which happened once or twice a week

when the afghan was too close to his chin, tickling it, or when
he had wrapped it too awkwardly around his wrists, causing
his fingers to go numb, or when he couldn't keep the other
end of the blanket firmly covering his toes, he would fuss
and turn and try out new arrangements until his shoulder
became sore on the thin foam pad covering the hard *banco*,
or his toes would get cold, and he would have to sit up and
fling the blanket off and get up and go back to work, with a
grievous sense of disappointment at having the most pleasant
moments of the day cruelly snatched from him again. During
his childhood, naps were considered a sign of laziness or lack
of imagination, especially long ones. He had never calculated
how many brief catnaps he had been roused from as a child.
Probably thousands. Time to mow the lawn, son. Naps had
become the one enduring luxury of being an adult. *Arbeit
macht frei*, his father would sometimes chant. It was some years
before Porter had decoded the layers of irony with which
the sinister slogan was uttered, and before he had finally
understood where it had come from.

But this afternoon he settled immediately into his woolly
cocoon as if into a familiar mold whose rough edges had been
worn away by habit, and in the secure warmth of the afghan he
felt his body slowly inflate to fill the entire room, incorporating
and transforming every object within it. A fly buzzing high
in the south window, the first of the season, became some
kind of motorized vibration that answered the steadier, more
insistent hum of the refrigerator in the kitchen, and the clouds
glimpsed through half-closed eyes as they drifted past the upper
panes of the south window were like fluffy sheets of paper
emerging from the noise of a copying machine, but slowly,
carefully, or perhaps some other substance, from some other
smooth gray object. The wind outside whipped and whistled
and then fell quiet for a moment, swirling around some huge

gray thing, and then there was water. His eyelids flickered as he found himself staring down into the brown water of the acequia, and he almost woke as he peered into tiny riffles and ripples, scraps of foam, twigs and dry leaves floating on the brown surface, soon joining a broad slow-moving flow, and then the ocean as blue as the sky between the clouds, the wind teasing up sharp foam-capped wavelets, the warmth of the sun suffusing the sky or the room or the back of his neck nestled into a pillow. Great structures of cloud and ice and mist rose higher and higher with faint orange backlighting, and he had to crane his neck back to peer up into the glowing heights, and there he floated on his back, arms and legs flung out, buoyant on air or in tepid salt water, the sound of distant surf, water tickling armpits and crotch, and his penis pushing firmly upward, expanding, buzzing, growing louder and louder.

A tickling sensation broke into his dream like an explosion. He gasped. He struggled to free his wrist from the seaweed and finally released a hand to grab at his nose. The fly buzzed away toward the east window. He blinked and rubbed his eyes. He was awake again, his nap rushing away from him into oblivion like the noisy wind outside. He adjusted the position of his legs to reduce pressure on what he called the sausage. He felt a pang. Always so sad, he thought, that it had to end, whatever it was. An image of Steph striding into the room and quickly massaging his penis flickered through his mind. But he could feel the thing retracting to become the naked little fledgling in a nest trying to keep from being noticed.

He sat up and disentangled himself from the afghan. He could feel the world rushing back in at him from all directions, all the things he didn't want to remember or think about. Get up, he told himself, get to work. Lazybones. He folded up the afghan and slipped on his boots.

But, he protested to himself, my naps are my work. They are how I make my living.

He could hear somebody saying, That doesn't make any sense. And then laughing. *Arbeit macht frei.*

He stood up. His workshop was only a few paces behind the house but it seemed miles and miles away. He began walking toward it.

CHAPTER 21

The Car Miser

Fabian Moro was considered by some to be San Marcos's wealthiest inhabitant on account of his collection of over a hundred cars and pickups, whose moldering, rusting shapes in a hollow below the highway, opposite the turnoff to the cemetery, were the first thing you saw of the village if you were coming from the south. The highway swerved and circled around the junkyard and looked down on it, a quarter of a mile before the dirt road that turned off to the elementary school.

Most drivers averted their eyes from the hulks, which sat in fender-high dry grass and brush, and from the leaning shed or barn whose wood had weathered to startling bands of black and gray, yellow and orange, and the low adobe house next to it with a flat green tarpaper roof, in front of which spread out an apron of dirt black with motor oil. Younger male drivers between the ages of fifteen and twenty or so, and even younger passengers, studied the junkyard carefully each time they passed, eyes fixed on the remains of a particular Chevy pickup or hardtop or an old Thunderbird or Grand Prix that they someday soon hoped to talk Fabian Moro out of.

His stubborn refusal to give up any of his hundred cars or pickups had only fed envy in others, the teenagers and young men of the valley. Man, he is so rich, that Fabian Moro. He wouldn't even miss one if we took it. They called him *el Avaro de Motores*. The junkyard was guarded by a fat, arthritic chow with deep, hoarse barks. It had been fattened on treats handed out by the latest generation of teenagers to steal into the junkyard at night to scavenge parts, during full moons.

But Fabian's concern this afternoon was not with the young *pachucos* who came and pestered him every month or so. He had heard at the store that the old man Abundio Moro had died sometime last night or early this morning and then he had seen the metallic blue hearse swing by on the curve above his junkyard. He was used to telling people that maybe they were related, maybe not. Fabian Moro had called himself the second oldest man in San Marcos for several years now, mainly because he found it an easy way to elicit compliments on how young he looked, not because he thought himself as really old at all, at seventy-eight, not like old Mr. Serrano or poor Mrs. Quintana, who weren't ever going to get up out of their beds again. He had thought about the problem ever since hearing the news at the store, when Onésimo had looked at Fabian and said, I guess that makes you the oldest now.

Fabian had said nothing. He never thought old man Moro would actually die, only that people would gradually forget about him, to the point it wouldn't matter whether he was still alive or dead and shriveling up and drying out in that cave of his, and that therefore he, Fabian Moro, would go on forever being the second oldest man alive in San Marcos.

And of course he wasn't the oldest now. Old Mr. Serrano and poor Mrs. Quintana were older than he was, or at least they certainly looked older, and there were probably a half dozen other *viejitos* besides sitting on couches all over

San Marcos watching the soap operas every day, at least until tonight, when they were going to shut off the TV translator because somebody hadn't paid the light bill.

No, he could go on being the second oldest man in San Marcos for some time now, perhaps even the rest of his life, at least for those Anglos who pulled into his yard every couple of months to ask about the old Cadillac, the one with those great tailfins, over in the corner. They never seemed to notice his limp or the way he kept his left arm at his side as he shuffled out of the shed and greeted them with a big smile and his right hand held out, almost shouting, Fabian Moro is my name. I'm the second oldest man in San Marcos. He would listen carefully at how they would exclaim over his healthy shock of silver hair and how he had so few wrinkles and how he stood so straight, almost as if at attention, patting him on the good elbow. No, I can't sell that one, he would say. That one has very special sentimental value, you know. Then he would mention some outrageous figure, half expecting one of these rich Anglos to reach in a pocket and pull out a wad of bills and give him what he asked. Look at those shiny new cars they all drove.

But even if they met his offer, which nobody ever had, he still wouldn't sell. Each one of those cars and pickups and old flatbeds was something he needed to have, either because he liked the way it looked or remembered how it drove way back then when it still had tires and a windshield, or the strange comfort they all offered when he pushed his way through the grass and pulled open the door to one whose glass was still intact, to be greeted with the warm fragrant odor of old seat covers and grease and oil, with the dogs peeing on the hubcaps and tires. He couldn't remember how many cars the Salcedos had brought to him. The Salcedos like to pick up old luxury sedans and hardtops on their last legs, Buicks and Oldsmobiles and Cadillacs, and run them until the transmissions went out or the engines threw a rod or the front ends got so loose you couldn't steer them anymore, things that either weren't worth fixing or for which they didn't have the money anyway. They took food stamps. Sometimes they took in trade a junker Fabian had picked up in Santa Fe for almost free and which had nothing really wrong with it, and which the Salcedos would run for six months before towing it back for good. They never drove anything newer than twenty-five years old, except now and then some tinny Japanese import. But Fabian never took imports. He took only good solid American cars and trucks, preferably GM. They really last out there, he had explained to a recent visitor with a sweep of his good hand. Kings of the road.

Fabian had started the junkyard after the war, for parts to keep the village cars going, and the oldest items were windowless, doorless, hoodless, paneless hulks from the 1930s and 1940s, with only a few still festooned with bits of chrome. If he spent enough time staring at any one of them eventually he could remember who had owned it for how long, whether they had bought it used or new, and what year it had ended up in the field in front of the shed that used to be the repair garage of the town, at least up until his stroke when he had to stop repairing cars for food stamps. Despite the Salcedos's derelict cars and those of a few other families like them, Fabian regarded General Motors cars as signs of prosperity and self-esteem, because that's what the best gangsters drove in the movies, the owners of Ford products being untrustworthy and immoral because of the other kinds of characters who drove them in the movies, and drivers of Chrysler-made cars and trucks as dangerously stupid or foolhardy because of the way the safety glass in all of their 1930 cars turned opaque in the sun, like mica. For twenty years he had expected the government to ban the import of all Japanese cars and pickups. They're made of paint applied to tin foil, those things, he invariably said to his Anglo visitors. My advice to you is to walk home.

Not a single vehicle in Fabian's junkyard had ever belonged to old man Abundio Moro who had just died, for the simple reason that he had never driven. He was perhaps the last man to have never learned that skill, which somehow reflected the fact that he died apparently unrelated to anybody else in the valley.

After coming back from the store, Fabian pulled an old tubular chrome kitchen chair out of the shed and set it against the south-facing wall, joining his snoozing chow. A breeze was blowing in his protected hollow, but not enough to disperse the warmth that was collecting on the *resolana* side of the wooden wall. His chair gave him a view out across the domed shapes of his cars and trucks emerging from the grass, like a herd of motionless cattle.

The old man didn't drive, he thought as he stared into the light. But he had something to do with one of those hulks out there, one of those dully reflecting rusty shapes. Idly, he identified them. A 1948 International Harvester pickup, which Mr. Morales bought new and then two years later totaled when he straddled a rock brought down by a landslide in a September downpour. Some kids shot out the windshield with a BB gun in 1975 when Fabian was in Santa Fe one afternoon. A 1963 Oldsmobile hardtop sedan, a Salcedo car. Thrown rod. Powder-blue hood half-open. Who's been wandering around out there? He felt the urge to get up and limp out there, supporting himself with his good hand on the warm roofs as he squeezed between the old cars, and open up the hood wide and lean over the greasy black V-8 and inhale its rich oily smells and remember its throaty rhythms. Hydramatic and power everything. But the sun was making him sleepy and he stayed in his chair. The 1949 Willy station wagon, but two-wheel drive, Onésimo's father's, never ran well, kept breaking down, finally just gave up on it in 1960 or 1961, no engine or transmission.

Somewhere in there a car, no, a pickup, old Abundio Moro had something to do with. But which? And what? Then it came to him. It was a '52 Ford pickup that had taken Abundio to the hospital when he had suffered a burst appendix. The time in the hospital had been so distressing that he walked, or limped, back to San Marcos, taking five days. There was nothing left of the pickup now except the doorless, windowless cab and the bed.

Up on the highway, a big government sedan rounded the curve, heading south, with one tire scrabbling at the edge of the pavement pocked with small potholes. Fabian raised his right hand in a sleepy wave.

I am Fabian Moro, he muttered to himself, dozing off. Second oldest man in this place. Not oldest. Second oldest.

It came back to him then, almost as a dream, how old Abundio Moro had once tried to pedal his red Schwinn bike the eighty miles all the way to Santa Fe, and how he had run off the road and broken his leg. But what was the car that took him to the hospital? Was it the Guerreros' 1952 dark green Ford two-door? Or that old Nash sedan, '48 or '49?

One or the other, maybe. Or maybe not.

CHAPTER 22

The Mistake

For Porter Clapp there was a moment in the afternoon before which it seemed always a little too early to undertake major tasks but after which it was then suddenly too late for more than minor ones. A change in light or temperature or the first stirrings of hunger usually announced the dividing line between too early and too late, a narrow band of time that on some days seemed to last only seconds.

As he pushed open the plywood door of his adobe workshop behind the house and switched on the fluorescent light, he knew that today was one of those too early and then suddenly too late days. The L-shaped workbench, which went around the walls, was littered with boxes and clumps of rounded wooden shapes between a drill press near one end and a small lathe near the door. Against the far wall a row of wooden packing crates nailed together served as benches for a table saw and a band saw. Everything in the room was coated with a mellow veneer of sawdust. The un-insulated corrugated tin roof rattled against the rafters. The sun gleamed through nail holes in the rusty metal.

Like a teeter totter the moment tilted into the too late. Porter pulled the door closed. He wondered whether he should put on the electric heater. Now that it was too late, that would depend on whether he was just visiting his workshop, to check in for a few minutes, or whether he might actually straighten up his tools before calling it a day.

What he could do, he realized, was update what he called his "tallies" on a dusty newspaper-size sheet of sketch paper spindled on two long nails up on the north wall, listing by the week the number of beers and bottles of wine drunk, joints and cigarettes smoked, and painkillers, mainly aspirin, downed. An unlabeled category was sex acts coded *S* for Stephanie and *M* for masturbation. The week went from Sunday to Saturday, and from what he could remember of last week he added twelve bottles of Schlitz in the form of two lots of four vertical strokes crossed over by two diagonals and two more verticals, plus two bottles of wine—Steph had drunk another two bottles—but only three joints and ten aspirin. He and Steph had not made love last week, a bad sign. He reluctantly drew two strokes under *M*. Both in the bath.

He had been keeping his tallies ever since moving to San Marcos, in the hope of controlling what he saw as his addictive tendencies, one of which was perhaps keeping track of such things. Behind the current sheets lay a padding of a dozen older sheets. Sooner or later he would have to take them down and make a master tally of the past ten years and then put up a new sheet and start afresh. He dreaded knowing these grand totals, even though as he wrote new ones on the current sheet the point of the pencil often punched through the thin paper, telling him it was time to take them all down. The grand totals would tell him the obvious, that he was addicted to everything.

Tallies entered, he looked around the workshop. The wooden shapes revealed nothing. Take us or leave us, they seemed to say. Either way. His eye passed over all the defects he would need to rasp and sand away, the roughness in the

tail of a whale, a line of dolphin mouth not clearly enough
defined, too much grain raised on the back of a manatee. He
pulled up a metal stool and sat down. Through the solitary
south-facing window of the workshop, which had once been
a barn for both chickens and goats, he could see the driveway
up the road. The sun was shining through the dusty glass,
casting a warm trapezoid onto the blotched workbench, a
definitive sign of the too late. In another half hour the roof
of the house would cut off the sun. He leaned over the bench
and stared into the light. It was warm enough in this one
patch. He wouldn't have to switch on the heater, which was
expensive to run.

With a sudden jolt, he thought of his other life, the life
he had not lived, the life he had veered away from living, the
life he sometimes imagined the people who bought his pricey
hand-carved toys to be reveling in, a comfortable middle-class
existence in a suburb somewhere, enwrapped in a soothing
blanket of possessions and insurance and stock market
accounts, where the most important labor was to keep from
being bored. It was a life he should have lived. He had
been gently herded up and down its chutes until that fateful
moment one night in the dark, amid the chanting, in the
middle of Shattuck Avenue, in Berkeley, a few minutes before
the TAC Squad rounded the corner, when he had held up
his Zippo and sparked the flame alive and, trembling hands
raised high, touched it to the corner of his Social Security
card. He could still hear the voice shouting in his ear. Hey,
man, what are you doing that for? That's not your draft card.
A chill touched his skin whenever he thought of that moment
when by accident he had become a radical, the blue and red
printed card burning down to the tips of his fingers. Then
he had fumbled through his wallet and found the draft card.
But he felt nothing when, later, he burned it and then a few
dollar bills for good measure. Then somebody had snatched

away his Zippo in the dark and that was the last he had seen of it. Now he regretted the absence of those last articles, the dollar bills and the Zippo, more than the symbolic ones. He could sense their presence still in his palm, still between his fingers, the smooth, brushed-metal shape, warm and scented with naphtha, and the almost slippery new dollar bills.

The Mistake, he called it. For years he told no one about it. Shame, not fear of the legal consequences, which he later discovered to be none, as the Social Security card could be easily replaced, drove him to twist his life around in such a way that he would never have to use his Social Security number. Lately at the few parties he and Steph went to in Santa Fe, he had taken to joking about what he imagined to be an intergovernmental task force assigned to track him down and make him accountable for the past twenty-some years of his life. The IRS would be part of it, perhaps even the organizers. Why had he failed to file a return, report any income, pay any taxes since 1969? If he had died, why hadn't he told anybody? The Social Security Administration would have similar questions. Why were there no entries to his account after the age of twenty? The Aid to Dependent Children program representative would be there, probably a woman, claiming to represent his first wife Natasha and her daughter Alexas. He was not Alexas's father but Natasha claimed he was, an arrangement they kept alive by mail and the occasional probably illegal visit. There were those years he ran up parking tickets all over California and in Santa Fe, none of which he ever paid. The police from two states would be there too, with their photocopies. Then there were whole days of phone calls made in the eighties on a corporate credit card account, number supplied by an underground Detroit newspaper. General Motors would have a team of lawyers dressed in expensive suits at the table, lawyers who lived that other life Porter had stumbled out of.

He could see himself through their eyes when they would finally catch up with him in thirty or forty years, the old hippie, bent with age, gray hair standing up except where he had tied it down with a rubber band into a crooked ponytail, shambling across the carpet to take his place at the table. Mr. Clapp, one of them would say with official politeness. Porter would look around the table. He was really on their side. He was inherently a truthful, honest man who had stumbled accidentally across a line. Law abiding. He loved abiding with the law. He wanted to be one of them, clean shaven, well trimmed, glossily suited up. Mr. Clapp, one of them would say softly.

He now remembered what he habitually forgot, a trip to Mexico paid for with a less-than-straightforwardly obtained credit card. He had sent in an application by mail, and they had sent him a card right away. It was really their fault that they didn't check his application carefully enough. It was not his fault that there was another, perfectly reputable Porter Clapp living in the southern end of the county, probably enjoying the fruits of a solidly middle-class life. A Porter Clapp who had never demonstrated at the corner of Shattuck and University Avenues and Telegraph and Haste and who never burned anything without carefully inspecting it first. Or when he made mistakes was someone who would quickly and loudly beat his breast and own up and get on with it and not go hide in a hole for twenty-some years. Porter argued with himself that he was not to blame for the credit card people having confused the two, though he suffered twinges on behalf of his unknown namesake. Did the other, the real Porter Clapp, have to pay the charges that he, the fake Porter Clapp, had run up in Mexico? Would the real Porter Clapp be sitting at the table too? With his expensive lawyers? Mr. Clapp, someone would say. But who? Which one would they mean? The other one, of course, the real one. They would call him Mr. For the imposter, they would use just his first name. Porter, they would say sharply, like the nurse at the doctor's office when he was late. Or worse, simply You.

Porter had moved to San Marcos because it was far from everywhere else, because it was cheap, because you could hide out there and nobody could readily find you, certainly not bill-collecting bureaucracies operating on shrinking budgets, and for whom it was no longer cost effective to shake down the renegades of San Marcos for what they owed in taxes or what they filched in welfare benefits and food stamps, which included perhaps half the population. Porter knew this. He had reasoned it through countless times. Yet his creditors still remained enshrined on the high ground of his consciousness. For so many years they told him that he could not at any given moment simply check back into the system, to the point that by now they were at last right. He was locked out forever, however much he might want back in, during those dim and uncertain moments of the day or night.

The village was his fortress, his citadel, his secret valley, like one of those hidden paradises or oases that now and then used to turn up in old black-and-white cowboy movies, discovered first by greedy, bad gunmen but then rescued and restored by the good guys. The Chicanos of the valley had a long tradition of expecting the government to feed them and educate them and even help them build their houses and pay their medical bills, a not quite fair exchange for having taken away their Spanish land grants and for exporting generation after generation of sons to fight the gringo wars and dig in the mines and work in the pea fields of Colorado and the orchards of California and on the railroads. Porter knew his Spanish-speaking neighbors were natural allies who had earned their cynicism about the uses of power and who automatically distrusted all those who represented it. But here, yet another debt, because Porter knew that he had not earned his renegade status in quite the same way. The government had failed in its attempt to send him off to war; it had not tried to change his native language. Instead it had offered openly and generously to this son of the middle class what it only rationed to people in small places with different kinds of last names and darker skin. He had blurted out no while really meaning yes. He had been stoned. It was dark. All a terrible mistake.

It was surging up. The pink meeting announcement had done it. The letterhead of the State Water Office. The sheet of paper tacked to the phone pole in front of Moro Mercantile. They were coming. They would want to sit him down at a long oval table. One of them would lean forward with a thin smile. They would be wearing suits or sports jackets and ties. The men, at least. The women would have ruffled blouses and little gold pins. Now, Mr. Clapp.

Their acre of land and their adobe house were in his and Steph's names. He had taken a chance, figuring it was safe for his name to appear on the records of a small county whose courthouse was located in a distant mountain valley.

The house of cards, he thought, was about to collapse. But no, the image was wrong. His house, his life, lacked precisely that, cards of any kind.

And this new invader, peering over the rim of the ridge above, down at the idyllic valley filled with springs and pools and flowing water—and, he remembered, Anglos dressed in buckskin and made up to look like Indians, with dyed black hair, in one of those first Technicolor movies he had seen as a kid. The other group, the uniformed gunmen on their horses would swoop down, waving rifles. All right, ladies and gentlemen, nobody's going to get hurt if you just sit down and fill out these forms. He could see one of the cavalry men slipping to the ground and grabbing the prettiest squaw by the elbow and leering at her. What was the name of that movie? Or was it two movies? With Roy Rogers, or who? All we want is your water, Miss. Let me go, she screams and shakes her elbow free of his grasping black leather glove. Dale Evans?

For generations they had come into the valley for the sons for their wars. Now they were coming for the water, the only thing the place still owned of value to the outside world. There would be public meetings, arguments, hearings, and the people of the valley would all end up in court, one after another, together, then one after another again, in Santa Fe, in Albuquerque, in public, names appearing again and again in summonses, hearing notices, fine-print legal ads, final decisions and final decrees.

His last stand. Or was it his first? The first, the card, wasn't really a stand. It was a youthful prank, an accident, the Mistake. But he knew finally that he had no choice but to take a stand. Clear headed, stone sober, sooner or later, he was going to have to stand up in front of everybody and say what he had to and ignore the quavering in his voice and the trembling in his hands. The enemy was here at last. And after all these years in which he should have been preparing, he had only continued to run in search of the warm enclosed spaces where all threats could be forgotten and he could hide through whole days at a time.

Even as these thoughts thundered through his mind, he reflected to the side on the oddity of a bunch of Anglo actors dressed up like Indians and speaking perfectly pronounced English devoid of a few participles, in deep voices. What did real Indians think of those movies? What was the real Porter Clapp going to think?

You fill this out, Steph, he had always said when some form arrived in the mail, of the sort that couldn't be avoided. His face seemed to swell and his chest tighten and his vision grow red if he tried to study the lines and boxes and squares and arrows, which had been invented by another race of beings, those who lived in that other life, the life of the real Porter Clapp.

A thought pierced him. When the time came, whenever it came, would he be allowed to die legally?

He looked around the workshop, aware again of where he was. Relax, he told himself. You're only a toymaker. You have chosen that most innocent of occupations.

The round wooden shapes jiggled as he shifted from one elbow to another, moving himself into the trapezoid of sun, which had crept left and was folding itself into an angular lozenge.

Touch us, they seemed at last to be saying. Take us into your hands.

Porter reached up and switched on the gooseneck lamp that hung from the wall. He picked up a wooden duck sitting at an angle, feeling a slight roughness with his fingers. It still needed a bit more sanding.

Under the duck lay a slightly flattened joint. What luck, he thought, picking it up and patting his pockets for the lighter that should be there somewhere.

CHAPTER 23

Wrecks

The only room of Lalo Moro's adobe house on the remains of the old plaza that didn't leak was the kitchen, which he had subdivided into four small compartments by means of old sheets tacked to the ceiling vigas. The rare visitor was likely to be ushered into the gloomy space with an introductory tour that consisted of the host flailing around in the sheets and calling out, This is the living room, no, sorry, this is *el comedor*, this is the bedroom, I think, hey wait a minute, then pausing to cough out the dust he had inhaled. Breathing momentarily restored, he would kick at a gray mattress on the floor. Bedroom.

An electric hot plate sat on the plain white enameled wood cookstove whose stovepipe leaned disconnected in a corner. Oven, Lalo would demonstrate, opening the squeaking, scraping oven door, and picking up the hotplate and thrusting it inside. *Mira, horno.* Followed by a high-pitched whinnying laugh.

Lalo Moro had inherited the adobe ruin from a great uncle who had lived to nearly ninety, leaving the house to the then fifteen-year-old because nobody else in the family wanted anything to do with that old *cabrón.* That was before the gringos started nosing around and asking how much people wanted for everything. How much you want for that nice pile of *basura* you got out there, nice trash you got.

Lalo had been passed from parents to step-parents, to aunts and uncles, and to Tío Baltazar, and finally to the solitude of the decaying mud walls and leaking dirt roofs of the ancient four-room house on the west side of the plaza, where he lived among piles of car and girlie magazines passed to him by a cousin who worked at a thrift store in Santa Fe. Lalo subsisted on a meager allotment of food stamps, part of which went on large boxes of Wheaties, the Breakfast of Champions, and the rest of which he turned over to the Santa Fe cousin in exchange for anything from bottles of vodka to rolls of toilet paper, at a cost of about a third of the face value of the food stamps. A cousin of the cousin's wife was a checkout clerk in a supermarket managed by her cousin, who was easily able to convert the food stamps into cash, ten percent of which he pocketed as a service fee.

One of Lalo Moro's most frequent requests was for a couple of gallon cans of Coleman camp-stove fuel to mix in with the occasional five dollars of gas he had to pay cash for at Moro Mercantile, to fuel the old Pontiac gas guzzler that had finally replaced the Ford Torino he'd wrecked two years ago. Considering the discount his food stamps suffered, this ran the price of his fuel to three times the going rate. His almost annual car wrecks since the age of sixteen were moments of glory that floated through the back of his mind as he thumbed through the old car magazines again and again. Mostly he had just run off the road and rolled over a few times down embankments. The crashes all blurred together now as a thunderous spinning sensation, to the sound of doors flying open and being crushed, the sharp little snaps of glass shattering, the gasp of tires hitting the earth, and then the fragrant rush of hot fluids dripping and squirting out of smashed crankcases and sumps and torn radiator hoses and cracked batteries. After a while they would come, all the *gente*, scrambling down the embankment and sticking their heads through the open doors and smashed windows and asking him where it hurt, could he feel anything, could he move his fingers and toes, would he like a drink of water? Soon the flashing lights would appear above, and when he was lucky they would pry open a door with the Jaws of Life, and then they would so gently ease him onto a stretcher and stagger up the slope, panting and coughing. People were so nice. They always treated him so nice. He always loved the moment when he heard some girl, some prima, gasp and say, Oh my god, you know who that is, that's my cousin Lalo Moro. He would try to open a swollen eye and give a little smile, whoever she was. And pretty soon, after the ride in the ambulance, sirens screaming, and after the emergency room where he would squeeze his eyes closed and pull back his mouth and howl how much he needed something for the terrible pain, he'd be back in the hospital bed again, all cleaned up, all bandaged up, casts in place, and they'd bring him nice warm food and even wash his clothes and let him keep the toothbrush and comb and even the soap, and he could take a shower sooner or later, and take a crap in a real toilet. And then because he didn't have any money, they'd spend a lot of time with him in the office trying to get him to promise to pay something, anything, even twenty dollars a month, for which he would offer to go rob a bank on the spot. Maybe even just ten dollars a month, Mr. Moro? You think I'm a millionaire, you know. Five? Just five dollars a month? Sure, you loan me the five dollars, and I'll give you five dollars a month. A dollar? For me, money doesn't grow on trees, except sometimes when I find a penny on the road that some rich person threw out the window. The sessions usually ended with his request to stay another day or two until he could find somebody to come and get him and drive him back home. And then when he finally got back home he'd get somebody with a camera to take a picture for his collection of him standing all bandaged up in front of the wreck in his backyard where it had been towed. As soon as he was recovered enough he'd start selling parts off the wreck to add to some food stamps to pay for his next car.

The Pontiac, which he hadn't wrecked yet, had belonged to him only three months but it was now sitting in Leandro Salcedo's front yard because the alternator had gone bad and the battery was dead. Lalo had been waiting all morning for Leandro to come by so they could decide whether to sneak into Fabian's junkyard tonight or tomorrow night or exactly when. The moon was supposed to be full tonight. Leandro told him that the alternator on the Guerrero Oldsmobile that they had sold to Fabian last year was still good when the transmission blew up. Lalo and Leandro could probably whip it out in five minutes if they had the right tools. Leandro would get the treats for the chow.

Lalo and Leandro had made a half dozen nocturnal forays into Fabian's junkyard over the years, as had most of the younger men of the valley during their teenage years. The tested routine was to shoplift some hamburger or hot dogs at Moro Mercantile to feed Fabian's increasingly overweight dog, which would often fall asleep at the feet of the intruders after being fed. Since his stroke, Fabian never ventured into the junkyard at night, though now and then he was known to prop his shotgun up against the side of the shed and discharge a shot into the sky, in the general direction of the schoolhouse, usually about nine o'clock, just before he went to bed. Word was also out that when the state police cruiser roared through town just after midnight on Friday nights, the cop shined his floodlight down on the junkyard as he drove around the curve above.

Lalo's main worry, as he sat waiting for Leandro, was that somebody had already got to the alternator first. Fabian's junkyard was such a popular nighttime hunting ground, with kids often starting at ten and eleven years old to burrow under the thick network of rusty barbed wire that Fabian had fortified his boundaries with. They foraged for hubcaps and cigarette lighters and easily detachable bits of bright work, mirror heads, lenses to tail lights, license plates, and other useless or worthless bits by which the young made the first claims to automotive manhood.

Leandro said he didn't know, he hadn't been back into the junkyard since the night after his uncle had sold the car to Fabian. He had had to go in that night to get a bag of weed he'd stuffed behind the rear seat fold-up center armrest. That was three or four months ago.

In his mind Lalo could see the alternator still there, in the orange glow of an old flashlight, as they worked away bent over, hood lowered and resting on their shoulders in the dark, dog snoring at their feet. It would be there. He could feel its heft as he lifted it out of the engine compartment and Leandro snipped off the wires and they squeezed back out of the space and half crawled and half walked through the damp grass toward the hole in the fence and then waited at the edge of the highway, below it, until their ears quieted and they could hear a car coming a mile away. Then up and across the pavement and then up the dirt road to the schoolhouse toward the moon shadows of a grove of cottonwoods known as the Lower Shooting Gallery where Leandro had parked his car. It would be as simple as that. Half hour at most.

Lalo Moro could hear in his mind his car starting up again, the long grinding of the starter, engine catching, then dying, finally catching and idling roughly, blue smoke from the rusty exhaust wreathing the landscape. He could feel himself getting ready for another wreck, a really good one this time, maybe a head-on with another Pontiac, after just a couple of beers up at the cantina in Los Martinez, just a couple, not too many, maybe with a shot of vodka to seal the deal. Always seemed a waste, those guys who go get so drunk they can't see straight, wandering all over the road, nothing worse than a real drunk driver, real stupid. Just enough to kind of take the edge off it, that's the way to do it, as you ease over into the other lane, into the oncoming headlights, or head for the gap in the guardrail. Though then he thought, looking up from a five-year-old copy of *Car & Driver*, maybe nighttime wasn't so good for that, because maybe the headlights would be a semi, and that would be bad, too bad, or you'd go over the edge and nobody would find you for a couple of days.

No, daytime's better. Late afternoon, lots of people on the road, coming home from work, lots of *gente*, lots of cousins.

But where's Leandro? The sheets swung in the breeze. Without Leandro he couldn't do it. You always needed two, one to hold the flashlight and the tools, otherwise you dropped them in the grass and Fabian's dog would want to lick you in the face. He threw down the magazine and pushed through the sheets to the door and stuck his head outside.

Dust swirled around. Two cars rumbled by slowly on the highway beyond, neither of which he recognized. It was cold. Maybe too cold outside tonight to do this, he thought.

He pushed the door closed and angled his way through the sheets to the wood stove and switched on the hot plate and held his hands out above the burner, as if toasting them.

CHAPTER 24

Comic Book God

The Cristianos didn't see Lázaro Quintana when he drove up. All four doors of the maroon Chrysler were wide open, as were the doors of a Ford sedan parked nearby. Mrs. Castaneda was collecting her things from the backseat of the Chrysler. Mr. Castaneda had his back to the driveway and was staring into the sky, hands on hips, jacket flapping in the wind. Glenda Louise Serrano's plump behind was emerging from the front seat, while her cousin Benny was behind the wheel of his old Ford, racing the engine.

Lázaro Quintana had pulled up into the western side of the rumpled, barren patch of ground that served as a turnaround in between a newly pruned apple orchard and Manny Serrano's double-wide mobile home from which he hadn't yet removed the broad plastic banner stretching diagonally along one end and that read Crestview Victory Medallion Deluxe. The popping of Lázaro's door alerted the Cristianos to his presence. As he fished out the rake from the backseat he called over gruffly, *¿Cómo estamos?*

Lázaro Quintana didn't much like their destructive god, so impatient for the end of the world and so ready to be done with the human nonsense. I like to grow little things, he had told them on their last visit to the house, when he had finally barred their way to Ramoncita. You know, the bushes and the flowers.

They will be taken care of, Glenda Louise had tried to assure him as she flipped through pages filled with drawings of a world racked by earthquake, fire, flood, famine, drought.

I'm not so sure about that, he had snapped back, tapping the pages with his index finger. Not when those things are happening. They were probably happening, he thought, because *la gente* had stopped taking care of their gardens. Worse, Glenda Louise's father, Jorge Serrano, never paid his ditch dues or only paid a little bit every now and then, just enough to make them believe that he was finally going to turn over a new leaf and become a proper *parciante*. Benny's mother, also a Cristiana, was worse. Why pay? World's ending, she had told him once. The Castanedas were recently back in town, but they still hadn't paid a penny on *delicuencias* they had run up by being away for thirty years. If they wouldn't believe in his acequia, he wouldn't have anything to do with their comic book God.

How's Mrs. Quintana doing? Glenda Louise called over. Is she doing any better?

El mismo. Just the same. No better. No worse.

He turned, hoisted the rake up on his shoulder and gave them a perfunctory wave with his free hand before sidling his way through a narrow space between a barbed-wire fence and the east side of the mobile home. The skirting had not yet been installed to conceal the stacks of cement blocks and boards upon which the structure was poised, nor had the wheel-less axles been removed yet. Lázaro was suspicious of mobile homes without knowing quite why. Maybe it's going to fall off its blocks sometime in the middle of the night, he thought as he made his way up the weed-grown slope toward the ditch bank, that's what's probably bothering me. He liked to live in a house firmly connected to *la tierra*, not balanced on piles of blocks so that when you walked around inside it everything jiggled and bounced.

He followed a dog track along the feeder ditch that ran down to Manny's apple orchard. Manny was never at home in the succession of mobile homes he had traded in, one after another, for bigger and better models over the past ten years. The only thing he had got done around his place was to prune the apple trees in the front yard, though this year he hadn't managed to clear up the plum-colored prunings yet. The back field was empty of all but last year's standing dead weeds and bright green clumps of alfalfa coming back to life. The same rusty tin cans and the same brown beer bottles the weather had stripped of their labels littered the rocky feeder ditch, the same ones Lázaro had noticed the year before, and the year before that, even for as long as he could remember.

He reached the base of the high ditch bank and began climbing the worn track, digging his heels in sideways for traction, reminding himself to come back down carefully so as not to trip again. At the top, across and above the channel, the foothill junipers and piñons hissed in the wind, cold now like the cold of winter. He had left his gloves in the car. The wind seemed to be trying to pry his fingers from the rake handle.

The brown water was flowing swiftly. The ditch channel dropped steeply through here. It had cut a deep channel in the rocky slope, and the water ran so fast that even a large branch broken off into the channel would not have held against it. There were never any breaks or floods along here. The flow was sufficient to tell him that in all probability the ditch between where he stood and Lalo Moro's place upstream was running without hindrance.

When Lázaro got back to his car the Cristianos had left. Manny's new Chrysler sedan they'd borrowed sat gleaming in the hazy sun, a veneer of dust on its maroon paint. Lázaro

walked past it close enough to glance in at its tufty leather seats
and strips of imitation walnut and little panels and consoles
of buttons and switches. For a car like that, he thought, you
would have to have somewhere to go. He didn't have
anywhere to go to, just back and forth through San Marcos.
Maybe to town once every three weeks, maybe not. Not far
enough for a car like that. Besides, he said to himself as he
opened the door of his old red Nissan, yanking it past the
point where the metal of the door caught on the edge of the
dented fender, no money for that kind of thing.

He drove back down the driveway through the leafing
apple trees and then out onto the highway heading past
Arturo Mesta's place, another one whose land was mostly
neglected through the perpetual absence of its owner. Then
an alfalfa field down below where the Vizarriagas kept their
cows, and then the road dipped and went over a knoll just
before the turnoff to the school, after which came the long
curve below which lay Fabian Moro's junkyard first and then
the five-acre field owned by Arturo Mesta, who rented it out
to the Vizarriagas to grow more alfalfa on. The field usually
soaked up the last of the water from the acequia but for times
when they needed to cut the hay there was a channel that ran
past it and back into the river. This field was the main reason
Mesta had been on the commission for years, to make sure he
got water to it.

Lázaro parked in front of the barbed-wire gate and rolled
down the window. A culvert carried water under the highway
at this point, where it shot out of the far end and dropped
down into a large rocky hole ten feet below, from which it
flowed along the upper edge of the field. But the water hadn't
yet arrived. Lázaro would hear it from his car when it belched
out of the culvert and plunged into the hole. All going well, he
wouldn't have to do more than just get out and walk over to
the gate and peer down below, watching the water thread its

way down the narrow channel back toward the river. Mesta or the Vizarriagas always burned the ditch banks down there, and then the cows browsed and trampled down what was left, and as a result there was little in the way of brush to catch any floating debris.

The wind rocked the small car. The bird-like jabbering from the schoolhouse above the highway was muffled by a gust of wind. Soon the orange school bus rolled down the dirt track, disappeared from sight behind some cottonwoods to emerge at the highway and head on up through San Marcos toward Los Martinez. It was filled with brightly dressed kids Lázaro suspected of throwing trash into the ditch—candy wrappers, tin cans, even old tires, whatever was handy.

He pulled out a packet of cigarette papers and pinched a solitary sheet with his numb fingers, then from a small muslin sack of Bull Durham dribbled sweet-smelling chips of tobacco into the paper trough, licked the paper, and rolled it into a creased cylinder. He felt the heat of the lighter's flame on his face, then a sharp serpent within his lungs, which grew with each puff warmer and softer. Seventy-five and not dead yet. Not bad, he thought. Maybe I'll get to eighty. Maybe even ninety. A hundred? No. I don't think so, not a hundred. *Cien años.* That's too much. Be all alone in the house, small and stiff, and probably blind, and deaf for sure, and bent double, like that oldest Moro who just died. Lázaro could see the face like a leather mask pulled down tight over the bones, in the coffin, nestled by the shiny satin material. The collar would be too big for the tiny neck. They wouldn't be able to figure out how to make it tight.

The crash of the water was so loud he flinched. At that instant he remembered the mouth of the culvert on the other side of the highway, which he should have checked but hadn't. He climbed out. A thick ribbon of muddy water arched out of the projecting end of the culvert and splashed into the rocky pool ten feet below, where it swirled around vigorously, generating a ring of dirty foam before setting off to the south, down a channel along the high side of the greening field. In the distance the silvery gray cottonwoods were fringed with light green, marking the course of the river, the ditch water's ultimate destination. Lázaro watched the water track its way by fits and starts down the channel, a foam-tipped worm, the striving member of a dog or horse, filling the banks as it went.

With luck his day would be done. Rake in hand he trotted across the asphalt and looked down into the mouth of the culvert. It was clear. A high line of dampness on the gray cement buttress told him that it had blocked briefly, but the water had pushed whatever it was, tumbleweeds and twigs probably, all the way through the culvert with the loud splashing surge that had given him a start while he was smoking in his car.

He climbed back in and swung out onto the highway. The enclosed warm space cradled his weariness and carried him along toward the center of the village, the car's easy movement a momentarily miraculous relief from his day of trudging up and down ditch banks and across fields and through rusty strands of barbed wire. The thought suddenly came to him that the Cristianos might have got into the house. If she were still there, would they have talked Isabel Moro into letting them in to see Ramoncita? They could have. Isabel Moro might do it because it would be easier than trying to say no. Mrs. Quintana, that Glenda Louise would say, please make a sign if you know we're here and if you still believe. . . . He would come home and find their little comic books on the white bedspread, perhaps even slipped into the fingers of her entwined hands. He wondered why they did it, especially the ones like Glenda Louise, who was too nice and plump, too young, for the end of the world. They should send tough old wheezing ones like me to scare them, he laughed to himself.

He almost drove past Onésimo's store. He braked, glanced in the mirror, and swung right into the lumpy dirt parking lot. The door popped as he pushed it wide open. He felt the stiffness of his legs as he walked, slightly bent, across the oily dirt to the door. He pushed through the chattering screen door and the wooden door behind it.

You need to fix that door, he called out to Onésimo without looking up. *Viejitos* like me aren't strong enough.

He picked up a pouch of tobacco and dropped it on the counter. *¿Qué tanto?*

Onésimo rang up the sale. Five people had told him to fix his screen door today. He was keeping count, a little tally on a scrap of paper next to the cash register, a tangible statistical proof of human perversity. Unfortunately nobody who owed money on an account had told him to fix the screen door, so he had so far been deprived of the line he held ready at the tip of his tongue, Pay your bill, *primo*, and I'll fix that screen door. Lázaro Quintana, who never ran up bills, received a sullen stare. No words accompanied the exchange of rumpled bills and the pouch of tobacco and a packet of papers.

Lázaro pulled open the wooden door and pushed through the reluctant screen door and called back to Onésimo. *Ya hay agua*, but tell the people they have to pay their *delincuencias* before they take any.

Among the people were Onésimo Moro himself, who hadn't paid last year's ditch dues because he didn't trust Lalo Moro, who he claimed was stealing money from the ditch treasury to pay off his bills at the store, because where else could he get it?

Lázaro drove slowly the rest of the way home, casting an eye eastward at first, up the slope, past fields and adobe houses, on the unlikely chance he might catch a glimpse of some sign the ditch was blocked and overflowing somewhere or that somebody's ditch gate had been left open. When the ditch passed under the highway, he squinted into the sun to the west and looked down on the fields below. At the Motts' driveway, Porter Clapp's rusty white Chevy Carryall waited for him to pass. He almost pulled over but then saw it was Porter's *mujer* behind the wheel—he could never remember her name, *la Señora Clapp*—so he drove on.

He turned into his driveway just after the acequia went back under the highway again, and he pushed the gear lever into second and bounced up the narrow dirt track toward his low adobe house with gray rafters sticking out over its weathered mud walls. Fresh tire tracks the wind had not yet obliterated in the sandy dirt told him that probably Isabel Moro had come and gone not too long before. He shut off the engine and climbed out and extracted the rake from the backseat and carried it over to the porch, which ran the length of the west side of the two-room adobe, and leaned it next to the front seat of his last pickup, which he had unbolted and pulled out before having the rest of the old Chevy towed to Fabian's junkyard.

Inside, he switched on the light. The kitchen stared back at him. The old green gas range on its bow legs, the bulbous Frigidaire, the glazed green walls and white-and-green patterned linoleum, and the warm bread-like smell that he remembered more than actually smelled—the space embraced him with a sharp pang, almost like a reproach, like one of those moments in the now remote past when he had stepped inside with muddy boots and Ramoncita had shrieked at him to pull them off before taking one more step. He looked down. They were clean and dry.

The posole was on the stove in a covered enamel pot, still hot. Isabel Moro had left some fresh flour tortillas on the table under a dishtowel. He pulled off the lid and dipped his finger into the mix. It was warm enough. He unlatched the cupboard above the sink and pulled out a plate and a bowl and ladled the posole into the bowl and slid the tortillas on to the plate.

There were no comic books on the bed or between her hands. With his boot, he pulled a chair away from the wall and worked it over toward the bed, balancing plate and bowl in his hands. He sat down next to the bed.

¿Tienes hambre, eh? Seguro que sí.

He dipped the spoon into the posole and then held it up and leaned over the plate and bowl. Then, gently, he blew across the steaming spoon toward her nose.

Tienes hambre, cierto, he said softly. He blew again.

¿Más?

He kept blowing again and again, pausing now and then to tear off a piece of tortilla, blowing its aroma in the direction of the softly breathing form. He blew until the bowl of posole was finally cold and the tortilla torn into a dozen scraps. A clear plastic bottle hung from a metal pole on the other side of the bed, and a clear tube ran down the pole and over to her arm. The bottle was still almost full. The nurse must have come. He stood up and worked the chair with his boot back to the wall.

Bueno, he murmured as he shuffled out of the room, pulling the door not quite closed with his free hand. He dumped the *posole* back into the pot and turned up the heat. Nibbling on a tortilla, he waited standing, staring out the dirty window over the stove. The wind was still blowing. Some clouds were building up in the east. It would be cold again tonight. It might even snow.

CHAPTER 25

Crestview Classic Medallion Deluxe

Manny Serrano roared up his driveway in his new black Ford Super Cab XLT pickup and pulled in next to the maroon Chrysler LeBaron that already looked almost old-fashioned after just six months. He noted that StarShip Classic Mobile Homes had not yet come and put the skirting on his new Crestview Classic Medallion Deluxe like they'd promised—yesterday they said they'd do it even though it was a Sunday or today at the latest—so it still sat there two feet up in the air on cement blocks and wood shims with its plumbing wrapped in thick insulation exposed, which undercut the effect of the arched windows and white mullions and the white plastic trim over the blue-gray pressboard of what the brochure called its "Distinguished Manor Style."

Manny had got the double-wide for less than wholesale from the dealer, with a good trade-in price, low interest rates, and a long payment plan, with no first payment for six months, by offering a discount himself on the satellite dishes or cable service that StarShip threw into every mobile home deal, for which they were able to charge double the going rate by salting the charges away in interest rates and things like warranty service charges. Most of the young couples who bought these things were already overextended and were terrified at being turned down on the finance package, so they usually averted their eyes when signing the contracts, and yes of course they needed the cable or satellite dish for the kids and would switch to the supposedly cheaper service to start out with. The older couples who bought these things usually wanted all the bells and whistles and didn't care what they cost, yeah, and throw in the satellite or cable for the grandkids, why don't you?

Manny Serrano used to like coming home to San Marcos after a long day or two in town, where he often spent the night. There was something soothing about the place, at least for a few minutes. But lately he had become almost frightened. He could feel it, whatever it was, as soon as he reluctantly switched off the ignition. Maybe it was in the trees, the old apple trees that crowded in on his driveway and, surrounded the mobile home, in the shadows, the stillness and quiet and cold, the wind sluicing through the branches. He knew the house would be empty. Brenda May would be out somewhere until late in her almost identical XLT, breezing in at midnight, supposedly playing bridge or something with her relations up in Los Martinez, though he knew better. She and Manny had a game going. For how many years now? Who could get home latest, who could leave the house earliest.

He hadn't been home this early in years, middle of the afternoon, and didn't know why he had impulsively made the drive all the way home from town after taking delivery of the new pickup, six months newer than hers, another kickback deal having to do with Fleet cellular phone service, which he also had a finger in, and though the discount had been good, better than he had hoped for, the thing had cost almost as much as the mobile home. Their insurance was going to go through the roof, even though he had a way to get some of that taken care of too. He wasn't sure how much she brought home anymore as a computer consultant and suspected that she was hiding some of her money in a secret account. He and Brenda May had another game going on too, to see how much each of them could put on their credit cards each month, and now with two Ford Super Cab XLTs, the Chrysler LeBaron, the Crestview Classic Medallion Deluxe, and seven Visa, MasterCard, Discover, and American Express Cards to make payments on every month, in the Ford dealer's finance manager's office while they were all yukking it up over some stupid dirty joke, he had realized that he and Brenda May were in way over their heads.

He opened the door of the pickup, exchanging the warmth of its new car smell for the icy wind that cut through the tan material of the summer-weight suit he had mistakenly put on this morning. The door closed with a soft, satisfying clunk that yet hinted of too much plastic. Why was he here? Brenda May wasn't home, her XLT was probably parked in her latest boyfriend's driveway, probably somewhere in Santa Fe. And even if she were at home, she would be the last person to turn to for advice or comfort. He would turn to his girlfriend first. He'd driven past her apartment on the way home but decided not to stop. She was like another credit card. Why would she want to hear him whining about money?

So he had got out on the highway, excuse to drive the new pickup, and found himself driving back to San Marcos and down the driveway for lack of anywhere else to go. But once here, then what? He decided he would go inside and pee and then come right back out and drive back into town, where he'd arrive at Buster Lopez's Lounge just as the gang would be dribbling in after work, and after a couple of drinks and another half pack of Marlboros everything would be all right, what the hell, and then maybe a steak and fries and some coffee to get him back on the road or at least over to Lydia's apartment for an hour or two. Then he'd be ready to come home and shower and sleep in one of the new bedrooms while Brenda May snored in the other one. He wondered why they even bothered.

StarShip hadn't installed the permanent steps either, in place of the flimsy wood and wrought-iron ones, which wobbled as he climbed up them. The door was unlocked. He stepped inside the living room. It was too quiet. A track of footprints indented in the orange shag carpeting led from the TV set around the sofa in brown-and-black plaid toward the kitchen. A bowl of Fritos, half empty and surrounded by crumbs, sat in the middle of a coffee table. Manny picked up the remote and switched on the TV. He hated being in houses or offices that were quiet. But no music or voices came on as he walked toward the bathroom, only a dull hissing.

He urinated profusely into the bright pink bowl. Just in time. What he was afraid of back here, he realized, was not what there was, which was nothing but trees and dirt and wind and people sitting around trying to get old really fast, but what there wasn't. He loved pushing into crowded restaurants and bars in town, to that corner or table where he knew all his friends would be eating and drinking and smoking, and the girlfriends they passed around to each other, and the tiffs and fights they had, and driving from place to place, making his rounds through the city and county and state offices, the car and mobile-home dealers, the banks and finance companies, swimming day after day through the amber social liquid, where people took care of each other and passed tidbits back and forth, and then schemed to take them back, betrayed each other, and then learned to trust again, for a while at least. He loved the padded leather booths and stools and benches and chairs, the dim lights, the drinks, the glass shelves of glinting liquor bottles from all over the world, the music, the shouting, the risks, but he feared being found out or going over the edge or being a little too daring, a little too sleazy, or being thrown out of the whirl, back into some cold, empty, windy place like this. He feared becoming like Jake Márquez, with five years in the pen for embezzling ahead of him. Good old Jake. He'd bought them lots of drinks with the taxpayers' money over the years.

He zipped up his fly and trotted back down the hallway to the TV, thinking to turn it off before he went out the door and drove back to town. Oddly there was no picture on the screen, only snow and hissing. He switched channels. Same thing. The satellite control box readout displayed no messages of distress. It was working OK two nights ago or whenever he had been home last. Perhaps the wind had unhooked something.

He strode through the kitchen and swung open the back door and peered out, craning his neck upward. What was the ladder doing there? Strangely the platform on the roof to which the small satellite dish had been bolted was now empty. At the far end of the back field where Manny's father had once grown chile, fifty yards away, the figure of a young man dressed in Levi's and a padded brown jacket was staggering up the ditch bank with an arm wrapped around the gray satellite dish, wires trailing behind.

Hey! Manny called out. He suddenly felt overweight and wrongly dressed. A picture of him running through dead weeds in suit and tie, panting, face red, did not please his vanity. And the suit was worth more than the dish. Hey, stop!

The figure reached the top of the ditch bank, turned around and glanced back before leaping across and vanishing into a plum thicket on the other side. Manny had no clear view of the fellow's features. He watched with appalled fascination the round gray dish, which had apparently snagged on the plum branches, being tugged this way and that until it finally disappeared into the vegetation like a face sinking beneath the surface of the water.

Goddamn, he shouted. His grandfather's far richer imprecations in Spanish swirled around in his head in bits and pieces without ordering themselves into coherence.

He stepped back inside and slammed the door behind him. A branch blowing in the wind was scraping along the siding of the north wall, a long scratching noise, then a pause, then resuming, as the branch blew this way and that. Should he call the sheriff? The state police? His insurance agent? That would all take time. He'd have to sit in the house waiting for somebody to show up. He couldn't see himself sitting in a room like this without the TV on, not this early. Later, very late at night, maybe with the stereo on, sure. He looked at his watch. Later, tomorrow or the next day. He would get his secretary to make the calls.

He locked the back door and strode through the living room. The TV was still on blankly. He left it on and latched the door and pulled it closed behind him.

The snout of the new black pickup, parked on a slight incline, greeted him expectantly like a dog waiting to be taken on a walk. His fingers grazed the perfectly smooth metal of the fender. The new machine would take him back to the lights, the plump leather booths, the laughing faces of his friends, the pouting lips of the women, and to the double margarita he knew he now deserved.

He climbed inside and inserted the key in the ignition and turned it. The engine fired to life instantly. All roads led away from this moment. Perhaps he would never come home again.

CHAPTER 26

Imperfections

They don't want my love. All they want is my paycheck, Steph was saying.

She and Carrie Mott were hunched over the kitchen table, chairs pushed out far, which gave their cross-legged leaning forward an acute angle. Steph's gaze was fixed on the brandy bottle and heavy tumbler. A pot of tea was still emitting steam from the spout, and the mid-afternoon sunlight through the kitchen windows was picking out individual droplets swirling up from the mugs.

So Len Mott imagined. He was sitting in the next room pondering the order for Santa Fe. Carrie had not closed the swinging kitchen door, a sign. Nor had she led Steph off to the bedroom, another sign that usually meant that he might soon be called in for advice concerning the probable evolution of the current Clapp crisis, which usually had to do with money. Probably Porter was oblivious as usual, and perhaps it might pass without him ever becoming aware of it at all. Consumed by his own convoluted reasoning, he rarely noticed Steph's more public eruptions.

Steph had arrived all breathy about planting a flower garden at last but then had dropped back into her more habitual despair over the cost of seeds and bulbs and plants. She loudly wondered why she had quit her job in Santa Fe as a secretary in order to give more time to the kids—and to Porter, she added hesitantly. And why she had thought she could depend on Porter's toymaking business, which of course was not prospering as planned and had even declined of late and was bringing in even less money than usual for this normally low time of the year. The five-day-a-week drive into town for three years running had been awful, but worse was sitting at home with Athena and Krishna coming home from school every afternoon with semi-official demands for money. Apparently these days to get an A you have to be prepared to spend money, her voice rang through the kitchen into the living room.

Len studied the order and the lists of supplies he needed to pick up, his coffee sending up its own misty signal from another ray of sun through the living room window. The order form and supplies list were on a clipboard he had picked up and set back down on the glass top of the coffee table a half dozen times since retreating to his armchair. Please stick around, Carrie had urged him while through the kitchen windows they watched Steph climb out of the big rusty baby-blue station wagon. There was something in her manner that spoke of the continuation of the chronic Clapp crises, hair blowing over face, chin up, oddly cheerful defiance in her green eyes.

I'll stop by and see Carrie, I said to myself, she had said to Carrie, dropping her purse on the table, and we'll talk about my garden and get drunk together.

Can't, said Carrie. We've got a big order to get on the truck this afternoon for Santa Fe.

I know, I know.

Len had not been addressed during her entrance. He quietly finished making his coffee and stepped into the living room. For Steph, he was a member of the enemy species.

The only way for men to negotiate with her sullen attractiveness was to flirt with her, something a succession of lovers and husbands had perhaps grown weary of, thereby slipping back into nonbeing. Len suspected this was what was happening to Porter, as inevitably it would. Exhausted by nonstop courtship, he had ceased to exist in Steph's eyes. Either you were the Male or the Enemy or a Nonentity. Len sipped his coffee, half listening while contemplating his nonbeing, as the two women talked in the kitchen in gradually lowering voices. Carrie would be drawing her out, offering the sympathetic word, the suggestion, glances passing from the brandy glass to the clock and back. She knew that they had to start loading soon if they were to leave before dark. It would not be pleasant in the wind.

He's been talking about moving farther south, Steph was saying, her voice raised again, where there's nobody at all to find him out. Between Lordsburg and Deming, where half the people are already illegal. He loves it down there. All that empty flat space, mile after mile. Where you can see some-body coming from ten miles away. I couldn't stand it.

This was the first Len had heard. He was jarred by this talk of defection. And puzzled that Porter had never said a word about it. Yet, he reflected after a moment, one of the subjects that he and Carrie had been drawn to during the long winter months was not whether they should sell out and move on but how much they would get for their place and the nursery business if they ever decided to do so. Everyone had been scandalized—or thrilled—by how much one of the old Salcedo places on the way up to Los Martinez had gone for to that couple from California who hadn't moved in yet: scandalized, the locals, if they had sold a piece of land or old adobe to a newcomer Anglo in the past twenty years, calculating the difference between what they had got then and what they might have gotten today had only they hung on. Or thrilled if they were still in the possession of saleable property.

He leaned back and looked at the ceiling vigas and planks, dark with sticky varnish. There was not a level floor, plumb wall, or ceiling or lintel beam that did not sag anywhere in the house. He had become used to thinking of their old adobe house as a collection of construction mistakes and lessons on how not to build things, though it was solid in its way, even somewhat overbuilt. It was as if the house had been put together over several generations without the benefit of a spirit level, T-square, or tape measure, and probably with the strange carefree happiness of those who believe that sloppiness and inexactness have no consequences—as apparently so far they didn't in this house, as long as you shimmed the refrigerator and bathtub and hot water heater to make them level and didn't expect to open and close doors and windows in a hurry whenever the weather changed.

Whenever he felt the hopeful flush of prosperity from the nursery and landscaping business, Len Mott imagined all the ways he would bring the old house into the code of his more exacting standards by replacing floors and reframing windows and doors and even defying old Mr. Guerrero's injunction never to change the kitchen, by tearing up the linoleum floor and replacing it with Mexican tile and putting in a restaurant-grade range and a new refrigerator. There were the walls and ceiling to insulate, the windows to double-glaze, and the old iron plumbing nearly dead with arteriosclerosis to tear out and redo right with copper tubing, and the rusty tin roof to replace with some of that new painted metal roofing material. He fed these fantasies with a subscription to an architectural magazine that specialized in lean and efficient interiors with thrillingly clever fixtures and design systems at prices he and Carrie were years, even decades, away from affording, though he was afraid to think that they might always be beyond their reach. Some of the houses in the glossy photos were much like the houses of their landscaping customers in and around

Santa Fe, and their clients' money came from investments, professional fees, and the lucrative work of brokering, jobbing, wholesaling goods and symbols and information, far from the sweat and grime and physical exhaustion of manual labor, and their clients' wealth depended on the difference between what they got for their services and what he and Carrie could hope to charge for theirs. His and Carrie's prices were high, otherwise they couldn't stay in business, and they could obtain them only from those clients who treated them as fellow professionals, essentially as equals, not mere laborers, though he often felt they were perched on a particularly precarious ledge.

The sale of the latest Salcedo place might be a sign of encroaching affluence but also perhaps of something else. Also badly designed, or rather totally undesigned, the Salcedo adobe was of some age and surprising solidity. The new owners had made a fuss of how charming it all was and how little they were going to change it. Since then Len had begun to look at their own house through somewhat new eyes, or perhaps the eyes with which he had first seen it ten years before, when both he and Carrie were at first taken by its chunky, awkward character, though they didn't and would never call it charming, a character that said at the time that it welcomed ordinary people who should feel free to do whatever they wanted within its idiosyncratic spaces, not dictating that you be insanely neat and tidy, as so many efficient new interiors seemed to command, or that you ransack the earth for goods and possessions to store in whole walls of cupboards and closets, or that you dress up and entertain and eat and drink from dawn to dusk. The old adobe had said simply, you are inside now, this is the indoors, you are out of the rain, the cold, the wind, the dark, and please feel welcome here as long as you need before resuming your real work, which is outdoors. It was a house that would tolerate a small radio or

TV and a telephone and a computer in a corner somewhere but not anything as grand as an entertainment center.

Now he wondered whether his fantasy plans for the rebuilding of the house were not at odds with its real character and the perhaps confused or contradictory intentions of its several generations of builders. He and Carrie were in the business of perfection—they sold people on the idea of the perfect front yard, the perfect courtyard, the ideal patio, even the perfect vegetable garden—yet he knew how illusory it all was. Once achieved, what inevitably followed was degradation, decay, the maddening weeds of imperfection, the cracks in the expensive paving, trees that grew too tall and trees that refused to grow fast enough, trees that failed to blossom at the right time, trees that gave fruit that wasn't quite what was wanted or that came all at once, too much to deal with. Yet, the persistence of imperfection gave them a steady stream of repeat business, to revise, expand, uproot, replant.

And maybe the house was so imperfect that it could never be put aright, or that in trying to do so, in leveling the floors and making them smooth he might then fixate on the lumpiness of the walls, which in fact didn't bother him yet. And it would be that the house, in insisting on its imperfections, was in fact trying to say that perhaps it was easier to live in a world you accepted as imperfect rather than to strive futilely to bring it up to some standard of levelness and squareness and smoothness that in fact could be maintained only by him being in a state of constant exasperation. Perhaps this is why he had stopped envying the almost perfect houses of his Santa Fe clients, even while continuing to trot out the compliments.

Such thoughts, he realized, would be bad for business, if he pursued them too far. He stood up and tucked the clipboard under one arm and picked up the empty mug and ambled into the kitchen and did the male thing.

Steph, he interrupted, why don't you take Porter into town one day and sign him back up. It probably won't hurt. The Social Security people probably won't bother to put him in jail.

She looked up at him. Her eyes briefly focused. Then he added to Carrie, We do have to get that order onto the trailer.

The two women sat without moving. There are couples, Len thought, who have in common only what they don't have in common. Their lives together consist in endless negotiation of the irreconcilable. Which is, after all, one way to put order into chaos.

Steph shook herself and stood up. The kids will be home, she said absently. Wanting something. And tomorrow, tell yours to get off at our place.

I'm calling in an order the day after we get back, Carrie said. They won't bill us for a month. Will that help?

Steph smiled wanly and nodded and picked up her purse and tugged at the door. Then she turned around and said, Bye, Len.

A little absently, he thought, but better than nothing. He was partially relieved of his Nonentity status. He leaned over and helped her pull open the door.

CHAPTER 27

Heaven on Earth

The picture went dead on Esmerelda Vizarriaga's TV during one of those confessional shows in which unhappily married couples complain about each other, fortunately not during her favorite soap opera. The picture blinked and went snowy and the whining voices gave way to a loud hissing. Remote in hand she sat on the sofa expecting the picture to return. Then she remembered that this was supposed to be the day they turned off the electricity to the TV tower or whatever they called it. The thing up on the hill that improved the reception.

Esmerelda Vizarriaga kept sitting there, waiting for something to happen. She was a little woman, and her feet barely touched the carpet. The faded floral house coat with its pattern of flamboyant pink roses blended in with the nondescript orange flowers of the sofa slipcover, whose rumpled material she was smoothing with her left hand. She listened for sounds of Juan coming up the back steps. As soon as she heard the door open, she would call out, Juan! Fix the TV! The TV needs fixing! But there were no new sounds over the hissing. She pressed the mute button. The hissing stopped. In the whitish flickering of the screen she could make out the faint shadows of the whining couple. They should never let people like that on TV, she thought, talking about things like that. Dirty underwear. Smelly socks. Sex.

Juan would still be out in the back digging ditches or something. Her joints ached too much to do a garden this year, she had told him. Time to let the weeds grow. But the vision of the ragweed and *quelites* and pigweed shooting up and taking over in the garden patch out the backyard, becoming a dense clingy mass you could hardly walk through, first green and sticky, then dry and scratchy, did not please her. And then there would be the *cabritos* sprawling over the dry corners with their reddish vein-like branches that hugged the earth and their oddly pretty tiny leaves and tiny yellow flowers, which gave birth to nasty three-pointed stickers Juan would track into the house and which would end up entangled in the chenille bathroom rug, to ambush her late in the night or early in the morning with a piercing sting that would last the rest of the night or day, though she sometimes thought they might be good for her arthur-itis, as she called it, like bee stings. Then there were those other stickers, what were their names, that suddenly sprang out of what looked like nice ordinary clumps of grass, little balls with stickers all around them, they liked to latch on to your shoelaces and ended up on the cuffs of Juan's pants and even the hems of her dresses and sometimes even on the sofa, like that time, who was it, Mrs. Morales maybe, had sat right down on one, *Eee, que bárbaro*, she had screamed, not thinking it funny at all, served her right. What did those stickers want to come inside the house for anyway? There's no dirt here. Not one speck.

But without the garden they'd really come inside the house, first those little bitty ones from the first weeds, that grass, they would get in her slippers so bad she sometimes had to throw the slippers out in the trash, and later those long black things with little hooks on one end, and then the big brown burrs from what's that plant, she knew the name of that one, that plant that looked so pretty with its big drooping broad leaves and purple flowers, what was it. Burdock, in English, one of the *vecinas* had told her. Pretty until it was all of a sudden covered with dark brown fuzzy burrs.

Maybe she could talk Juan into mowing it all down and planting grass there or something. He hadn't said anything when she said she didn't want to plant this year, he'd just looked away and walked outside. It wouldn't look good to have a bunch of weeds growing around the house, she knew, the neighbors would think they were finally getting too old to take care of the place. Well, maybe they were.

The kids kept saying, Move to town, you can live with us, we'll build you a little casita in the backyard so you can have a life of your own. Who needs a garden anyway. We got Furr's, Albertsons, Smith's, Osco. But whenever she went to town, Santa Fe or Albuquerque, and stayed for more than an hour or so in one of the kids' houses, even with their nice big TVs, she kept looking out the window to see more than just cars and other houses and cement brick walls, and then they'd get in the car and drive to the malls and go shopping for clothes for the grandchildren, everybody all excited, and it was nice, and such a fine selection, prices so cheap, but when you came outside it was all those cars again, the traffic, when all she wanted was to be sitting on her own sofa watching her own TV next to the window where she knew she could look out of at any time of the day and through the apple trees to the hills and the mountains behind, not another house in sight and not worrying about who lived in them and whether they were happy or not or hungry or miserable or mean to their kids or had enough money or not.

What does it matter where you watch TV, Grandma, one of the kids had asked. It's the same wherever you watch it, isn't it?

It's not the same at all, let me tell you that, she had snapped back.

She didn't like to watch it anywhere except at home, certainly not at the kids', and not at the neighbors' or at any of her relations in San Marcos, and not even with Juan sitting right next to her asking stupid questions, as if the picture couldn't be watched by more people than one. I want to watch this, she would tell him in the evening after dinner. You go take your paper over to your chair or into the kitchen, why don't you. *Vete!* Go on now. And he would stand up stiffly and shuffle into the kitchen and pull up a chair next to the wood cook stove, light to his back, and read through every word on the page.

Watching TV wasn't like going to the movies with a bunch of other people sitting in the theater, like she and Juan didn't do anymore. It was something private and personal where time stopped and all her worries about the kids and grandkids and their cranky old relations in San Marcos evaporated, and she didn't have to worry about what her long-dead parents thought about anything, or her dead sisters and brothers, aunts and uncles, who all would have said, Turn that thing off, it's no good for anything. Whenever she remembered, she took the phone off the hook and put it under a pillow when she turned on the TV after breakfast and settled in for the day on the old sofa. She didn't dare tell anybody, but she knew that's where she would go when she died, into that bright happy-unhappy world where everything was clean and bright even during the most tragic moments, which never lasted too long and which people forgot about so quickly, a matter of minutes, and certainly by the next episode, and where they were so busy that they never nursed grudges and grievances for fifty years running, like some people she knew in this place. People on TV came and went all the time and survived the most awful experiences without any smelly messiness; they died suddenly and cleanly, and then reappeared on other shows a month later in different makeup and clothes or in the always cheerful ads, where even the dirt didn't look dirty, and where nobody certainly died even from doing ridiculous stunts driving cars or jumping off cliffs or eating too fast, like they did every day in San Marcos.

These people would take her in when the Good Lord decided it was time for her to go and they would clean up the mess, because there was always a mess, and she would join the chattering bright world, in English or Spanish, she didn't care, she didn't listen to Mrs. Morales when she chided her for watching all those Mexican soap operas with their bad Spanish. She hadn't liked the Mexican soap operas at first because she didn't like the pushy way Mexicans spoke, right up there in your face, ratatatat, which seemed too bold and aggressive like the way most Anglos talked at you, like you were deaf, not at all like the quiet almost muttered Spanish of *la gente*, so much more dignified. But she got used to the way they talked too much and sometimes she thought *¡Mentiras, Mentiras!* was her favorite show now, though she kept hoping those people would slow down a bit, she didn't know whether she could talk as much as they did when she finally got there.

She stared at the nearly white screen of indistinguishable figures. She knew the Anglo priest who now and then came to perform mass wouldn't understand this, or how she saw Jesus and Mary being the official greeters who would open the doors into the bright world of happy never-ending drama where most everybody got what they wanted with only a little suffering, and there was always lots of company. Like Mickey Mouse and Donald Duck waving to you, *como en el Disnilandia*.

But she wondered what would happen to her window. Would she be able to see her view once she had vanished into the world inside the TV set? She turned sharply, twisting her head to the right. She could see nothing but a blur, she

realized, because she didn't have on her glasses, which was OK
for TV but not for looking out the window. As she dug into
her sewing basket at the end of the sofa, she wondered how
many years she had turned toward the window and simply
imagined what she knew was out there without actually seeing
it. The glasses were there, smudgy with disuse, or because she
hadn't bothered to clean them. She breathed on the lenses
and rubbed them clear with the hem of her housecoat and put
them on and turned to the window.

The apple trees were mostly leafed out. Their piercing
fresh green played in the wind and sunlight. And the first pink
buds were beginning to open. As the leaves flicked in the wind
she could make out the tan clay flanks of the cliffs to the west,
remembering that's where *la gente* had gone for generations to
dig out the special white clay, *tierra blanca*, to plaster the inside
of their houses before there was paint. Now why should she
remember a thing like that? And beyond, in the far haze, the
gray peaks still lined with snow.

She was surprised and then irritated to find Juan suddenly
standing in the room.

Juan, she snapped, fix the TV. That TV needs fixing.

He turned and stared at the snowy picture. He said something but she turned back to the window and stared through
the trunks of the apple trees to the barren patch of ground
that had been their vegetable and flower garden for the past
fifty years. What was going to happen to it when they took her
away into that other world? Would she somehow still be able
to look out at it?

She turned back toward him. Then she reached down and
picked up the remote and turned off the TV.

I'll put something on for dinner, she said, turning away
from him and stepping into the kitchen. She still wanted to
think about the garden. Maybe she should plant it one more
year. She could just go and do it without saying anything, as if

they'd never had that conversation in the first place. That way
Juan wouldn't cluck, See, I told you so, see, I told you you'd
change your mind, just like you did last year and the year
before that. See?

CHAPTER 28

The Anthill

Myrna Clippenger usually took her evening walk down to the river just as the light began to fade. Her adobe house was perched on a clay bank above a small arroyo whose ribbons of sand meandered in turns too tight and narrow to allow the passage of four-wheel-drive pickups down the half-mile stretch to the river below, though recently she had come across the first nubby tracks of those motorized three- and four-wheeler ATVs some of the local kids rode around on.

The wind and the cold of the day brought her out on her walk earlier than usual. The sun beginning to lower in the sky but the light still strong. Her lavender down winter coat, which she hadn't worn for weeks, felt puffy and binding, in an unwelcomed return to a state of bundling up that she thought she had left behind for the spring. She clicked her tongue for the dogs, who emerged stretching from the woodshed back of the house where they usually dozed through their afternoons outside, Venus and Aphrodite, sibling collie mixes whose long hair was unsuitable for this burry landscape. They frisked around her and ran down the bank into the arroyo, leading the way, tails held high and waving with excitement.

Water flowing down the arroyo in occasional summertime floods had carved a channel eight or nine feet deep, and as a result whenever Myrna walked down its serpentine track, well below the level of the tumble of rocks and gravel and sage-brush, the dumpings of earlier geological flows, she felt she was entering a labyrinth. Today its depth offered protection from the wind most of the time, at the cost of sand occasion-ally blowing into her eyes. The dogs preferred the low way, as she called it, with its blind corners and overhanging clumps of squawberry bush and chamisa, to the more direct and faster higher track that was negotiable by pickups and that ran more or less straight over open ground down to the long gallery of cottonwoods that lined the river. Each time the dogs paused and sniffed studiously at the blackish little deposits of coyote and fox scat, as if they were fascinatingly new and different every day, which to them they probably were, and thrust their noses into bushes where other dogs or creatures had mictur-ated, a word she preferred over the Anglo-Saxon *peed*, before reclaiming the spot with their own hasty dribblings, delivered squatting.

Myrna regarded her low way down the arroyo as her secret passage through the landscape, invisible to anyone on higher ground. The familiar wavy tread of her walking shoes told her that no one else had used the path but her, no other human, and that the animal tracks were mostly of her collies. In this wind nothing much would be out. As if to summon them, she amused herself recollecting the animals she had seen on her morning and evening and sometime noon walks down to the river, the coyote turning away and stealing back into the willows on the other side, the skunk, often the skunk, where the arroyo broadened and opened out and rose where its channel thrust out into the waters of the stream. For most of these encounters the dogs were well behind her, exploring

their favorite side channels, particularly the one above which
a packrat had amassed a great pile of twigs around the base
of a squawberry bush. Once she had come across a small
rattlesnake slithering slowly across the sand. She paused to
wait for it to pass, and then in the days after she had carefully
stepped across its faint S-track in the sand. In October she
could count on seeing at least one tarantula migrating from
one place, perhaps damp and cold, to another warmer and
dryer, or whatever it was they sought at the change of seasons.
From afar she had glimpsed what she guessed were a bobcat,
a weasel, a fox, and most certainly in the water a beaver. Then
there were the hawks, an owl, and all the bird life she had seen
over the years down at the river itself.

Her favorite sight was an anthill next to a fire-blackened
juniper post from which hung two sagging strands of rusty
barbed wire. The anthill indicated that she was halfway
down to the river, and the post a property line to the lower
portion of a Vizarriaga field that wasn't irrigated anymore
and had been left to turn back to chamisa and cactus, now
inhabited by ground squirrels and little brown towhees. The
anthill stood a foot tall under the wire, a graceful pyramid of
fine gravel which she had heard people used to shovel into pails
to take to their chickens for grit. Myrna didn't particularly like
ants, especially the large biting black and red ants that made
such monuments, though she would occasionally tolerate the
explorations of the smaller black ants that didn't bite, the ones
that scampered over rocks down at the river with such restless
energy and dragged carcasses of dead insects for seemingly
interminable distances.

But she loved this particular anthill, whose red ants
were beginning to stir, at least during the warmer hours
of the warmest days, bringing up from the depths of their
excavations yet more gravel to add to their mountain. She had
noticed it on her first walk down the arroyo five years before.

It had changed little in that time, growing no larger, or not that she could detect, nor any smaller. She didn't care what it was for. It probably had something to do with warming or cooling the burrow, or keeping rain and snow out, or maybe it served as a little tower from which the new queens flew away after the summer rainstorms.

Nobody bothered it, probably because there was nobody around to pay attention to it except her, though she had come to notice anthills near the highway that seemed undisturbed for years on end. She regularly reflected as she walked past it, how long it might have been there, wondering if there was an internal clock that caused anthills to die out after a few years or decades, or whether they could be eternal, or eternal in relation to human lives. Was the anthill older than the fencepost? Was this same anthill around at the time the village was first settled by the Spanish in the late 1600s? Was it an anthill that the Indians had watched and had carefully walked around for hundreds of years, perhaps occasionally approaching to gather a few grains of gravel for a gourd rattle?

The anthill stood at roughly eye level where the arroyo swung around away from it. She nodded as she passed. They would all be inside, tending their eggs, the disagreeable red creatures who yet could construct and maintain such a perfect shape, a lean yet sensuous breast rising up from the earth. Perhaps, she thought, the fate of us all in the end, to become ants maintaining the perfect cone, from inside, from within its darkness.

She walked on. Though she warmed to the thought of a political organization of one female being tended by thousands of males, how that was about as perfect as you could get, except the poor queen had no female company, except briefly, when the summer showers ended and thousands of young queens were dispatched into the cool breezes, most of whom would fail in their quest to land on the perfect bit of ground where they could dig a new burrow and begin laying the eggs of a new colony. How sad.

That would have to be redone, of course. The queen should keep the young queens to herself and send out all the males, letting them crash onto barren ground, their wings falling off, to die in the emerging sun, gobbled up by birds. Myrna had long ago decided that males of the species, the human males, should be exterminated in a grand battle in some unscenic place, Antarctica perhaps, so that women could get down to the business of living without constantly being distracted by their always importunate claims, especially since they were too far gone to labor in the dark, like the male ants. The snow and ice would freeze their sperm, to be gathered up and thawed as needed.

She abruptly found herself at the river, the sun lower on the horizon to her back, the wind having finally dropped. The dogs slid down the gravelly bank and drank from the muddy water. It had risen an inch or two from yesterday, she noted from the shape of a familiar boulder, though with the cold weather the water would probably drop for the next few days. She guessed that the river would flood mildly in a month or two, its silty waters fanning out among the cottonwoods and willows, meanders lengthening or contracting depending on which trees were undercut and felled and what was floated down from the mountains with the brownish, reddish silt that gave it its name, the Río Sucio. (dirty)

Some days she turned left and followed the track of the river south, toward the canyon from which it exited the valley, and other times she risked turning right and following it upstream a half mile or so until it came to a dirt track down another arroyo that dead-ended at the stream and where, if there was nobody around, she picked up the beer cans and bottles, the fast food cartons and cups and wrappers, even occasionally disposable diapers and sanitary pads, though she just kicked dirt over the condoms, and carried it all home in a plastic shopping bag.

But the wind was gusting again, and the clearness of the sky told her it was probably going to get colder tonight, and she turned back up the arroyo, ignoring the urgings of the dogs to go downriver, into the wind, which brought rich hints of what was to be found down there. She clicked her tongue and they turned their necks around at her and stared a moment, tongues lolling, before they swung around.

It would be dark in two hours, three at the most. Night always came as a relief, perhaps less to her personally than how she imagined that night came as a relief to the earth. People would go inside and fall asleep, traffic would die down and then stop or almost stop, and the earth, protected under its blanket of darkness, could go about its business undisturbed, or less disturbed. The beavers could come out and resume work on their dam down near the mouth of the canyon, and the skunks would take over the paths again, the coyotes and foxes and bears, too, perhaps, which had occasionally been sighted down by the river, perhaps even mountain lions and deer. In the dark they would repopulate the world the way it used to be before there were so many people, with all their cars and guns and bulldozers and chainsaws and everything else they used, men used, to turn everything into desert.

She strode back past the anthill into the sun as it was approaching the clay cliffs to the west. No ants were visible. She wondered whether they came out at night, in the dark, when it was warm, like all the flying insects that whirled around her porch light in August and September.

The dogs were far ahead now, remembering the house again, and in anticipation of the plates of food she would soon ladle out to them, and the old blankets next to the stove and behind the couch where, like humans, they would sleep through the dark night while the earth healed itself.

CHAPTER 29

Excrement-Smearing
Liberals

Len asked Carrie to check what he had loaded into the pickup and on the flatbed trailer against his list while he showered and packed his work clothes. Once in Santa Fe they would park the trailer where it would be safe for the night, at the small exclusive private school which had contracted with them to plant a display of native vegetation, of the sort that had presumably been cleared away when the estate that was later to become the school had been built fifty years before. Trailer parked, they would go have dinner with the Perrys and spend the night at a motel down on Cerrillos Road. It would be a demanding day. The older schoolchildren, fifth and sixth graders, were going to help them plant trees and shrubs and flowers. Spoiled kids, most of them, sons and daughters of the wealthy. But Carrie knew she could handle them. She had been one of them herself.

The project was first conceived as a little area out back of the school demarcated by a circle of rocks and featuring one small juniper, one small piñon, a cholla cactus, a yucca, a chamisa bush, a sagebrush, and a tuft or two of native dryland

grasses. But one of the board members had inflated the idea
to a whole "bioregion ecosystem display" large enough to
attract native birds and other creatures, or so it was hoped, and
the project had expanded to a half-acre of former Kentucky-
bluegrass lawn, the watering of which was the school's second
highest utility expense. The lawn was stripped away and the
area recontoured with gravelly clay into several mounds
featuring outcroppings of "native" flagstone and basalt and
various boulders and slabs of geological interest, including a
two-ton basalt boulder students would be allowed to graffiti up
or generally alter in any way they chose, short of dynamite. This
last did not sit well with certain board members, who argued
that it would suggest to the young that it was okay to deface
natural features, with a slim majority taking the position that
the Rock, as it became known even before it was installed by a
giant skip loader that inadvertently knocked down the "historic"
west portal or verandah of the grand old adobe that served
as the main school building, that the Rock would present the
whole environmental dilemma in symbolic form to generation
after generation of tender young minds. Some would want
to scribble all over it in spray paint, others to paint it white
or purple, and the next class would want to sandblast it clean
and pure, the next to urinate on it or smear excrement all over
it—at which point the board meeting exploded into shouting.
The Rock is the world, the headmaster had quoted the board
member as saying, and how our kids treat the Rock will be how
they treat the world. If only it were so simple, Carrie thought.
While awaiting the plantings that would complete the project
and pending a second board vote on the matter, the Rock sat
enwrapped in a sheet of heavy black plastic, for fear that a
student, or even a board member, might take matters into their
own hands before some kind of consensus had been worked out.
After one meeting a board member had been outraged to

overhear out in the hallway another joking that he "felt like smearing a little excrement tonight."

The trees and plants in the trailer, some in large black plastic pots and others with root balls wrapped in burlap, tallied with Len's list, plus the rolls of drip irrigation tape, fittings, boxes of tags, rolls of woven weed barrier, sacks of potting mix, and lengths of plastic pipe. She moved on to the camper shell on the back of the pickup, inside of which lay the right number of flats of grasses, native penstemons, and wetlands plants that would grow around the artificial spring in the middle of the small park, plus a dozen shovels and rakes, tampers, stakes, and three hand trucks and one four-wheel cart and two wheelbarrows to move the heavy pots into place and mix up whatever needed to be mixed, and the usual buckets and hoses that were always supposed to be on the work site but were often too short or leaked or had been loaned out the day before. Everything seemed to be there. Len was thorough in his preparations but often fell apart at the beginning of the job, not knowing where to begin. Her main function was to point him in the right direction and then to keep him organized the next two days, along with a dozen fifth and sixth graders, and probably a few board members and teachers as well, and making sure everything got done right with nobody hurting themselves, while keeping a list of supplies and plants they used and the hours they spent at it all.

She went back inside the house, and called into the bathroom, Do you think anybody told the kids to bring work gloves to school tomorrow?

Of course not, he called back.

She thought that they should probably pick up a dozen pair of cheap cloth work gloves on the way into town. Otherwise the kids would grab shovels and rakes and two minutes later would plaintively hold out a reddened hand and whine, I've got a blister. She would double the retail price to the school as part of their service, their thoughtfulness, and as an element of their overhead. The school was already impressed with the way they had adapted to the ever-changing and now controversial project. The spearheading board member had reached into his sufficiently deep pockets to cover the sky-rocketing estimates.

Carrie scribbled "gloves" on the list on the clipboard. Their clothes bags sat on kitchen chairs. A long note for the kids was on the table. The kitchen radio alarm was set to go off loudly at six-thirty in the morning. The living room lights were on. Their lunches were already made, wrapped and ready to go in the fridge.

Len emerged from the bathroom with his shaving kit.

Let's get out of here.

They stepped out the back door. Len checked the latch and pulled the door closed. A gust of wind made the woven shade cloth flap vigorously as they walked over to the pickup and climbed in. Carrie knew what Len was thinking, that probably the moment they drove away its moorings would break and the next two days it would beat at the saplings below. She said nothing.

She realized as she climbed into the pickup how tired she was and that she no longer looked forward to this long-anticipated drive into town and the challenge of working with school kids and hypercritical board members over the course of two whole days. All she wanted to do was to go back inside and cook up a simple dinner and go to bed. She felt the soft stretching warmth of the sheets and comforter, or rather the absence of them within the confined hard space of the pickup cab, its little prison of plastic and metal. She drew her arms and legs together and shivered. Len started the engine.

The wind had worn her out. Then there had been the Cristianos, so earnest, so deluded, and then Steph needing some kind of comfort and assurance, a different kind of bolstering than Porter usually asked of Len, and then the always exhausting business of loading the truck and trailer, so demanding that she and Len had no chance to talk over the events of the day, and now she feared she would be too tired to do so as they made the two-hour drive to town. And then the Perrys, who they always looked forward to spending time with, but who also always somehow disappointed Carrie, usually because somewhere in the middle of the evening after the third or fourth glass of wine Mel and Robin would take to rubbing salt in some old wound, and then she and Len would have to spend the rest of the evening trying to keep them apart and restore peace. She wasn't up to the effort tonight.

We need to stop for gas at Onésimo's, Len announced as they pulled up onto the highway. She looked out the back window to see that everything had survived the steep ascent and the tire-skidding transition on to the pavement.

Len had given signs that he regarded the job tomorrow as a harbinger of much bigger contracts, and he had resumed talk of moving the nursery out of their front and back yards, getting the business out of their personal lives and where it should be, on a couple of acres leased or bought just outside of Santa Fe, with its own proper office and full-time employees—a real business, in short. Meaning of course that she would be expected to present the plan to her father for ratification, because he would be the one to bankroll it, as he had the first stages of the business, including the purchase of the San Marcos property.

They had moved to San Marcos for something like a "way of life," which they defined more as a messy collection of positives and negatives, his and hers, than any carefully thought-through plan. To raise the kids away from the smothering values of mainstream America, a positive, in a narrow little valley whose sweeping vistas to the north and south continued to thrill them, another positive, and away from the undermining influence of her family's wealth, a negative, and away from his family's conservative middle-class tendency to look down on the values of any other culture, another negative, and to live among a people who by circumstances of geography and history had been marginalized for hundreds of years and who furtively nursed their ailing culture, not knowing whether it was in its death throes or was about to spring back to life, maybe a positive, which she had believed in her first years in the valley, but not quite as positive as it used to be, and perhaps someday a large negative. She was no longer certain.

And Len's hopes and plans for the business that would enable them to stand on their own financial two feet someday, certainly that was a positive, except that as the business expanded it drew them deeper and deeper back into the moneyed culture she had tried to free herself from, in the form of their Santa Fe customers, and required greater and greater financial participation in the business by her family, a magnetic pull against which she instinctively dug in her heels but against which she couldn't yet imagine any countervailing force. Just say no? Voluntary poverty? she wondered. The kids would not be easily brought along, not to speak of Len.

They had to wait at Moro Mercantile until a pump was free. A half dozen cars were scattered around the parking lot. Getting the truck and trailer in and out of the long narrow space would be a challenge.

Should have done this before hooking up the trailer, Len mused.

An untended pickup sat next to the pump on the side they needed to get to, a new black Ford extended cab.

You don't have enough to get to town?

No.

Carrie sensed that Len was probably as tired as she was. The board member of the school whose idea it had been to expand the small garden into a park had taken to calling him every other night and complaining about the other board members in between throwing out new ideas for something even bigger and more elaborate. He was the one the conservative wing of the board called among themselves the excrement-smearing liberal. One night he had suggested a snag in the form of a dead ponderosa leaning artistically to one side, for woodpeckers and owls. Len gently protested that they specialized in live trees, not dead ones, and that the leaning trunk would cost a fortune to anchor, while still presenting a falling hazard in the park area. And too much of an invitation for the kids to climb, Carrie had suggested afterward. Len was now so used to saying, Great idea, but . . . , that the phrase had become a refrain between him and Carrie.

Eventually a chubby man in a tan suit and a loose flapping red tie swung out the door and climbed into the pickup. Carrie studied the faint outlines of his thick neck and wide shoulder pads. He was vaguely familiar. She had seen him around the village, always dressed in a sports coat and suit and tie. Somebody in politics, she thought.

Len eased the pickup into the space and climbed out and began pumping. She leaned over and rolled up his window to keep the smell of gas out. Perhaps she would feel better, she thought, once they were on the road. About halfway to town they could turn on NPR, where the reception got good enough to make out most of what they were saying, and she could lose herself in other people's worries and problems.

The store was busy. People were stopping on the way home to pick up little things they had forgotten to get in town for half the price, and for the Coke or snack they needed to sustain themselves between here and any one of a half dozen villages that lay farther up the highway. She looked out the window, away from the store, so as to avoid catching the gaze of anyone she might know. Finally Len came out of the store, crossed the dirt and climbed back in, started the engine. There was just enough room ahead of them to squeeze between two parked cars and get back on the highway.

They rumbled through the village, around the slow curves, down past the school turnoff and Fabian's junkyard, the cemetery turnoff, the little adobe house down by the arroyo where Myrna Clippenger lived, past the last structure in the village, the burned-out adobe shell of the Cantina Feliz, to the straight stretch where Len gunned it to keep up speed through the cut in the hill that took them up and out of the valley and out into the rolling hills, the edge of the Great Plains, that lay between them and Santa Fe. The heavily laden trailer tugged against their progress, with a back-and-forth rubberyness.

She slumped down and closed her eyes. The magnetic force was money, and that was what was pulling them to Santa Fe. The counterforce, with which she had tried to resist the pull of money since moving out to the little valley, was something as vague yet as palpable as her own physical labor of lifting things and planting and transplanting cuttings and flowers and grasses and shrubs and trees. Her labor was the labor of resistance, of resistance to ease, to letting others do it all, to being tempted back into a life in which others far away, faceless and dark, labored for almost nothing in wages, labor that brought a good return on the investments that provided a life of choice and ease and security for those who owned them, investments that could bring you everything you wished for if you were cunning with money and lucky and rich. Thoughts of an excrement-smearing liberal, who just wanted to spoil the fun. She had cautioned Len never to repeat the phrase in the presence of her own family because they would thereafter tar her with it, to the end of time.

She was physically weary, and the force was not strong, the magnetic force, and she wondered whether perhaps it had all been a sham, a self-deceiving sham, their years in the village, as she struggled to fight that which she secretly knew would sooner or later overcome her, through her father, or Len, or eventually the children, when they finally became aware of the situation, of the magnetic pull.

Len's silence as he drove she knew to be an expression of it, of the force of the pull, like her own fatigue. In sleep lay the only flickering hope.

The heater was now full on. She nested her head on her rolled up work jacket and submitted to the jerky forward motion of the truck, the laboring engine, and to the warm liquid of relaxation as it spread through her body.

CHAPTER 30

Post Office Box
Number One

Mr. Morales signaled the closing of the post office for the day by stepping out the back door and walking around to the northwest corner of the cement-plastered adobe and untying the lanyard and lowering the tattered American flag straight to the dusty ground and unhooking its fasteners. On windy days like today he held it in place with his foot while he worked at the stiff snaps. This was sacrilege, he knew, at least according to the training he had received during his two years at the junior high military academy in El Paso, where he and other boys had been shouted at nearly daily during the ceremonial raising and lowering around the blazingly hot athletic field in heavy gray wool uniforms. The blond crew-cut red-faced gringo drill sergeant, Wallerheim, bellowed how the flag, the colors, Old Glory, must never be allowed to touch the ground, though he never spelled out any details of the terrible consequences of that event, which he claimed had never once happened since the Alamo. When he reached the point in his harangue when every one of the twenty-five recruits of his squad knew he was about to thunder out the words,

"The Al-a-MOW," and then to turn to one of the darker Hispanic faces and draw close, raise his fleshy chin, and look down through his red-rimmed blue eyes at the trembling twelve-year-old, at whom he would bellow out the syllables yet one more time. Fifty years later Mr. Morales could still feel the explosion of the sergeant's tobacco breath upon his face and the cold drops of sweat dripping down from his armpits inside the prickly uniform. The memory could make him shake with fear and rage at his own cowardice for failing to correct Sergeant Wallerheim's pronunciation. *Álamo*, he kept saying to himself, accent on the first syllable. ÁL-a-mow, not Al-a-MOW.

This afternoon he swirled the flag around in the dirt a few times for good measure, then picked it up and gave it a good shake, and stuffed it unfolded into a large JCPenny shopping bag. Though the squad had spent endless hours learning how to fold the flag properly into a triangular pad like a sopapilla, Sergeant Wallerheim had inadvertently failed to test them all at the end of the semester. He had discovered new opportunities for intimidation in the hygiene class he had temporarily taken over when the school nurse suffered a nervous breakdown, issuing with relish thundering pronouncements about how squeezing pimples would cause the pus to go straight to the brain and make you drop dead on the spot. His booming voice still echoed through Mr. Morales's mind on the evils of masturbation, how it would cause your pecker to drop off, your fingers and toes, your ears and nose, and then make you blind and deaf. Most of the boys were too young to know what he was talking about and make any connection between the long, obviously dirty word, and the furtive solace of wet dreams and the first hesitant fondlings of the nightly erection—or at least Mr. Morales had no idea what the word meant, having been sent to the school by a rigidly puritanical mother, to lessen his exposure at that tender age to his often drunken father. And that first day, when the new students stood in a long line in their baggy underpants, shivering, to be issued uniforms and bedding and towels, that was also when they each had to stand in front of the barrel-chested Sergeant for the first terrifying time. The Sergeant had taken pleasure in their blundering responses or embarrassed silences as he dismissed them one by one with one of several puzzling queries. Now let's see, private MORE-ALL-EEZ, have you got your balls firmly attached? Concealed by the heavy load of clothing and bedding and towels he was hugging, he wet his pants.

The flag brought back those fifty-year-old memories far too often and far too sharply, no matter how hastily or brutally he lowered the tattered rag each day and took it back into the building and threw it in its bag into a corner. But today at least some small measure of justice had been rendered in a related matter, or even more than justice, something like justice with reparations. From remarks overheard on the other side of the partition he had gathered that old Abundio Moro had finally died, confirmed later by conversations with the busybody Isabel Moro when she stopped by to pick up the mail and who was absolutely certain, having seen Abundio Moro twice that morning, early when he was still alive, or barely alive, and later that morning when she went back to his cave to check on him, when he was dead, just before Zip Zepeda's hearse came and got him. There could be no doubt about it, old Abundio Moro was finally *difunto*.

Abundio Moro's main ambition in his prime, in the decades before Mr. Morales became postmaster, was to become the holder of the prestigious Post Office Box Number One. He had achieved his goal by following newspaper obituaries and by memorizing everyone's post office box number, not a difficult task in the old days when most people got their mail through General Delivery and there were only fifty PO boxes, not two hundred like there were today. Upon

the death of the holder of a lower PO box number, Abundio
would immediately apply for it. Word had it that it had taken
him twenty-three years to realize his ambition. And perhaps
as his last official act four years ago, when he could still more
or less see and hear, he hobbled into the village one afternoon
and lurched up to the post office window and pounded at the
plywood panel with the insistence of a dog wagging its tail.
When Mr. Morales finally opened it, revealing the toothless,
grizzled, furrowed face, Abundio Moro flung out a bony palm
to which he had glued a $20-dollar bill with honey, *Así que no
la pierdo*, so that he wouldn't lose it on the way. *Por la caja*, he
explained after catching his breath. *Renta. Número Uno.*

Claro que sí, Mr. Morales had sighed, gentle peeling the
sticky bill from the old man's palm, surprised that the old man
had been able to act so fast in response to the previous holder
of PO Box 1 and even to make it to the post office on the same
day as the death.

But now Abundio was finally dead himself, and *Número
Uno* could be Mr. Morales's for the rest of his life. Mr.
Morales's parents had suffered a series of reverses over the
course of their lives, one of which had rescued him from
Sergeant Wallerheim and the military academy when they
could no longer afford the tuition and room and board, and
every time things got bad they would have to give up the
modest luxury of having their own private post office box and
go back to general delivery, for sometimes years at a time. His
mother was of very proud *gente*, reluctant to ask for anything
from anybody, even their own mail during their spells back in
the village, but particularly from any of the Salcedos who had
served as postmasters for two generations. As a result, over the
course of his childhood they had tumbled down from PO Box
7 all the way to PO Box 123.

His mother would be proud to know that her son had
finally risen to the rank of PO Box 1. To make it official and to

cut off anybody else who might have their eye on the number, Mr. Morales sat down and filled out both the application form and a change of address form and then loudly stamped them with the date and an "Approved" stamp in rich maroon ink, and then slipped the forms into PO Box 1 with a snappily efficient gesture. Sometime that evening, after dinner, he would sidle up to Mrs. Morales and announce to her that they were at last *Número Uno* in San Marcos. It might take her a while to figure out what he was talking about. When she finally did, he would allow himself a tight little smile.

CHAPTER 31

UPS

San Marcos was separated from Los Martinez, its nearest neighbor to the north, by five miles of two-lane state highway, whose twisting hairpin turns followed the serpentine course of the Río Sucio through a narrow canyon of steep cliffs of red clay. Thirty miles an hour was the best you could do. There was nowhere to pass safely on the five-mile stretch, though most drivers who lived in Los Martinez and the villages upstream now and then managed to pass slower cars and trucks on one of the more open curves. The road was paved three decades ago, and since then several dozen drivers had failed in foolhardy attempts to pass and had landed upside down in the stream below or on the rocks on the way down in the many small gullies and side canyons around which the road twisted. Seven drivers and passengers had paid with their lives. The sites of most of the fatalities were marked with *descansos*, small wooden crosses wired to the guardrail and painted with names and dates of the victims and festooned with ribbons and plastic flowers and the occasional small American flag.

Over the past three years Ronny Vásquez had come to know the five-mile stretch through the canyon as intimately as any long-time driver, well enough to know that there was no place he could count on being able to squeeze past a slower vehicle in his boxy brown UPS van and make it back into the right lane in time. The best he could do was tailgate slower cars, the ones going much too slow, and let his wheels drop into potholes along the edges, which would cause the sides of the tall heavy truck box to boom and bang, in a way certain to make the offending car ahead aware of his presence.

But this afternoon the way was clear ahead for once. He leaned into the curves sharply left and right, the large black steering wheel shaking under the pull, tires gasping on the rumpled pavement, the box booming behind him, and three undeliverable parcels sliding back and forth on the metal floor with each turn, the hand truck rattling in its confining straps, and the old clacketty engine and its flat unglamorous exhaust roaring away. His delivery day was almost over, and during the drive back to the warehouse he could let go of all the details of muddy driveways with nowhere to turn around, wrong addresses, and dawdling customers. This last two hours on the road was the sweetest part of the day, when he could just drive, not think, just drive as fast as he could make the old box go. He loved the thundering clatter of negotiating the curves, at least when no one was in front of him.

His route for the past three years had been San Marcos Abajo first and then seven miles higher, San Marcos Arriba. A major challenge was sorting out the Moros and Salcedos and Quintanas who lived in Arriba from those living in Abajo. A church schism in the early 1800s, he had heard, had divided the original San Marcos, the Arriba, and a good third of the population had moved downstream out to the edges of the Great Plains, where they defiantly claimed the old name, San Marcos, for their new adobe church and new settlement. To add to the confusion, their zip codes were only two digits apart.

After the two San Marcoses came Los Martinez, and the upper villages of Los Osos, La Floresta, and Piedras Negras, the second route he had had since joining UPS, and he now knew many of the mountain villages on this side of the range, and a passing acquaintance with hundreds of their inhabitants. Oddly this had whetted his curiosity, and he began each morning at the warehouse going over the day's delivery route in the hope that some box or large envelope or tube would lead him at last down a dirt road high up in a mountain valley where he knew there was a clutch of old adobes and newer mobile homes but which he had never delivered to. His curiosity was scoffed at by the older cynical drivers, who would often pull him aside at the end of the day, if they happened to check out of the warehouse at the same time. Hey, Ronny, you'd love this one. Old guy lives across the ditch but it's all flooded because it froze or something so his pickup has been frozen stuck in the middle of his drive since December. He wants me to pull it out with a chain. And back up down his road for a good mile. You know, muddy, slippery, icy, with a ditch running right beside it half the way. Sorry, *primo*, I told him, I'm not Triple A.

There was also the strange power of coming on people unexpectedly, catching them in the act, particularly in the summer. He classified them as those who didn't see him at all or those who simply ignored him, like the hippies standing naked in the stream near the plank bridge, or two Chicano guys shooting up next to a pickup parked in the trees along the road, or he didn't know how many teenagers probably smoking weed in the same spot after school, and up in the canyon down below the highway a couple screwing in a low-rider, a bare rump ballooning up and down, a gringo couple having at it on a back porch one fine afternoon, the guy even pausing to wave at him as he dropped their parcel at the back gate, a woman chasing her husband around a garden with a rake.

Then there were those who viewed him as only an extension of the big brown truck and saw only the uniform, not the face, and shied away from human contact. Others wanted to know his name and to grill him in Spanish about who he was related to, at which he would smile and explain that he grew up in LA and his parents didn't want him to learn Spanish and would never talk to him about his New Mexican relatives. The old ones would cluck disapprovingly. They would persist. What's your name?

Vásquez.

Are you related to the Vásquezes in Los Martinez? There are lots of Vásquezes there. There are no more Martinez in Los Martinez but there are lots of Vásquezes.

I don't know. Maybe.

They should tell you those things, your people.

They don't want to, I guess.

Que bárbaro.

He would smile and climb back into the truck. Gotta get back on the road, he'd say. Lots of stops left.

They would stand there, watching him as he settled into the high seat. One of them would call out, Why so soon?

He couldn't remember how many times he had had that conversation with some old couple way up in the mountains, a stooped old woman with a bandanna tied around her head, a gray-haired old man with a cane, sometimes alone, sometimes together, out in a dusty or muddy driveway, as he handed them a holiday or birthday box of candy or fruit or something else sent out from a large mail-order company, by distant children or grandchildren. The old people's hardened looks told him that they felt abandoned to a lonely old age at the edge of the forest. They seemed to be silently calling out with their questions that he would do as their absent son or grandson.

People were so lonely, he often thought after some of his stops. They showed it in funny ways. Then there were people who were quick to see if there was some advantage to be had in his acquaintance, like that fellow down in San Marcos who would stick his head in the side door and ask, Hey, what do you do with all those things you can't deliver, huh?

And each village had its own distinct character. There was the one where the kids threw rocks and even aimed BB guns at the truck, and the dogs snarled with genuine viciousness. There was the one in which there always seemed to be some medical emergency requiring an ambulance and police cars and fire department pickups with emergency lights flashing, all rushing out toward the highway. The inhabitants of one sloping, slightly crowned highland plain never seemed able to keep their horses, cows, goats, and pigs confined to field or pen, and their sullen owners persisted in driving their aging low-riders and high four-wheel-drive pickups down the middle of the road until the last minute, and they often gave him the finger. Another place was all broad smiles and friendly waves and six-packs of beer before the Christmas holidays, like out of some TV commercial.

The canyon opened out abruptly and the road straightened briefly as it cut through a grove of old cottonwoods and crossed the river and headed south and rose up into the first adobe houses of San Marcos. San Marcos had a different character from the more isolated mountain villages and valleys but one he couldn't quite put his finger on. It was easy to deliver to because most of the houses were close to the road and people seemed to be at home more than at some of the other places nearer town. He had only delivered one package earlier in the day though as he slowed down for the curves just before the store, he could no longer remember where. He stopped at the nursery at least twice a week but didn't think he had earlier in the afternoon, and then there were always deliveries to Moro Mercantile, around whose hairpin turn he now slowly rumbled. He wondered whether to stop for a snack but thought better of it.

He picked up speed through the rest of the village, and though it seemed early he flicked on his headlights as he rose up out of the valley and passed through the cuts in the hill and gained speed out across the rolling plains, leaving behind the memory of something like a vast puzzle to which he had fitted together only a small number of the oddly shaped pieces. He knew he would never learn more than what he saw from the high seat of the boxy truck or from peering out the sliding side doors when he stopped momentarily for a delivery. It would always remain a somewhat confused jumble.

He looked ahead. There would be a quick shower, a beer or two and TV, and maybe Lorena would clatter in and throw something on the stove, and they would eat and fall asleep on the couch with the TV still going, and they would wake up and crawl into bed in the middle of the night, maybe make love, and then he would climb back out of bed at five and start all over again, and find himself back on the road at nine-thirty after packing the truck at the warehouse and heading back up toward San Marcos and the higher villages. He wondered how he could possibly look forward to it again, starting a new day before he had even finished this one, yet he did.

CHAPTER 32

Lunch Box

Isabel Moro piloted her silver Buick around the parking lot
and behind the store and into the garage with its automatic
opener not long before the late afternoon rush began. Once
inside the garage and the door closing with the whirring of
the electric motor, she opened the trunk and pulled out a large
black plastic garbage bag. Leave it here or take it upstairs, she
wondered. The blankets inside stank, they would have to be
washed, the threadbare synthetic blankets she had loaned old
Abundio Moro. She untied the bag and pulled out a casserole
dish and an aluminum pan and the blankets and dragged
them over to the washing machine and stuffed them inside,
adding a double amount of detergent. She turned the knob
to Super Soak and pulled it out. The machine clicked and
hummed to the sound of gushing water.

The rumpled plastic bag sat on the cement, next to the
open trunk. A hump in its shape indicated something was still
inside. She knew perfectly well what it was. But each time she
touched it or moved it since discovering it under the old man's
bed, the world had changed a little. She wished she had not
driven out to his dark little cave. She wished she could leave the

plastic sack just lying there on the garage floor and walk upstairs into the house and close the door and forget all about it.

With a loud click the washing cycle started, a rhythmic groaning and sloshing. How long had she been standing in the garage? This was silly, she thought, returning to herself, her efficient business-like no-nonsense self. You find a box under the bed of a smelly old *difunto*, and what do you do? You pick up the box and take it home and then you open it up and see what's inside, that's what you do, that's what anybody would do. *Claro que sí.*

She peeled back the plastic of the trash bag, exposing an old metal lunch box, the kind with a domed top and probably with wire clips inside to hold a thermos bottle. The dented rusty metal had been painted dark green and was streaked with traces of unthinkable substances. A small hasp and latch were screwed to the box, which was locked closed with a large brass padlock. It was this last feature that had begun to alter Isabel Moro's world when she heard it rattle under the blankets as she hoisted the sack into the trunk of her car.

She picked up the box out of the bag by the handle. It was heavier than she remembered. But then she remembered that when she had picked it up the very first time, it was heavier than she had expected it to be. With the other hand she took the plastic bag over to the washing machine and dropped it in front of it. Then she climbed the stairs and opened the door at the top landing and pushed her way into the kitchen and carried the box into the living room. Where should she put it? Where could she put it down? Should she hide it? Put it on a shelf somewhere as if it was part of the house? It grew heavy as she stood next to the old mahogany dining table pushed into a corner and the roll-top desk next to the hole in the floor through which she could hear the faint gabbling of voices and a warm draft brushed against her stockings. She put the lunch box down on her desk and sat down in the oak swivel chair and leaned back and stared at it.

She had spent half the morning fretting whether or not she should drive back out to Abundio Moro's cave and see if there was anything she could do, but thinking what did it matter, he was dead, Onésimo had passed the news up through the hole in the ceiling, and that was that, but then she worried that since he was so old maybe nobody would go up there to pay their respects, though who would she pay her respects to since nobody would be there anyway. What finally decided her was the recollection that she had lent him a couple of old blankets during a nasty cold spell last winter, and that's the sort of thing you never throw away. Then there were some dishes she'd left, a casserole dish and an old aluminum pot he'd never returned. They were probably down with all the spiders and mice below the basin, the dishes anyway.

She had gone downstairs later in the morning and snapped at Onésimo to start getting people to pay their bills because they were dying like flies around here, though Abundio Moro had passed with a clean slate at least. They'd like that in heaven. She stood for a long time staring at the display of new aerosol room fresheners before choosing Woodland Berry Bouquet over Forest Meadow Mint and Flower Garden Garland and Herbal Sachet Essence, which all smelled the same to her anyway. Those blankets would stink, she knew. She pulled a black plastic garbage bag off the roll under the counter and went out to the garage and climbed into the Buick. Afterward she would come back and pick up lunches for old Mr. Serrano and poor Ramoncita Quintana.

She was surprised to find the hearse parked in front of the cave with the Zepeda kid asleep in the front seat while waiting for his uncle to come and help him get the old man out. The uncle, Rudy Zepeda, drove up in a long black funeral home car just as she was getting out of her car. He jumped

out, lit a cigarette, woke his nephew with a joke about how
business was suddenly booming. She explained her presence
to the two men dressed in rumpled dusty black suits. I brought
him something to eat every day, *pobrecito*, though we're not
related. She pushed her way through the door into the dark
cave, waving the Woodland Berry Bouquet spray this way and
that over her head. The undertakers followed with a stretcher
that barely fit through the doorway and nudged the old man
off the bed and on to it, cigarette dangling from Rudy Zepeda's
lips the whole time. She made a point of not watching, at
least not directly, except when they began wheeling him out
the door and neither of them had a free hand to pull off the
blanket that had caught on his foot. *Es la mía*, that one, she
said, leaning over to free the blanket. *Y la otra pa'ca*. And some
of the dishes, they're mine, too.

While stepping back into the dark space and leaning
over to free the other blanket from the tangle of stinking
bedding, her foot banged against something under the bed.
She stepped back and crouched down. Light fanning in from
the open door illuminated the old brass padlock dangling
from the rusty lunch box. She turned. Backs to her, the two
men were struggling to push something out of the way so they
could slide the stretcher into the back of the hearse. The older
one was swearing. As she crouched there, knees protesting,
her eyes fixed on the padlock and the dented lunch box to
which it was attached, she felt the first slight shift of her world
beginning to change. She reached under the bed and pulled
out the surprisingly heavy box. The men still had their backs
to her. She unfurled the garbage bag and stuffed in one of the
blankets and then lowered the box down on top of it, covering
it with the second blanket, on top of which she stacked the
casserole dish and the aluminum pot.

Es tan feo, she said, staggering out of the cave, holding the
sack in both hands, but not finishing what she was going to

so u g h y

add, *la muerte*, because the two men were now clowning at the back of the hearse, the older one delivering mock punches to the stomach of the skinny younger one. They stopped abruptly as she walked by. The older one nudged the back door of the hearse and it closed with a slam.

Pobrecito, she said, shaking her head and opening the trunk of the Buick and swinging the sack inside.

So now there it was, sitting on her desk, a big brass padlock like she thought they used to use on the railroad. Around it her whole room was changing. Should she hide it? Should she tell Onésimo about it? Get him to pry it open? Nobody ever came upstairs to visit them, but now suddenly she imagined all kinds of people tramping up the back stairs and tapping on the glass of the back door, which was also the front door, since the upstairs apartment had no front door, and wanting to come in and have a look around. She could see them walking straight through the living room and into the dining room where her office was and looking at the hole in the floor and then at her desk piled high with bills and papers and the dining room table crowded into a corner next to the matching buffet, both of which Onésimo's father had taken in payment from the Salcedos to pay off an overdue account, and then their eyes swiveling around and landing on the old lunchbox and its large brass padlock. They would ask one by one, pointing at it, *¿Mira, qué es eso? ¿Qué es eso?* Where did that come from?

Voices were surging up through the hole in the floor. Onésimo would need help. She strode into the living room and snatched a towel from the rack and returned and draped it over the box, a disguise that made it even more conspicuous. That was the way it was becoming in her head. The more she tried to push it out of her mind, the more she couldn't stop thinking about it. What was happening to her?

She returned to the kitchen and clattered down the stairs, gripping the handrail tightly. This was no time to trip and fall, she thought, with that thing sitting on my desk. She pushed through the back door to the store and slipped behind the counter with a sense of relief of a sort she had rarely known, to face a small crowd of people milling around the counter as Onésimo punched away at the cash register. Everyone in the village was used to her appearing at Onésimo's back at such moments, slipping in behind him with a scowl, looking down at the counter, bony hand reaching out to bag the goods spread out there. Instead she looked up and smiled—straight into some squabble little old Esmerelda Vizarriaga was having with Manny Serrano, who was looking shifty-eyed and sweaty as usual in a rumpled tan suit and red tie.

You turned off the TV station, I know you did, Esmerelda was saying, chin thrown back and eyes flashing, you turned off the TV station so you could sell more of those things, what do you call them? All you care about is stealing money off the people. *Sin vergüenza*, some people I know, that's what they are, not mentioning any names, she said, poking a finger into his chest. She threw her head back even farther and kept poking him above and below the six-pack of Coca Cola he was trying to defend himself with. Not to mention any names.

Isabel Moro couldn't hear his reply, an attempt at low-voiced confidentiality, because he had turned away from the counter, and the *güero* Mott was waving two twenty-dollar bills at her, saying, Twenty-four dollars even for gas. Onésimo was counting out change as loudly as he could to Manny's back. Hey, *vecino*, your money's here on the counter.

We're on fixed income, she heard Esmerelda snap. You know how many years Juan worked before he retired?

Manny had regained his composure. But you get cost of living, Esmerelda, you get all the benefits, I'll bet you even get commodities, don't you?

Isabel Moro turned away. That would get Esmerelda, she thought. Sure they got commodities, all that nice free surplus cheese and butter and bacon and flour, even though he received a good retirement, Juan, and their kids helped all the time.

Esmerelda Vizarriaga turned her head around to make certain nobody was listening, or at least to see that everybody who was listening intently was pretending not to. Those commodities, she said, just make you go to the bathroom all the time.

So, Manny persisted as he turned and scooped up his change, what's nineteen ninety-five a month for a clear picture and two hundred channels? Think about it. A different channel for every day of the year, how can you go wrong with that? He lowered his voice. And there's some other stuff I can throw in, you know, for the *viejitos* on fixed incomes. Even for the ones like you who don't look a day over fifty. Talk to Juan about it.

She appeared to lose interest and turned away from him, depositing a box of sugar on the counter. *¿Qué tanto?*

Suddenly the store was empty. The vision came back. Isabel Moro could see the lunch box sitting on her desk covered with a kitchen towel. She could see Onésimo shuffling into the room, yawning loudly, and then looking down at her desk and asking, *¿Mira, qué es eso?*

He was saying something.

What?

He was standing only a foot away.

I said, he said much too loudly, *dije que,* what are we going to have for dinner?

You don't have to shout, she replied. I'm not deaf, you know. Did anybody pay their bill?

CHAPTER 33

Spaghetti

They can wait, Stephanie Wachler said to herself as she climbed out of the station wagon, leaving the front door open. A path parallel to the driveway angled up the hill to the two garden terraces that lay between the house and the steep embankment atop which ran the highway. The air was cold, almost wintery, but the wind was blowing in only fitful gusts, perhaps promising a calm night. She headed up the path.

She would look at the garden first, hard as it might be to leave the wound of her absence open another few minutes. The kids would be in the house. They would have heard her drive up. They would be waiting for the sound of the car door slamming. Yet they would still probably be trained for her much later return from work. They could wait.

The previous owner had created two garden terraces, wide scallops that curved out toward the house below, the banks held in place by flat rocks stacked up to form low walls. She and Porter had never managed to plant more than the lower terrace, the always unsatisfactory vegetable garden, with a few flowers around the edges, marigolds and zinnias, with a patch of yellow iris in a far corner. Just below the highway embankment there was a row of gnarled apricots and peaches.

Everybody liked to point out how badly pruned they were. The weeds had already made a good start everywhere. Why hadn't she got Porter to get to tilling the garden sooner?

She'd quit her job only a month ago and had slipped into a mild depression a few days later, which seemed like years ago. She wondered whether the kids would be looking out the windows at her standing on the edge of the garden looking down at clumps of grass and dandelions and the feathery fern-like weeds that would soon sprout tiny lavender flowers. The kids would be hungry. Right away they would want something to eat, they would want something to be fed to them, not because they were helpless, but because they wanted to be mothered. Then dinner, she would have to fix dinner, something warm and dramatic and steaming, otherwise they would all feel cheated. Then she would have to browbeat them to do the dishes and they would whine about having to do homework. Maybe she should be more forceful in bargaining with them. I won't complain about cooking dinner if you promise not to complain about washing the dishes afterward, promptly, thoroughly, spotlessly, putting them away afterward, every last one of them, exactly where they belong. Or exactly where you think they belong. The kitchen was always a mess.

She felt her face growing flushed and her chest tightening. The brandy at Carrie's was probably a mistake. This was not what she came home for, she chided herself, shuffling across the lower terrace to the low stone wall of the upper terrace, which came up to her knees. She peered across it to the fruit trees, now fully leafed out and beyond pruning again this year.

She turned around and glanced at the house. No faces pressed to glass at least, though a plume of bluish smoke was spiraling out of the chimney on Porter's workshop behind the house, which meant that perhaps he had actually got to work today and might even decide to work late. He would eventually straggle back to the house and into the kitchen and smile down on his plate of food on the table as if it had dropped from the sky and how fortunate it was that he lived in a house where food dropped from the sky, warm and tasty and abundant. And then after dinner he would want to carry on for hours about what had bothered him today, probably that meeting announcement which Carrie said Len was also worried about, while the kids made little pilgrimages back and forth between their rooms and the bathroom and the living room with a growing list of needs, until finally bed was the only solution, after more bickering. Maybe then she'd have five or ten minutes before it would become clear that Porter's sluggish hormones were beginning to bestir themselves and he would want to pull the cushions off the couch and lay them down in front of their woodstove and he would want them to slip off their clothes and get into their bathrobes in case the kids woke up, though she had refused him for over a week now. And then, unless she refused him again tonight, he would want to enter her and stretch himself out on top of her and just lie, not moving, just lie as his breathing became steady and deep and she felt increasingly smothered and trapped under his weight, locked in place by his swollen penis. If she allowed him, he could lie like that for hours. The rigor mortis position, she privately called it.

She took a deep breath of cold air. Her temples were pounding again. The garden, she reminded herself, she was out here to think about the garden. She climbed up on the upper terrace, a thick mat of orchard grass coming back to life. They would have to get somebody with a tractor to deal with this, perhaps Juan Vizarriaga down the road, if it wasn't too late. Water was dribbling down from the leaky ditch gate into the trees. She realized she didn't know anything about garden design except to plant tall flowers behind shorter ones. Carrie had tried to tell her something about that. She would have to go back and ask her to explain it all again. Something nice ought to grow in between the rocks in the walls.

She turned back and walked down to the wall and stepped down into the lower terrace, whose earth was still soft and spongy. Between the end of the lower terrace and the driveway there lay a patch of flagstone in between stunted lilac bushes that someone had once tried to organize into a landscaped area in some way. Beyond, the old station wagon with its front door open, nose pointing at the adobe house with its steeply pitched rusty roof of corrugated iron, and beyond that the adobe shed that Porter had made into his workshop.

She knew what she wanted now, not at all clearly, but clarity would come sooner or later, by accident, trial and error, and in this for once Porter and the kids would help her do what she wanted. Bit by bit, gesture by gesture, she would turn them around and point them in quite another direction, toward her garden, the one that they would all be out there planting this weekend, rain or shine.

She walked over to the station wagon, picked up the plastic sack with the carton of milk in it, and walked up to the back door and stepped inside.

There's nothing to eat, Krishna said by way of greeting. He was sitting at the kitchen table.

Steph pushed the door closed with her shoulder and set the carton of milk down in front of him. Open it the right way, she said. Where's Porter?

Krishna shrugged. Working, she hoped, out back. She rummaged around the cupboard above the stove, high up, where she hid crackers and cookies from the kids. There was still a half box of those cheese-covered things. She set it down on the table.

This milk is warm, Krishna commented blankly between gulps.

Athena drifted into the kitchen. Hi, she said. She brushed minimally up against Steph, who drew her closer with a pat. Athena would be sealed inside her own world this afternoon, a place she had learned about from Porter. Since she was about eight she'd been able to turn off and on the world around her. From the vacant look of her green eyes, Steph knew that the world was now off. Steph had had the same coloring at her age, straight blond hair against almost dark skin, and the same hollows under the eyes. Athena would look like her when she grew up. Krishna had the rounder features of his father, though set on a lanky frame, suddenly growing, yet still with the oblong narrow head of a young boy. The tension of the long days in their absence went slack when she was reunited with them at the end of the day, and suddenly everything became simple again. Cook, eat, clean up, bathe, set out clothes, sleep. Though from now on she was going to hold something in reserve. For Porter their return home from school meant quite the opposite: distraction, interruption, crisis, evasion. She wondered whether he would be that way were they his own kids. Holding a handful of the yellow crackers up to her mouth, palm to chin, Athena shuffled out of the kitchen back toward her room.

Mrs. Morales used my dictionary to look up a word, Krishna announced from the table.

Steph thrust a large pot under the tap and turned on the water. She wondered what Krishna was talking about. What word?

Krishna was going through a phase where he took pleasure in eating things in tiny bits, almost crumb by crumb. Lips curled up, head thrown back so he was looking down his nose, he was methodically slicing tiny bits off a cracker with his front teeth. From what she had gathered from Krishna's cryptic accounts of the class, Mrs. Morales had some theory about the local Spanish, the main effect of which seemed to be to discourage talking of any kind in any language.

She put the pot on the stove and turned on the burner and poured a half teaspoon of salt into her palm and dumped it

in the water. Tonight was spaghetti night. During her working days in town, they had a regular menu. Steph thought it
helped them all get through her time away. If she were late
then at least they would know what to look forward to for
dinner. Weekends were leftover nights, or spur-of-the-moment
nights, and sometimes eating-out nights.

Why do they call it Thousand Island dressing?

What? she replied absently, opening the tall pantry door.
They off and on bought organically grown spaghetti sauce by
the case and she thought there ought to be two or three bottles
left from the last purchase.

Thousand Island, he repeated.

There was only one bottle left in the bottom of the pantry.
She lifted it up and set it down on the counter. An image of
a lightly salmon-colored dressing, faintly lumpy, entered her
head. Why indeed?

Well, what do you think? she asked.

A new cracker was being slowly aimed toward his chattering teeth like a piece of wood toward one of Porter's saws.

Maybe that should be your last one, she suggested. He
ignored her.

She heard Porter come in the back door and stamp his
feet on the mat, and then the door closed. He'd probably
gone back outside to brush the sawdust off his pants legs and
shirt and perhaps even out of his hair. Once the house had
become so filled with sawdust, it was on the couch, even on
and inside their bed, in the sink, all over the rugs, that she
threatened to leave him unless he figured out how to stop
tracking it inside. Then he had taken to changing into and
out of overalls and a hat for a while, but lately he seemed to
be reverting to his old ways. It's in the eye of the beholder,
he had claimed one night. It certainly is, she had shot back.
And it's in the bed of the beholder, and in the bathtub of the
beholder, too.

He stepped into the kitchen. She went up to him and looked him over. There was a faint yellow fuzz on his left shoulder, but not enough to worry about. If it fell, maybe it would fall into his plate and he would think it was Parmesan cheese.

Hi, he said. Did you just get home?

The water was boiling. She pulled out a packet of spaghetti from a drawer and slit open the end with a knife and slid the contents into the pot.

With Krishna there she couldn't say she'd driven almost all the way to Santa Fe and back, otherwise he would want to know why she went and then why she didn't take him with her, and she didn't want to go into the whole tedious business of the leaking milk carton and Porter's charging gas and not telling her, at least not yet, not until after dinner when the kids were in bed, so she shortened the trip into a visit to the store and a long stop at Carrie's. To talk to her about the future garden.

Porter said he couldn't figure out why they called it Thousand Island dressing. Finally he ventured a theory.

Because they have to chop everything up into a thousand little bits.

If you don't know, why don't you just say so, Krishna retorted sourly, as if to say that he was no longer just a dumb kid with time to waste sorting through stupid answers. Porter retreated to the living room to light the woodstove.

Athena wandered back into the kitchen.

No more crackers, Steph said. Why don't you set the table, dumpling.

Athena paused in the middle of the kitchen and looked around and then turned to the silverware basket on the drainboard. From the living room came the muffled sound of fire crackling and popping, and the faint odor of pine smoke. Steph stirred the spaghetti sauce, into which she had tipped onions and carrots chopped fine.

The word was *dump*, Krishna announced.

And how do you say that in Spanish? Steph asked.

I don't remember. *El dompe* or something like that.

Porter came back into the kitchen and sat down at the table. The word *dump* always conjured up visions in Steph of the village dump up an arroyo, a stinking trench frequented by wild dogs and cats and even vultures, with small fires eating away at all the stuff people dumped there from the backs of their pickups, the acrid smoke blowing this way and that. And the waste of all that perfectly good stuff that could be reused or recycled somehow, the old refrigerators, probably perfectly good, the old stoves, aluminum cans even that people threw away because they couldn't be bothered to take them to the recycling bins in town.

She turned down the burners and bent down and opened the lowermost drawer next to the sink, once a junk drawer until last year when she cleaned it out and turned it into a place where she stored flower-seed and bulb catalogs Carrie and other friends had passed to her. She plopped the stack down in the middle of the table.

That's what we're having for dinner, she said.

Both Porter and Krishna turned to make sure that something was still cooking on the stove. Athena finished setting the table and slid into her seat and picked up the top catalog and leafed through it.

What we're going to talk about over dinner, Steph selaborated from the stove. The great big flower garden you're all going to help me plant this weekend.

You said I could spend Saturday night over at—

Of course, after you help.

She picked out a strand of spaghetti and tested it. Almost, but not quite. Keep calm, she told herself. This was what they do to me all the time.

Are you hungry? Are you all going to help me with this or not?

These are pretty, Athena chimed in, her nose to a page of bright splashes of color, some detail of which she was trying to see better. Steph felt a rush of gratitude—that Athena was simply who she was, sometimes able to read the needs of others without going through all the bargaining around her, which she was usually oblivious to. As soon as the spaghetti was ready, she dished up Athena a plate and carried it over to the table.

Krishna, whose voracious hunger was usually served first, stared pointedly at his younger sister, who ignored the food to turn the page.

Next? Steph called from the stove.

Me, called out Krishna.

I think somebody's missing the point, Steph muttered into the pot. Maybe I should just throw it all out, if nobody wants to work as hard for it as I do. She urged herself to remain calm and firm, pretend she was in control of the situation. I am in control of the situation, she repeated to herself. This is my spaghetti. I own it until the price is paid.

Porter turned and blinked. Is it bad or something? How can spaghetti go bad?

As ever, Porter was missing the point.

Can you rototill the garden tomorrow and get Juan to do the upper terrace also with his tractor?

I think it's going to snow tomorrow.

Well then, I'll freeze this and we'll eat it after it snows and the ground dries and then you can get the garden rototilled. Is that OK? She had lost it, or was about to lose it. She could see herself stomping out the back door and heaving the kettle of spaghetti at the lilac bushes.

Porter was wide-eyed. There was something almost

innocent in his incomprehension. It would take her days to
explain, patiently reason through what had become clear to
her, about the garden, which wasn't really about the garden at
all, but about who her life really belonged to. Herself? Him?
The kids? Yet she had at last caught his attention. Just say yes,
she said.

Yes?

Just say yes, I will till the garden tomorrow at the very, very
first moment I possibly can, no matter what.

Sure, he said, but what's the big deal?

Krishna?

He was sulking. I said I would, he said archly.

No you didn't, not out loud, she said, sliding the plate in
front of Porter. His upturned look said, Now what? You didn't
say you would offer cheerful willing help in the garden on
Saturday or else you wouldn't dream of asking to go to Alvin's
for the night.

Yeah, he said after a long pause during which she pressed
her nails to her palm to keep in check an urge of foolish
generosity. Cruel, food-withholding mother, she berated
herself. Blackmailer.

Yeah, what? she almost sobbed.

Sure, I'll help, he said as softly as he could. Then more au-
dibly he added, Ricky Salcedo wants me to come over tonight.
Dad can drop me on the way to the meeting.

Homework? Don't we do homework tonight?

We're going to work on algebra together.

I can never win, Steph thought. But she didn't mind
Krishna spending the evening at Ricky Salcedo's. They
had the nicest house in town, a big rambling adobe built by
professional builders, not the local amateurs. The Salcedos
both worked in Santa Fe; he was a contractor of some kind
and she taught at some private school.

Sure, go.

Oh, I get it, Porter said cheerfully after the first bite. You want to plant a flower garden this year.

Athena looked up from the catalog pages and stared at him as if he was out of his mind.

CHAPTER 34

Un Nip

Lázaro Quintana stepped out of his small adobe to have the last smoke of the evening, the spring-loaded screen door closing with a sharp bang that could be heard a quarter of a mile away on a clear, still night such as this. The wind had finally dropped. Ramoncita had never allowed him or any of his friends to smoke in the house. I don't want nothing to do with that second-hand smoking, she had called out the door not long before her stroke. You take that second-hand smoking a long way from the house.

He lit up leaning against the west-facing wall, which radiated some warmth. A faint orange light still hung in the west sky, soon to be replaced by the colder, brighter light of the rising moon, full or nearly full tonight. There was an iciness to the air that made him think of the high mountain forests where he used to go cut wood for the woodstoves, the cold of the last days of autumn before the first snows that would close the narrow dirt tracks into the woods for the rest of the season. It would be cold tonight down here, like up there, and maybe the fruit would freeze.

Lázaro's eyes weren't good enough anymore to make out any individual stars, though he remembered the clear starry nights in the middle of the summer when he had slept out on the flat dirt roof of the house before they had covered it up with the rafters and the corrugated tin of a pitched roof, when he was still a boy. The stars were up there as a faint blurry haze, dimmer than the blank TV picture he had stared at off and on throughout the evening, waiting for the picture to come back on, which it never had. Manny Serrano must have finally run off with all the TV station money to pay for all those cars and pickups and that new mobile home of his, taking all the TV pictures with him while he was at it.

Even though he couldn't see any stars, he could still feel the immensity of the night as it settled around the yard, in the stealthily settling air, into which the smoke of his cigarette drifted away and disappeared. Ramoncita would go at night, he guessed, and he himself would also go at night, their warmth slowly evaporating into the night like the stones growing cold when the sun goes down in the evening or the kettle on the stove in the morning, after the fire goes out. What they would bury at the *camposanto* at the other end of town was what would have been left to grow cold, that's all, long after the warmth, the warm thing, whatever it was, had floated up out of the chimney into the night sky to disappear into the haze that he knew were stars.

He didn't know where it went from there, no more than he knew where the smoke from his cigarette went. *Es como la vida,* he had once explained to some gringo who had nagged him about smoking, first you roll up this little thing and make it into a little *muñeca,* how do you say that, a little white doll, and then light a match to it and it comes to life and you breathe life into it, puff puff. Nice little glow, tastes sweet, you feel better, it's a good life, *qué no?* Then before you know it, it's all over, you're at the end, and it begins to taste a little bad, a little strong, you know, a little bitter. You want to try to hang on? You burn your fingers if you let it burn too long. So you drop it in the dirt, and that's that. *¿Como la vida, no?* That's why they give them a cigarette before the electric chair. So you can live your whole life one more time before they pull the switch. But don't ask me what happens next. I don't know anything about that. They know all about that down at the church. I don't know how they know about those things but they say they do.

He dropped the warm, damp stub of his cigarette and put it out with a twist of his boot toe. The sensation of boring in his left temple, Lázaro realized during the last shallow puff, was the beginning of a headache that a day out in the wind often gave him at this time of year. Within minutes the sensation flowered into the familiar sharp throbbing, dropping like a curtain over his forehead.

He groped back inside and rolled himself another cigarette and stepped outside and lit up. Sometimes that helped, sometimes not. Maybe the ditch was trying to tell him something, maybe the acequia was sending a message to his head that he needed to go have a look. Maybe something up at the *presa*, the diversion dam, at the headgate with its big iron wheel bigger than a steering wheel on a screw shaft that raised and lowered the gate and was getting so stiff he had trouble turning it by himself. Pretty soon he was going to have to get help to turn that thing. Maybe there was something going on somewhere down the acequia and his headache was saying, Go turn off the water.

He puffed on the cigarette. It was the same old headache. It was going to be the same, no worse, no better. Should he get in the car and drive up there or not? He didn't like driving at night anymore because he had to stop every time a car came in the other direction because he couldn't see through the glare and then he had to sit awhile on the edge of the highway until he could see good enough to start moving again, though there was only a short section of highway before the dirt road that turned off and went along the river though the *álamos* to the headgate, the Upper Shooting Gallery, as the kids called it. But then sometimes the Benji Guerreros and their *borracho* buddies would be up there drinking at night around fires and shooting off guns. They'd park so nobody could get by and then they'd try to talk him into having a couple of beers and then they'd try to get even about something by throwing empty beer cans in his backseat or pissing on the tires or getting him drunk enough to show them how much money he had in his wallet. No, he was getting too old for that kind of stuff, and they weren't getting old enough to stay home and just watch TV like everybody else. No thank you, maybe.

Maybe he should, maybe he shouldn't. Maybe it was too cold for them to be up there tonight. But it was still going to be dark, even with the moon, and the yellow glow of the flashlight with half-dead batteries. He told himself maybe he should listen to those ads for new batteries. He dropped the keys enough back in the days when he could see where they went, the ring with his car key and the key to the house, which he never locked, and the three padlock keys to the headgates. He could see himself dropping them in the dark and hearing them pinging off the concrete and splashing down into the water like a spooked frog. He could see himself lying down flat, aching knees and all, and leaning way over the concrete edge and reaching down into the freezing water to grope for the keys. And beginning to slip, arms thrashing, flashlight plopping into the water, then tumbling headfirst into the water and being sucked down into the gurgling culvert. They would pull him out like a dead rat the next morning. No thank you for that one, for sure.

His forehead throbbed. Maybe the best thing would be to go back inside when he finished his cigarette and open the cupboard under the kitchen sink and reach over the can of Drano and the bottle of Lysol, way back into the corner where he kept a bottle of bourbon for his aches and pains. Just a nip. He liked the English word. Less than *un dedo. Un nip.*

He put out his cigarette on the sandy ground, a little *camposanto* he would come across first thing next morning, a graveyard of gray bits of paper with singed ends and tufts of brown and blackened tobacco, some of which the wind would carry away throughout the day, scattering everything off into the hazy remoteness.

The bright warmth inside felt good to his cold hands. He shuffled over to the kitchen sink, bent down, clawed open the cabinet door, and reached over the intervening bottles and pulled out the quart of gold-colored liquid. "Kentucky Rose," its ornate label announced.

He inspected a red plastic tumbler on the windowsill for spiders, poured himself a good *two dedos*, two fingers, hesitated, then added a touch more.

Just a nip, he said to himself, to fix up that headache. *Solamente un nip.*

CHAPTER 35

Nest Egg

As soon as Isabel Moro heard the garage door downstairs rattle closed and the tires rumble across the dirt parking lot, she sat down at her desk and pulled Abundio Moro's old lunch box from her bottom desk drawer. Onésimo had gone off to some meeting or other, something about water. He was always going to meetings about water. If they had any more meetings about water then nobody would have time to irrigate. When she set the rusty box down on her desk, the big brass padlock clacked. A screwdriver, she thought. There was a big one in one of the lower kitchen drawers, and a pair of pliers. She returned to the desk with the tools, plus a dishtowel she placed under the box so as not to scratch the desktop. Inserting the screwdriver blade into the metal hasp of the lunch box, she pried with all her strength against the lid. With a snap, the small screws fastening the latch to the box sprang loose—and the whole assembly, latch and hasp and brass padlock, flew past her and across the room and crashed through a glass-topped end table. *Santo Dios,* she muttered, not knowing whether to clean up the broken glass first or to pry open the rusty box. What would she say to Onésimo? She would have to find some heavy object and claim she had accidentally dropped it through the glass. But what? A vase? But which vase? And why would she be carrying around a vase when there weren't any flowers yet? Well, she was getting ready for when there would be flowers, she would tell him. Lame, she thought, but he wouldn't notice. He'd only start thinking about how much a new piece of glass would be.

She inserted the screwdriver blade under the lid of the box and pried. It popped open. Under a layer of wrinkled waxed paper were rows and rows of old envelopes, each one folded tightly around something. She pulled one out and unfolded it. It was an envelope postmarked nineteen-0-something, with a stamp so old she'd never seen one like it, and addressed to Abundio Moro, San Marcos, NM. Only a bit of the return address was left, also NM. Inside, a tarnished silver dollar from the 1800s. She replaced the coin, slipped it back into the envelope and the envelope back into the place where it had been, and then methodically began going through each of them from left to right.

They were in three files, apparently in chronological order, or very close to it, the oldest in the upper left hand of the box, the newest in the lower right corner. The envelopes were from dozens of different addresses. They contained mostly silver dollars, plus a dozen or so five- and twenty-dollar gold coins and a few silver certificates, a hundred or more coins in all. The latest postmark was from a decade ago, suggesting to Isabel that Abundio had stopped adding to his collection about then, but until then they suggested that he deposited a coin a year in his little savings box. The last envelope contained two Kennedy half dollars, which was about the time the last Eisenhower silver dollars dropped out of circulation. There were none of those new miserable attempts at a dollar coin, which Abundio probably wouldn't have been able to tell from a quarter.

She thumbed through the envelopes a second time, wondering whether the stamps too might be worth something. Some of them had letters in them. She went back to the earliest envelope and pulled it out. Inside was a single page covered in fine delicate handwriting in ink. Long forgotten memories surged up of scarred varnished school desks with inkwells in the upper right hand corner and black wooden pen holders and scratchy nibs. The heading on the letter was *el Convento, 2 Mayo 1909* and it was signed *Tía Juanita.* The letter was in Spanish, very proper Spanish, but there was little of substance in it beyond reports of the weather, fruit trees blossoming, and the promise of better meals in the convent when the garden started producing. Isabel rifled through and pulled out more letters and read through them, through the teens and the 1920s, but they were all as formulaic: the weather, the garden, meals, rain, snow, drought, wind. Over time the handwriting became more angular and irregular and blotchy with ink spots. After 1928 the handwriting on the envelopes changed and there were no more letters, only sheets of paper wrapped around pieces of thin cardboard over the coins. For Isabel, the effect of the old letters and even blank pieces of paper was to plunge her back into her early years, speeded up in odd little flashes. So many more animals then, she thought, horses, cows, sheep. Her father had brought the first car to the village, a Model T Ford pickup, but the roads in and out of the valley were so bad that he rarely took it anywhere and had to bring gasoline for it in a big can on the back of a horse. People marched through the store to the backyard just to have a look at it. She was ten when she saw her first frightening gringos and black people on the train from Las Vegas to Santa Fe, telling her mother that she and her were just the right color, entre los dos. During the Depression and the long drought, a family nobody liked starved to death, or at least one of them did.

She slipped the letters back into their envelopes and back into the box and pushed it away from her and closed the lid. She had no sense of the value of the coins. Hundreds of dollars? Thousands? The stamps might even be worth more, she thought. But what to do? Put the rusty box back down in the lower desk drawer? He had no heirs. She had heard long ago that his funeral expenses were already covered. Somehow, someone might be able to find a distant cousin to take the tiny piece of hillside land into which his cave had been dug. Give it to the church? No, the church already had too much money. Besides the priest never came anymore, except for funerals and sometimes a wedding, usually some overfed gringo who didn't know a word of Spanish and who maintained that the bishop had ruled that there were to be no eulogies by *la gente* and not even any music.

With a start she remembered the broken glass. And the still unbroken vase. She found a heavy cheap clear glass vase on the upper shelf of the back pantry and brought it around to the living room and dropped it through the frame of the glassless end table. It hit the wooden floor with clunk but failed to break after three tries, forcing her to resort to a hammer from the kitchen tool drawer, the blow shooting splinters of glass all over the floor.

As she swept, she pondered the fate of the coins. What would Onésimo say? Nothing useful. We could pave the parking lot, he would say. We could put iron bars over the windows and doors, he would say. We could put an alarm system in. He would have lots of uses for the money they would get from selling the coins and maybe the stamps too, but as for the fact of her having found and removed the box from under Abundio Moro's bed, all he would suggest would be, Finders keepers. And maybe he might go as far as to say, We're Moros too—I must be related, maybe I'm even the long-lost cousin, the rightful heir.

But what, she wondered, if the coins and stamps turned out to be worth not a thousand dollars or so but a lot of money instead. Would that change anything? What if they were worth tens of thousands of dollars?

She slid the glass from the dust pan into a double-bagged grocery sack. What if somebody else knew about the lunch box and what if that somebody found out that she had gone back to the cave after they had carried away the body? What if somebody came to the door in the middle of the night and started pounding? We know you're there, Mrs. Moro, and we know you have it. Waking the Vizarriagas next door, lights going on all over the neighborhood, couples whispering to each other in bed, Well looks like they finally got Onésimo and Isabel, about time. They would be with the county sheriff, maybe even the state police. We have a search warrant, Mrs. Moro, open up in the name of the law, you are charged with grand larceny.

She slumped down on the sofa, lowering the sack of broken glass between her knees on to the floor. Was this to be the curse of Abundio Moro, the oldest man in San Marcos? She saw herself in prison, in a drab gray uniform, fingers wrapped around bars, like in that old black-and-white movie, what was it called?

But wait a minute, she thought, sitting up straight. How many years did I take Abundio Moro bowls of *atole* and posole, sometimes even little dinners when I was away in the morning? Twenty-two, twenty-three years, since he was in his eighties, from when he couldn't do much himself? Three hundred and some meals a year, twenty-some years, now that adds up. Some six or seven or eight thousand meals, grand total, plus the drive back and forth, two miles round trip each time, that's a lot of miles and gas and wear and tear on four different cars, helped wear them out, plus insurance, too, and registration each year, tires, batteries, plus that time she

backed over a rock near his cave and they had to call a tow
truck and tow the car all the way to Santa Fe.

She folded over the top of the grocery sack and carried it
downstairs to the barrel for store trash they kept in the garage.
By the time she returned upstairs to the living room, she
had it all figured out. On her next trip to town she'd take
the collection into some coin dealer and get it appraised.
Onésimo? No need to tell him, get him all worried or plotting
how to spend the money right away. It would be her own little
nest egg. She'd either sell the collection and put the money in
her own little account or else get a new safe deposit box and
store it there. After all, as long as she didn't actually spend
the money, she could think of herself as keeping it safe for
Abundio and any eventual heirs, not that there were likely to
be any. It would be a nice way to keep his memory alive.

The Abundio Moro Memorial Fund, she said to herself. It
had a nice ring to it.

But then she wondered why she had gone to the trouble
of breaking the glass vase. Onésimo would have accepted her
word, wouldn't have poked around in the trash. *Santo Dios*, she
muttered, a perfectly good vase, too. What a waste.

CHAPTER 36

Miranda's Memories

Ricky Salcedo's father had an evening county commission meeting to attend in town, so his parents decided to spend the night. Nothing stupid, his mother had said, nothing stupid, understand? Ricky was a perfectly behaved thirteen-year-old, at least to his elders, an A student, and passably good at sports. He was the pride of the family. His grandmother had boasted, *Salió bien blanco,* He came out nice and white, which was the only Spanish he really knew, probably Thousand Island Spanish at that. But among his companions he led a secret life as a prankster and clown. He had earned the nickname Streaker or Streaks through occasional late-night full-moon runs up and down the highway through San Marcos during the summer months with a ski mask on and with a pair of black briefs balled up in his fist in case of dire emergencies and Nike running shoes and white athletic socks. Knowing his parents would be away weeks in advance, he had bet his friends he would go through with it but was having second thoughts given the unseasonable coldness of the evening. The bet was for ten dollars. But he only had $3.75.

Ricky Salcedo was proud of his well-formed but still some-what soft body and had amassed a large stack of bodybuilding magazines for inspiration to harden his muscles. The images served as blurry mirrors to convince him that his physique was becoming more muscular and more richly veined than what he actually studied in the mirror—or what he imagined he was becoming on the strength of still minimal and fitful work-outs. The body he ran in while streaking at night was one of magazine images, or a collage of them. It had all started early last summer on a dare after a friend saw something on TV.

I'll freeze my balls off, he said to no one in particular as he and three of his friends settled into the La-Z-Boy reclining sofa and armchair to watch the tape of *Miranda's Memories* Ricky had picked up at the post office just after school before his parents got home from work. George Serrano Jr. took a swig from a quart bottle of Lucky Lager he'd smuggled out of his house and passed it to Krishna Wachler, who in turn passed it to Billy Mora, who issued a celebratory giggle before taking a swig and passing it on to Ricky, who took a sip and passed the bottle back to George and then pointed the remote at the TV.

This was only their second porn night, as Ricky had only recently figured out how to obtain tapes through the mail by disguising his status as a minor, with the help of the uncle he was named after. Aside from giggling Bill, the boys were very serious in a studious sort of way. The first video they had watched a couple of months earlier was so unrelentingly explicit that they had all sat there, mouths agape, pillows over crotches, not saying a word, and immediately afterward they had muttered good-byes and rushed outside in nothing more than thin T-shirts to seek the calming embrace of the below-zero night. But now they were experienced, adult, capable of a certain critical distance, participating in a serious ritual, or so they thought. Ricky had started calling them their Sex Education Workshops, which had sent Billy into a fit of giggling so severe he had vomited into the kitchen sink.

So tonight would be different. Ricky already knew he was going to be a film major in college. They would study the foreplay, the anatomy, the positions, the lighting, the furnishings, the quality of acting, the style of directing. They would be students, not horny teenagers. The next day they would tell their schoolmates, We watched some very superior porn last night. Really first class. Makes that other stuff look trashy. It's really a form of art, you know. But such thoughts immediately evaporated once the credits ended and clothing was ripped off right away in the first scene, literally ripped off, and bodies athletically crashed onto the mattress.

Billy giggled.

Don't throw up again, Krishna said, passing the bottle.

Throw pillows were discreetly inched into place.

Ricky had turned off the sound in order to hear a car driving up, in case of an early return of his parents. Other than a high-pitched hum from the TV or video cassette player and regular sloshing sounds from the beer bottle, the room was utterly silent.

An hour later The End was greeted with faint relieved expulsions of breath. One by one the boys got up stiffly from the sofa and went to the bathroom, Billy first.

What's taking him so long?

Then Krishna.

What's taking *him* so long?

Then George.

When they had all reassembled Krishna said, Well, Streaks, are you going to do it or not? If not you owe us ten bucks, me and Billy two-fifty and George five. Just do it, like they say, or pay through the nose.

What time is it?

A little after eight, Billy giggled.

Ricky parted the drapes. The moon was up, almost full. He wondered whether he could get away with only going halfway, not all the way to Moro Mercantile and back, which the bet specified. He could put the tape back on and maybe they wouldn't notice.

OK, yeah, I guess.

He trotted off to his room and stripped, put on the ski mask, found a pair of skimpy briefs and wadded them up in his left fist, slipped on his Nikes and darted out the back door. It was cold. He'd hoped that the cold would serve to deflate him but it had the opposite effect. He began running as fast as he could, the thing slapping back and forth from thigh to thigh. Go down, he ordered it, go down. But running with him were a quick succession of scenes from *Miranda's Memories*, one after the other.

The highway was deserted.

Why? he wondered. How? he wondered. Why the fuck? he wondered. Then he remembered the ten bucks. He hoped Billy and Krishna and George really had it on them.

Slap, slap, slap. Oh my god, he moaned. Lightning shot through his loins and up his spine and he veered off into some bushes on the side of the road, where he slumped and ejaculated into the grass. He crouched, shivering, for a few minutes.

When he emerged he stood on the edge of the pavement, wondering whether to continue on his run or go back. He had only run a couple of hundred yards. What should he do?

There he was, naked, cold, standing on the edge of the highway in the dark, in what now seemed like miles from the warm living room and his bedroom where his clothes lay rumpled on the floor.

He was suddenly more alone than he had ever felt before.

His mother's words echoed in his brain, Nothing stupid, son, nothing stupid.

Well here was something really, really stupid.

CHAPTER 37

A Tale of Two Alternators

J ust in time, Lalo Moro thought as he watched Leandro Salcedo angle the DISH TV satellite dish through the door, long wires dragging behind it. Where'd you get it?

Manny's new mobile home, Leandro replied, peeling off his ripped padded brown jacket and draping it over a chair, the .38 snub nose in its side pocket thudding against the wood. They left the ladder right next to it.

There's no TV tonight. Nobody paid the electric bill.

This will fix it, *primo*. You just watch.

Leandro perched the metal dish on the sink counter and stripped off insulation at the end of the wires and unscrewed the antenna led to Lalo's small black-and-white TV, fastened the new wires, and switched it on. He worked with the exaggerated confidence of the young as witnessed by a clueless elder baffled by new technology.

Snow, just like before.

Maybe we got to point it in the right direction.

Leandro picked up the dish and aimed it at various spots in the ceiling of sagging, water-splotched Masonite.

Didn't it come with some kind of box, you know, electronic thing?

I dunno. The back door was locked. Maybe if we take it outside and point it at the moon.

After ten minutes of holding the dish up to the night sky out in the yard and pointing it in various directions without result, Leandro gave up. This fucking thing is heavy. But, hey, Lalo, why don't you put it up on your roof anyway. That way your *pendejo vecinos* will think you're getting a hundred more channels than they are.

He brought it inside and lifted it up and set it on top of the refrigerator.

Though no longer young, Leandro was a pioneer in low-hanging jeans and in the habit of lifting his T-shirt and stroking his smooth stomach and chest, in part to reveal the pride of his body, a tattoo centered across his navel, the N straddling his belly button:

𝔏 𝔈 𝔄 𝔑 𝔇 𝔕 𝔒

He had acquired the tattoo during a two-week stay in the State Pen near Santa Fe, following a DWI arrest. The wreck had been the envy of Lalo: right through the front porch and living room window of a house just off Canyon Road. Mistaken identity had caused him to be transferred from the county jail to the state pen, where he joined an uncle and three cousins who didn't try to correct the error. The tattoo artist, a bald gringo, had approached him on day three, hinting it wouldn't cost him anything, at least until he got to the second letter.

I really get off on working on guys' bodies. You got real nice smooth silky skin, he had said. This is going to be worth two.

Two what?

Blow jobs.

After pondering the act for a moment, Leandro asked, But who for?

For me.

I thought only *chicas* did that.

You see any *chicas* around here? You're the *chica*, bro. Two blow jobs or I stop right now.

Maybe if he pretended he was Estampillas, his food stamp girlfriend in Santa Fe, who gave him blow jobs when she was sore, it wouldn't be so bad. But in the end he'd only had to do the first of the two as he was pulled out of the pen just after the tattoo was finished, when the administrative mistake was discovered. Aside from the blow job business, memories of which were reliably dissipated by a couple of beers, he missed being there with his cousins and the uncle who was a passenger in the car Leandro's drunken father drove off the road and rolled, killing him when he was thrown out of the car. The site was marked by a *descanso* in the form of a metal cross festooned with plastic roses between San Marcos Arriba and San Marcos Abajo. In Korea, Leandro's father had resented his commanding officer, who called him a Mexican despite his pointing out that, Hey, *gringo*, sir, I'm Spanish, not Mexican, a distinction lost on the officer. He wouldn't let him and his buddies speak Spanish either. At home Leandro's parents spoke mostly Spanish and were unable to help him with his homework. He finally flunked out of high school his freshman year.

He pulled down his shirt and said, Maybe this dish thing will keep things colder inside the refrigerator since it won't work with the TV, you never know. You got any beer?

Lalo opened the fridge. There were seven precious cans of Coors. No, he said, not much.

One will do, Lalo.

You owe me, then.

They popped the cans and guzzled.

Think it's late enough to go for that alternator?

It's dark, it must be late enough.

Vámanos.

Lalo had already wrapped a couple of wrenches and screwdrivers and wire cutters and dog biscuits and a flashlight in a plastic shopping bag, knowing that Leandro never could think far enough ahead to do so himself, other than make certain he always had his revolver on or near him, as if that would solve all their problems.

As they were about to go out the door, Leandro opened the fridge and snagged the six-pack carton.

Hey, protested Lalo.

Hey, man, it's cold out there, we're going to need some help.

They climbed into Leandro's aging Impala, which he had attempted to turn into a low-rider by removing the shock absorbers, but without success, the only result being so far that without shocks it bounced so badly over every bump in the road that he couldn't control it over thirty miles an hour. As soon as they turned onto the highway, they both popped new cans of beer. When Lalo realized Leandro was going to chug-a-lug as fast as he could, he did the same so as to keep Leandro from drinking more of his beer.

Just before the school turnoff, Leandro switched off the lights and they bounced up the dirt road toward the school, weaving back and forth, until they came to the long grove of cottonwoods known as the Lower Shooting Gallery and pulled into the trees, guided now by parking lights. Leandro had his favorite place over to the left, where they could leave the car hidden by clumps of willows. Up the road a half mile, all the lights were on at the school.

Before climbing out of the car, they pulled the last cans of Coors, and popped the tabs. Thoroughly agitated by the bouncing Impala, the cans sprayed beer all over the dashboard and headliner.

Holy shit! *¡Que bárbaro!* What a fucking mess.

They climbed out of the car, shaking beer off their hands, brushing it off their jackets, wiping their faces.

Funny, murmured Leandro, I smell pot.

That's beer, not pot, *primo.*

Yeah.

They peed into the bushes.

Lalo pulled the flashlight out of the plastic bag, but there was enough of a moon that they wouldn't need it until they got to taking the alternator out of the Oldsmobile. They walked back down the dirt road and then followed the highway along the junkyard fenceline until they came to the place where they could climb through. The hulks of nearly a hundred cars lay spread out before them, shapes dimly reflecting the rising moon. There was no light on in Fabian Moro's distant shack, a pretty good indication that he had gone to bed. They squeezed through the wires.

You remember where it is?

No, but I'll remember.

If you don't remember how can you remember?

Shhh.

Leandro led the way, pushing through the tall grass and squeezing through places where the cars had been parked bumper to bumper, the odor of beer on their clothes mingling with that of motor oil and rotting tires.

See that white top? I think that's it.

The hood was unlatched and they opened it up just enough to slip head and shoulders inside. Lalo switched on the flashlight, producing a dim yellow beam.

You need new batteries, bro.

Lalo felt around in the plastic bag for the wrenches and found one that fit and began unbolting the alternator.

El perro. Did you bring anything for the dog?

In the sack.

Leandro pulled out the biscuits and threw them on the ground for the chow, which had arrived, panting and wagging its large, burr-infested tail.

Five minutes was enough to unbolt the alternator and clip the wires and for the flashlight batteries to go dead. Before they left, Lalo peed in the trunk of the Oldsmobile, Leandro on a back door.

Let's get out of here, Lalo said.

They hiked back through the wrecks, regained the highway, then the dirt road. Halfway up to the cottonwoods where they had stashed the Impala, a car roared past them, lights off, and spraying gravel and throwing up so much dust they couldn't make out whose it was.

The Impala greeted them with a broken driver's-side window and the hood up. Sons a bitches! shouted Leandro. *Pendejos! Puta madres!* Lalo fished out his flashlight. There was just enough of a glimmer for them to see that the battery was gone. And the alternator.

Leandro pounded on the front fender, kicked the tire. Sons a bitches, sons a bitches, I'm gonna shoot those sons a bitches?

Who? asked Lalo.

Don't know who until I find them, *pendejos.*

Through the trees, a half mile up the dirt road, the lights were still on at the school.

Fucking broke, too.

At least we got a replacement alternator, Lalo observed.

Fucking broke, Leandro fumed. But I think I know how to take care of that. Let's go.

Where?

Up there. There's some meeting or other. I got my gun. All we need is a couple of wallets from those fat cats. Come on, let's go.

But first they peed into the bushes.

Leandro pulled out his .38 and reached behind his neck and pulled up his dark green T-shirt up over his head and up over his chin and mouth. There, he said, they won't know who it is. He was unaware, other than a certain draftiness, that when he pulled up his T-shirt the action exposed his midriff tattoo.

LEANDRO

Lalo asked, What do I do?

Just stand outside and wait.

They began hiking through the trees toward the dirt road that meandered up the slope toward the school, where a couple of dozen cars were parked under orange sodium vapor street lights, plus Zip Zepeda's metallic-blue hearse.

Sure this is a good idea? Lalo suggested. He realized he was still carrying his bag of tools and the alternator, which was getting very heavy. He was panting.

Sure it's a good idea. Best idea I ever had.

They paused at the edge of the parking lot to pee again.

CHAPTER 38

Ambulance Service

Zip Zepeda Jr. sat slouched behind the wheel of the Cadillac Fleetwood hearse, eyes half-closed against the glare of the sodium vapor lights of the school parking lot. For lack of any official county service, three generations of Zepeda hearses had doubled as ambulances in the farther reaches of the county for an annual subsidy, and Zip Sr. entertained the belief that at every public meeting in San Marcos inevitably someone got shot and even killed, on the strength of two events within living memory. In the first a Serrano decided to settle the feud with the Carrillos once and for all, but the victim was not the Carrillo but the Serrano, when the shotgun barrel, stuffed with peanuts by some rodent or a child, exploded in his face. The second was during a meeting called by the Forest Service to inform the residents of San Marcos that all their land was in fact Forest Service land, owing to a recently discovered surveying error. Toward the end of the meeting, a pistol slipped out of a pocket and hit the floor and discharged, causing Onésimo Moro's great-grandmother to suffer a fatal heart attack.

Zip Senior had ordered his son Zippy to go back up to San Marcos for the water meeting, which his aunt, Esmerelda

Vizarriaga had phoned about, despite the son's protest that he had a date that night, finally, with the tall blond *güera*. Take her along, the father had suggested. She'll enjoy the ride. Cadillac Fleetwood, how many of her dates are going to take her out in a Cadillac Fleetwood? Just tell her that.

It's a hearse, Dad.

Tell her it just looks like a hearse from the outside. Inside it's *puro* Cadillac Fleetwood. Tell her not to turn around, that's all. Sprinkle some of that air freshener inside.

So now Zippy sat, nose of the hearse parked up against the adobe wall of the gym, the time ticking away slowly, an hour gone, perhaps another hour or two to go. His father had got the meeting time wrong, so Zippy had arrived on time, not late as he had hoped, and had watched Mr. Molinas unlock the gym to admit the early arrivals, followed by a steady stream of inhabitants from San Marcos and upstream villages, perhaps almost a hundred or a hundred and fifty in all. In defiance of funeral home rules he was both smoking and listening to the radio, to mariachi music from the only station with decent reception.

He was dozing off when two guys approached the door of the gym, one with a sweatshirt or something pulled up over his head, exposing his midriff, the other probably older. The puzzling pair stopped at the door, gestured impatiently at each other, before the hooded one stepped inside. Zippy closed his eyes.

Latecomers, he thought, latecomers, before slipping into visions of driving the hearse, windows open, with *la güera* sitting beside him, radiant at being driven through town in a real Cadillac Fleetwood.

CHAPTER 39

Dust to Dust

Martin Caudell from the State Water Office wound up his presentation on the benefits of regularizing water rights by clicking on the last slide of his show, a view of a scenic river brimming with water and overhung by weeping willows and other trees he suspected were not native to New Mexico. The Old Man had assured him that the long slide show with scenes of flowing water interspersed with pie charts and bar graphs generally had a soporific effect on audiences, reliably mollifying and even pacifying the most recalcitrant. You'll have them eating out of your hand, son, he had told Martin, with a pat on the back and a squeeze of the biceps. They'll think this the greatest idea since sliced bread. Then guffawing, That is, if they've finally got sliced bread up in that valley.

The arrival had not been auspicious. A young man with elaborate tattoos on his forearms had offered to keep his tires from being slashed during the meeting for twenty dollars. Martin had offered him ten. So you want only two of your tires slashed, bro, is that it? He had caved. More water-cooler gossip back at the office, he could imagine.

The high school principal, Mr. Molinas, a short roly-poly

older man with a fixed maniacal smile of a strange coldness, had helped him set up the slide projector. Martin was puzzled by the white dust mask dangling from his neck. So, he said to Martin in a wheezing voice as they were testing the lamp, the people down south, *los tejanos*, want our water, is that it?

Well, replied Martin, it's a little more complicated than that. They already got our land grants, you know.

What?

They got our land grants first, the gringos, your people, he said, pointing a finger at him. You a lawyer?

Yes, uh, just passed the bar.

You lawyers got our land grants. Then the railroads down in the Plains they came up and cut down all the trees, you never heard of that?

The trees?

For how do you call them, the wood they put the rails down on.

Ties?

Ties, railroad ties. Then you come and take our muchachos, our boys, and send them off to World War First and then World War Second and then Korea and then Vietnam. You know how many *veteranos* we have?

No.

I don't either but a lot, let me tell you. Between Arriba and Abajo, a lot, let me tell you. Though there were a lot of draft-dodgers in down there in Abajo.

Mr. Molinas said all this with his fixed wide-mouth smile. Martin thought it best not to confess to the fact that his extended schooling had meant deferments through the last Vietnam years.

You don't know, do you, that this was all once the Anastasio Moro Land Grant, do you, by the King of Spain who signed the original papers, you can find them in the state archives, you don't know that, do you? This he said with a sweeping gesture of both arms toward the roof and presumably the heavens themselves. All, everything, *todo*, used to be ours.

And then you take all our money, taxes, taxes, taxes. With a second sweeping gesture at the wavy adobe walls of the gym, the sagging water-stained paneling that served as a ceiling from which dangled fluorescent fixtures, half of whose bulbs were dark, he asked, And what do we get? This is what we get, Mr. Lawyer. He paused to catch his wheezing breath. This is what we got left. Except our water, and now you're going to take that, too.

Martin was torn. Yes, one thing would lead to another, and yes, the state would make claims on the watershed, and yes, eventually the state would end up taking water out of the valley for senior downstream users and the ever-expanding cities. But, no, he wasn't here personally to actually do that, he was here to, well, sort of begin to pave the way. Yes, well, in fact, he was indeed part of the process. He stood staring at Mr. Molinas's Cheshire-grin teeth. Uh, he said, finally adding, but you know, it's going to take a long, long time.

Mr. Molinas turned away. On the wall behind the narrow stage he pulled down a once-white screen that had been attacked by what Martin imagined were fruits and vegetables over the years.

The first villagers were pushing through the double doors at the rear of the gym. Martin sat down on a folding chair below the stage and thumbed through his notes. This will not end well, he thought. It might not even start well. Maybe he should just stand up and say outright, I'm here to begin the long and torturous process of taking away your water, but it will be a lot easier if everyone just stays calm and we figure out how to work through the process with as little fuss as possible. Which he imagined is what rapists said. Whereupon he heard in his mind the voice of the Old Man. Fired, Caudell, you're fired. He broke into a cold sweat. The office had abandoned him to his fate. The Old Man had promised to send him a couple of other staff members. They had probably been ambushed on their way, tires slashed, windows smashed, briefcases and papers strewn among the cactus. Maybe they went to the wrong San Marcos.

He checked his watch. Another five minutes. The gym was filling rapidly with a noisy laughing and guffawing crowd, people shouting back and forth in Spanish.

Into an aisle seat in the third row slipped Porter Clapp, seized by a strange excitement, something that Steph had triggered. She was a different person over dinner, wouldn't let the conversation stray from her garden fantasy until dinner was over and the last dish and last piece of silver washed and dried and put away. And when the kids went off to their rooms she turned on him. And you, she said, when are you going to get your fucking act together and lay off the weed and put on some clean clothes and drive to town and fucking sell some of your toys?

When?

When? she repeated, When?

I have that water meeting tonight at the gym.

Then tomorrow. Agreed?

Tomorrow?

Tomorrow.

I don't think I have any clean clothes.

Then wash some, she said absently from the couch, flipping through a fruit tree catalog. There's a machine for that. It's called a washing machine.

His thoughts were cut short when Martin Caudell stood up and buttoned his suit coat and climbed the two steps to the stage and walked over to the podium and adjusted the microphone to his height. He tapped it but heard nothing coming out of the speakers.

Doesn't work anymore, someone called out. The audience tittered.

Okay, can we dim the lights and see the first slide, he shouted, realizing too late in the darkness that he had failed to introduce himself and explain why he was here. There were over a hundred people in the audience, he estimated. The Old Man had said only a handful would show up.

First slide, please, he repeated, nodding down at Mr. Molinas next to the projector, now with his dust mask on. As if, Martin thought, not to be infected by my words.

There followed a succession of bucolic scenes showing clear streams and waterfalls and lush forests alternating with slides of short, simple statements about where water comes from and who "owns" it and explanations of "beneficial" uses, including agriculture, with images of fields as large as the whole San Marcos Valley, and municipal development, showing new subdivisions under construction and sewage treatment plants and lush green parks and golf courses.

All of a sudden, it seemed to him, there were no more slides. He was shocked that he had come to the end of his formal presentation so soon. Uh, lights on, please. Now some of you may have a few questions. I'd be happy to try to answer them.

Español, español, someone called out from the back of the room. No speak English here.

More laughter.

Onésimo Moro and Porter Clapp stood up at the same time, Clapp waving an arm for attention. The time had come, Porter had decided, to bare his soul to the community that had taken him in and confess to the act that had led him to hide out in San Marcos. It would enable him to become a new man, pure and upright, someone who could stand his ground without fear of being undercut by past sins and omissions.

Someone who could defend and save their water.

Wait a minute, Onésimo said, I want to say something, amigos, I want to say something first. He looked around at the crowd. A quick instinctive calculation told him how many current and former customers there were, who owed a little, who a lot, and the faces of those who had never come into the store. He wondered how he could turn the gathering into a heartfelt plea to the *delincuentes* to pay their bills.

I just want to say something, Onésimo shouted.

Then say it, bro, someone called out from the back.

I just wanted to say that we should all just sell our water to, I don't know, whoever wants to buy it for a good price. That's all I want to say.

Peals of laughter. Someone else called out from the back of the gym, You no fuck with our water, see?

More laughter. A group of young people started chanting, You no fuck with our water! You no fuck with our water!

Soon people were standing, waving fists, shouting. Martin wondered if there was a back door. A vision of him crouching down in a clump of cactus, slide projector tucked under an arm, trying to hide, flitted through his mind.

The far entrance door opened. For a moment he thought reinforcements had finally arrived.

A strangely dressed young man strode into the gym, head bizarrely hooded, jacket hiked up. Martin couldn't at first make out the letters tattooed across his bared stomach. He was shouting something, moving closer to the last row of folding chairs. Finally Martin could read the tattoo on his bared stomach.

LEANDRO

Hey, Leandro, someone called out, what's with the hood?

Leandro pulled out a pistol and aimed it at the ceiling. Everyone abruptly fell silent, their eyes fixed on the pearl-handled revolver whose nickel plating was pitted and peeling.

Throw your wallets and purses and jewelry and food stamps right there on the floor, everybody, quick, quick!

More howls of laughter, but now everyone was turned away from the stage. Martin wondered whether he could slip away. But what about the slides, the projector? More water-cooler gossip. He had to abandon everything, they would be saying, slides, projector, even the Old Man's state car, took him two days to hike back to Santa Fe.

Hey, Leandro. Come on, Leandro, a bunch of the younger guys were calling out.

Leandro raised the pistol and fired a shot into the ceiling. The recoil threw him backward onto the floor. The impact of the fall caused him to fire a second shot into the ceiling near a corner.

Everyone fell silent. From overhead came the sounds of pigeons flapping and banging into each other, chortling in panic, followed by a crack. Starting at the first bullet hole, a section of the warped paneling slowly tore open, dumping a waterfall of gray dust and feathers onto Leandro and the last row of seats, to the sounds of coughing and shouts and screams and folding chairs collapsing and light fixtures hitting the floor. Dust quickly filled the gym. Abruptly more ceiling panels collapsed, dumping yet more decades of pigeon guano and feathers and fragments of nests and fledglings on the people below, while pigeons flapped blindly around the auditorium, crashing into lights and windows. All but the two fluorescent fixtures over the stage went out. Porter Clapp stood immobile, marveling at the pandemonium. The end of the world, he thought. Finally. At last. Until he too was engulfed in a falling curtain of dust that was advancing toward the stage, where Martin Caudell ripped the cord of the projector from the socket and jumped down from the stage to his chair and snatched up his briefcase before being dumped on as the last ceiling panels cracked open.

CHAPTER 40

Ghosts

Outside Zippy Zepeda was abruptly roused from a dream when the gym doors flew open and people all covered with white dust groped their way out and stumbled toward their cars, coughing, wiping their faces with handkerchiefs—a dream, Zippy thought, a dream of all the dead people he and his father had taken to the funeral home and then back to the rural cemeteries, there they all were, their ghosts, old, young, streaming past the hearse, a dream, a nightmare.

But he wasn't asleep, he finally realized, he was awake. He opened the door and got out, watched them file out, taking off coats and shaking them, coughing, sneezing, swearing, followed by gusts of white dust billowing out the gym doors.

A fellow in suit and tie burst out the door, slide projector tucked under one arm, briefcase under the other, and headed toward the state Crown Victoria parked a few cars down.

Late to emerge was a hippie with a dusty ponytail, smiling oddly as he shook the dust out of his shirt and patted down his Levi's.

A couple of guys carried out Leandro Salcedo, unconscious from a concussion. His right arm dangled limply at an odd angle.

Hey, bro, you need to take him to the hospital.

Zippy opened up the back door of the hearse and the three young men shoveled Leandro inside, then stood staring for a moment at the plush gray upholstery of the interior.

Last out of the gym was the principal, Mr. Molinas, who switched off the surviving lights before closing and locking the door behind him. He slipped the dust mask up over his head and gave it a good shake.

To no one in particular he said, I guess we showed them, didn't we?

CHAPTER 41

Reward

Ricky Salcedo was half running, half walking back toward his house when the first cars from the school meeting turned onto the highway and headed in his direction. The rules of his streaking called for him to not hide if cars came along, and so far he had been lucky in his adventures. But not tonight. One by one, cars turned on to the highway ahead of him, the lights growing brighter and brighter. He increased his running pace.

He could not know that as the cars passed one by one that their drivers and passengers would hardly notice the running naked masked figure with white athletic socks, occupied as they were with thoughts of getting into the shower and throwing their clothes into the washing machine. Though he avoided any chance of eye contact, after the fifth or sixth car a few quick glances made him wonder why everyone inside them seemed to have a ghostly pallor—and why nobody seemed to pay any attention to him.

He'd never do this again, he knew. Everything was getting too weird. Not even for ten bucks. Well, maybe for twenty, but not a nickel less. For twenty he could rent a couple of more tapes. Sure, one more time, but that would be it.

He almost cried with relief when he swung into his driveway and ran around to the back door and slammed into his room and switched on the light. He pulled off the black woolen mask and kicked off his Nikes. His room was bathed in a strange luminosity. The so-familiar details seemed to glow: the black-and-white movie poster reproductions on the wall opposite his bunk bed: *The Maltese Falcon, Sunset Boulevard,* the first Beatles movie. Schoolbooks stacked neatly on the left side of the small desk. The pile of bodybuilding magazines on the floor between the desk and the bunk bed. The bunk bed itself, its beams stained red to resemble redwood. The small stereo on a shelf above the top bunk, and on top of it two small plastic running trophies. The orange wall-to-wall carpet, his jeans and T-shirt and blue undershorts with white dots in a heap on the floor next to the bed. The dark pine paneling. He took it all in as if seeing it for the first time, as if he had just been dropped from another planet—into a warm, secure, comfortable place. He was convulsed by a deep shuddering sigh of something like gratitude. On the way to pick up his clothes he caught sight of his naked form in the full-length mirror on the closet door. He paused and looked at himself, a rather soft-bodied teenager without prominent muscles or veins, younger and more innocent than the one he habitually imagined himself to be. Quickly he slipped on his clothes, welcoming the embrace of the material.

He darted out the door in bare feet and burst into the living room.

Give me my ten bucks, he yelled triumphantly.

sleep

In the clear evening sky over San Marcos, the rising moon presided, its cool light undiminished by smog or smoke or cloud, a slight flattening on the lower side indicating that it was a day away from its grand monthly ripening. During its rise, in a loose unconnected way, those inhabitants who had not gone to Santa Fe or to the water meeting at the elementary school sat down to dinner at Formica tables, oilcloth covers, round and square oak tables, at kitchen counters, into dining nooks, where they ate silently watching the blank TV screens in the hope that a picture might soon emerge or listened to the radio or engaged in those telegraphic communications that passed for conversation among people who have spent a lifetime together. Children squabbled or excused themselves from the table or just got up and left to make phone calls to see whose VCRs were working that night and who had luckily brought home a new movie rented in town. The old and the very old listened to the passage of time in the motions of their own chewing and swallowing and rumbling stomachs and bowels. Out back doors dogs and cats pricked up their ears at the predictable waves of brittle metallic sounds through doors, and they sniffed at odors creeping out under doorways.

Out in the henhouses the birds settled onto their roosts and nests and lowered pale lids against the fears of all darkness. Inside pens and sheds, goats and pigs settled into warm corners. In the fields, cattle and horses chewed.

For some residents the time after dinner was the loneliest hour. The bright lights of the faraway cities were remembered, those of Santa Fe and Albuquerque, which had grown farther away in the dark, Las Cruces, Denver, Phoenix, Los Angeles, and even New York, Paris, Madrid, Rome, which seemed so distant as to be on another planet. Calculations were made about whether it was too late to drive to Santa Fe to a movie or a dance or concert, or whether a nearby friend or relative should be called on or summoned. But it was Monday, only Monday, and everybody had just spent the weekend seeing each other up at a wedding in Los Martinez or a funeral in Santa Fe, and nothing since had happened, the village had not yet had time to recharge itself with news and gossip, other than the death of the oldest man in the valley, about whom there was nothing more to say, since he had outlived his time. Phones had not yet started ringing about the water meeting at the school.

The village made itself comfortable in armchairs and sofas and couches, in bed, on carpeted floors, before newspapers and old magazines, and in front of TVs with VCRs and those few that had satellite service. This particular night there were no readers of books other than the Bible. The village yawned and grew drowsy, and one by one residents began nodding off, except one couple who pretended it was Saturday night and who dressed themselves in tight dark clothes and danced the tango on a tile floor to candlelight and a blazing fireplace— until he pulled a muscle in his back. In another house a mile away, a woman in a pink bathrobe sat astride a man stretched out on the floor on cushions in front of a woodstove and bounced up and down to the pulsations of an old Beatles song.

The moon rose higher and higher, seeming to grow harder and colder and smaller. There was the odd shooting star, which no one saw. Jets flew high overhead, signaling down with tiny blinking lights. Satellites glided across on light taken like the moon from the absent sun. One by one the villagers began making their way to bed, first the very young, then the old, then the middle-aged, and lastly the teenagers, who lingered before mirrors. They made their way down hallways, up stairs, in and out of bathtubs and showers, through doorways, switched off lights, checked stoves and heaters, locked doors, let dogs and cats in, climbed into bed in pairs and nattered to each other about the events of the day, or alone muttering to themselves, and fondled each other or themselves briefly before losing interest. Then they lay still, most of them, before setting out on the slow, groping swim toward daylight.

Sometime between nine and ten the community well went dry when too many former attendees of the water meeting ran baths and showers and washing machines, leading to the suspicion in not a few minds that the State Water Office had already begun cutting water off to the village and was already sending it down to Texas. A little later phones all over the village began ringing, forcing many residents to climb out of bed to hear first- and secondhand accounts of events at the elementary school, the volume of calls rising so fast that a circuit blew in the local exchange system, cutting off all service to San Marcos and five upriver villages.

Otherwise, there were no drinking parties in the cottonwoods of either the Upper or Lower Shooting Galleries owing to the coolness of the night. After the rush following the water meeting, traffic through the valley waxed and waned, became erratic and wandering. A state police cruiser with flashing red lights roared through the village. Then, well after midnight, the weaving and fitfully speeding and then

crawling cars of three drunk drivers returning home to San
Marcos from the cantina up in Los Martinez.

By one in the morning almost everyone was asleep despite
mice in attics and cupboards and under floorboards. By about
three a.m. consciences and memories and imaginations began
to wake up their owners all over the valley, or perhaps more
simply, acidic stomachs, full bladders, itchy noses, congested
lungs, aching joints, inflating penises, pulsating vaginas,
muscles seizing up in cramps, as the moon cleared rooftops
and angled down into bedroom windows. All over the village
people got up to urinate, blow noses, rub joints and muscles,
sip from glasses of water, turn up or down electric blankets,
turn up heaters, throw a log in the woodstove, squint at clock
faces, peek in on children, check the doors, let out dogs, and
worry. They worried that they were coming down with spring
colds or late cases of the flu, that the lump or ache was cancer,
that the heart was weak and clogged, that old age had come
up on them too soon, that their lives were over, that they lived
in the center of nowhere. Three in the morning was when
the dead were reproached for having died and when the
young feared they would die young and the old feared they
might never die, and when blasted hopes were most luridly
painted and when checking accounts could never be balanced
and credit cards never paid off and when there wouldn't be
enough food stamps to make it to the end of the month, when
neighbor feared neighbor and father and son feared each other
and mother and daughter exhausted themselves in jealousy,
when old resentments came back to life, and tallies were made
again of what was owed and what owing, lists of what had
been stolen by others, and stolen from others, who had been
faithless, disloyal, and who had lied and lied. Three was when
everyone except the young realized they would never win the
lottery or the jackpot at the new casinos and that all would be
visited by catastrophe in the form of war or flood or drought

or car wreck or heart attack. Old electric clocks wheezed. Newer digital alarms winked in numbers of red, blue, green.

By four the moon would be down or obscured by clouds moving in from the west. The sky would darken. A great collective snoring would rise within the adobe houses and mobile homes of San Marcos. Then the coyotes would sing and chatter from the tops of the clay cliffs as their night, which is their workday, came to a close, and sometimes they would be joined by foxes lower down in the valley, and from the smaller arroyos, all those who had been successful at the hunt, having carried off the prize of a field mouse or gopher or a jackrabbit or cottontail, sometimes even a hen or a duck. Dogs below would howl in response, plaintive and unsteady, admitting a kinship like none they had with the other creatures who slept inside houses, on mattresses, under blankets.

Beavers worked in the river until the first rays of dawn, chewing around the trunks of cottonwoods and nibbling at the gray-white bark of the higher branches they had felled into the water. On this night they brought no trees crashing down into the water. Skunks cruised the paths and roads and the gardens to which they would later return to raid sweet corn patches. Their smelly passage would distract the foolish dogs, who could never outwit the skunks' flag-waving, their quick-footed spraying dance. The acrid burning smell, onion-like, would pass right through walls, waking with a start the sleeping forms.

As the human noises fell silent in the darkness, so the hissing wash of the distant stream would grow louder, seeming to rise up toward the sleeping houses, then to fall back down and sink away as the sky turned rose and then pink and then orange and yellow to the east, and toilets flushed, faucets began to run, radios were turned on, toasters started ticking, and car and truck engines started, doors slammed, and a new day began in San Marcos, so little different from the one before, or the one to come after, that for most inhabitants it would soon fade into the wash and jumble of all days lived in this one place, and thus be quite forgotten.

ABOUT THE AUTHOR

Stanley G. Crawford is a writer and a farmer. He was born in 1937 and was educated at the University of Chicago and at the Sorbonne. He is the author of seven novels, including *Log of the S.S. the Mrs. Unguentine*, *Travel Notes*, *Gascoyne*, and *Some Instructions*, a classic satire on all the sanctimonious marriage manuals ever produced.

He is also the author of two memoirs: *A Garlic Testament: Seasons on a Small Farm in New Mexico* and *Mayordomo: Chronicle of an Acequia in Northern New Mexico*. He has written numerous articles in various publications such as the *New York Times*, the *Los Angeles Times*, *Double Take*, and *Country Living*.

Stanley Crawford is co-owner with his wife, Rose Mary Crawford, of El Bosque Farm in Dixon, New Mexico, where they have lived since 1969.